Also by Madalyn Morgan

Foxden Acres
Applause
China Blue
The 9:45 To Bletchley
Foxden Hotel
Chasing Ghosts
There Is No Going Home
She Casts a Long Shadow

OLD CASES NEW COLOURS

DUDLEY GREEN ASSOCIATES
PRIVATE INVESTIGATION AGENCY

MADALYN MORGAN

Old Cases New Colours © 2021 by Madalyn Morgan
Published Worldwide 2021 © Madalyn Morgan

All rights reserved in all media. No part of this book may be reproduced or transmitted in any form by any means, electronic or mechanical (including but not limited to: the Internet, photocopying, recording or by any information storage and retrieval system), without prior permission in writing from the author.

The moral right of Madalyn Morgan as the author of the work has been asserted by her in accordance with the Copyright, Designs and Patents Act 1988.

All characters in this publication are fictitious and any resemblance to real persons, living or dead, is purely coincidental.

ISBN: 9798724791731

British Library Cataloguing in Publication Data.
A catalogue record for this book is available from the British Library.

Acknowledgments

Formatted by Rebecca Emin
www.gingersnapbooks.co.uk

Book Jacket Designed by Cathy Helms
www.avalongraphics.org

I would like to thank editor Nancy Callegari and proofreader Maureen Vincent-Northam.

Thanks also to Jeanie McKinlay who was the highest bidder for a copy of *She Casts A Long Shadow* in the 2020 auction for Children In Read. As promised I have named a character after Jeanie. Thank you, Children In Read and The Authors' and Illustrators' for giving me the opportunity to contribute to such a worthy cause.

Old Cases New Colours will be auctioned for Children In Need this year.

Old Cases New Colours is dedicated to my mother and father

Ena and Jack Smith

CHAPTER ONE

Ena sat on the narrow step between the office and kitchen. As the Cold Case department, a top security facility of the Home Office, access to the kitchen was through an archway. Now, as the private office of Dudley Green Associates, Private Investigation Agency – advertised discreetly in The Lady Magazine and boldly in The Times – there had been a door fitted. To keep the attractive feature of the arch, Ena had designed a door in the style of a French-window with lattice squares instead of glass for windows. With panels on either side, she thought the door very stylish. It complemented the room perfectly and when closed added to the privacy needed for potential clients to talk about their investigative needs in confidence. Discretion was key. Like a doctor's surgery, anything discussed in the office of Dudley Green Associates would be confidential.

Ena leaned against the door and closed her eyes. Had she done the right thing? She had gone against Henry's wishes, *again*. Even though his name was on the brass plaque on the wall next to the front door, she had ignored him. She had also ignored the advice of her sisters who were unanimous in their opinion that it would be best to find offices in a different location for a new company. Like Henry, they'd suggested somewhere that didn't have bad memories. Ena sighed. She hadn't listened to Henry or her sisters. She had done what she always did, gone headlong like a bull in a china shop and done what she wanted.

Ena yawned, opened her eyes and looked around the room. It was empty but for two telephones on the floor where there were once desks and where, when delivered later, there would be desks again.

She liked the office. There was something about it that felt comfortable. She liked Mercer Street and Covent Garden, but it was more than the building and the area. It was, as always, the people. Ena had been fond of the men she worked with when it was the Cold Case department of the Home Office. She looked over to where her friend and colleague, Sid Parfitt, had worked and still wasn't able to think of him without emotion rising in her throat. Sid, being older, had been protective of her. During the war he had been a codebreaker, first at Beaumanor and then at Bletchley Park. He was a clever man. He was also a bit of a fusspot, which made him thorough.

It was because of the work Sid did on cold cases that he was killed. Ena had spotted Frieda Voight in Oxford Street; a woman she had worked with during the war and whom she had exposed as a spy. Henry had stated that it was impossible to have seen Frieda because they had been to the funerals of her and her brother Walter ten years earlier. When Sid got close to finding out the truth about Frieda Voight, he was murdered on Waterloo Bridge and his body thrown onto the Embankment. Ena wiped tears from her eyes.

Her other colleague, Artie Mallory, who worked with her and Sid on cold cases, was in his early thirties. He was tall, had dark, wavy hair, wore fashionable clothes – blazers and slacks and open neck shirts. He was also very good looking, which often got him into trouble. In contrast, Sid wore dark suits, white shirts, wouldn't be seen without a tie – and you could see your reflection in his shoes.

With regard to work, Artie had been as casual as Sid had been precise. Sid worked until he had dotted all the i's and crossed all the t's, whereas Artie was always ready to leave the office at five-thirty and head for The Salisbury pub, or a club in Mayfair. Ena laughed. Sid was never late for work while Artie often tipped up half an hour late with a hangover. Artie was a chatterbox who loved to gossip, Sid on the other hand didn't engage in rumour or hearsay. He didn't speak unless he had something to say. He was what Ena's mam would call, 'economical with his words' except when he and Ena were on their own. Only then did Sid relax and talk more. Similar to Ying and Yang in Chinese philosophy, her ex-colleagues complemented each other, they worked well together and, more importantly, they got results.

Ena looked around the room. 'No 8 Mercer Street has some good memories,' she said aloud. 'And it's the good memories I shall focus on!' Besides, she liked working in such a vibrant location as Covent Garden. The market was expanding, shops were springing up along Long Acre, as were cafés – Coffee Bars – cafés selling strong Italian coffee with music blaring out. Jukeboxes were the latest craze and in some of the coffee bars there was live music at night. Young men with floppy hair strummed guitars and sang moody love songs. Sometimes there was a duo, or a band of three or four musicians playing rock music and singing in American accents like Elvis Presley, Bill Hayley and Chuck Berry. Covent Garden, Leicester Square and Soho were full of life – and Ena liked being part of it.

Loud banging brought her out of her reverie. The builders in the flat above the office had finished their tea break and gone back to work. She pushed herself up, crossed the room and taking her handbag from the windowsill she pulled out a notepad and pen. Ena then turned the pad to landscape position and drew a square that almost filled the page. Adding double lines for the doors and window, she then sketched where she would place her desk and the rest of the furniture she'd bought – hoping, as the delivery people had promised – they would arrive early that afternoon. She smiled. There hadn't been a window when Sid worked there. Standing in exactly the same spot as Sid's desk had once been, light from the window would now shine directly onto her desk. He had been gone for more than a year, but she still missed him.

Ena wondered about the nature of work she'd be asked to do as a private investigator. Butterflies stirred in her stomach and she took deep breaths. She was excited to be starting a detective agency and hoped the work would be exciting too. When she first began investigating cold cases for the Home Office the work had fascinated her. She often worked long hours and sometimes didn't get home until late. Henry worked for MI5 at the time and his hours were equally long, the pair of them often too exhausted at the end of the day to do anything but eat and fall into bed.

Frieda Voight, the spy Ena had worked with during the war – and who had come into her life again the year before – was the last cold case she had worked on. Frieda had killed herself, which led to the personal assistant to Henry's boss at MI5, Helen Crowther, committing suicide and framing Henry for murder. Ena had been instrumental in the capture of Crowther's sidekick, a sociopath named Shaun O'Shaughnessy, as well as the ousting of a top German agent – Ena's boss at the Home Office, Director Richard Bentley. Bentley had recruited several German agents and promoted them to powerful political and military positions during the thirty years he'd been at the Home Office.

What would have been a huge scandal had been hushed up. Bentley was tried for treason, found guilty and hanged, the others had German passports and were in prison. Ena had been called in as a witness for the prosecution at Dick Bentley's trial. Although the trial had taken place behind closed doors, someone had leaked it to the newspapers and it made the front pages of them all. Ena had neither read the newspapers nor cared about Bentley's fate. It was too personal and too painful. For almost a year she had kept her head down, spent time with her family in the Midlands and then stayed at home. She needed to spend time with her husband – and she'd enjoyed it, but being a housewife was never going to be enough for Ena.

Henry had left MI5 almost a year ago and now worked for GCHQ. He often went in to the office early and worked late, so with the new decade of the 1960s, Ena decided it was time she returned to work. She was unaware of exactly what she wanted to do, but when she saw the "For Sale" sign on the wall of her old offices in Mercer Street, she knew where she wanted to work. It took her from New Year until March to gather the money together to buy the premises, late June to knock it into shape and refurbish it and a further month to decorate it. The latter she did herself because she'd almost run out of money. Now, in the summer of the new decade, she was beginning a new career.

The role of spy catcher, unearthing spies hiding in the shadows of respectability and exposing people who held senior positions in the country's security services, was too much responsibility for one person. The job made her feel grubby. She'd had enough of dishonest and corrupt people. Working on cold cases for the Home Office, she had no choice but to work on cases that landed on her desk. She had a dilemma. She was good at what she did, so, why not work for herself in a private capacity? However hard it might be until she got to grips with the business and establish a good reputation, it would be better than working for Spooks. As her own boss she could turn down cases if she thought they were morally or ethically opposed to her conscience, were illegal, or if the client was disreputable.

Ena took a long deep breath and smiled. She was determined to make a success of the investigation agency, and rather than reminiscing over the past, she would look forward to the future and everything a new venture was bound to bring.

Ena got to her feet. The banging from upstairs had quietened. Later she would go up to see how the builders were getting on, but first the new worktops and kitchen cupboards needed cleaning.

CHAPTER TWO

'Hello?'

Hearing a male voice in what she thought was a locked office, Ena looked up. 'Ouch!' She had forgotten the cutlery drawer in the kitchen cabinet was open. 'Artie?'

Artie Mallory, her colleague from their days working together on cold cases, sounded as surprised to see her as she was to see him. 'What are you doing?'

'Cleaning. What does it look like?' Ena touched the top of her head where an egg-like swelling had already begun to form. Thankfully, no traces of blood were evident on her hand, meaning she hadn't cut her head.

'I thought you were going to rent offices above the coffee bar in Maiden Lane. I went in there and the chap behind the counter said you'd decided against working upstairs so I popped into the theatre and the stage doorman showed me your advert in The Times.'

'It's been in The Times for two days. It's in The Lady too. Neither ads have brought in any business.'

Artie looked around the empty office. 'I'd say that's a good thing. You're not ready for business yet.'

'I should have been. The Home Office did everything at a snail's pace. The paperwork took an age as everything was tied up in red tape. Then, when everything appeared to be going to plan, the furniture people let me down. Anyway, we're back on track now.'

'You and Henry?'

'No, just me. Henry's at GCHQ.' Ena dropped the cloth she'd been cleaning the cupboards with into the bucket, dried her hands and put on the kettle. 'Which begs the question, why aren't you there?'

'I've resigned,' Artie announced with an air of grandeur, giving a wide berth to the area in the middle of the room, where the dead body of Helen Crowther, the mole at MI5, had been found the previous year.

As the kettle began to whistle, Ena looked over her shoulder to ask Artie if he wanted tea or coffee. She laughed. 'I scrubbed the floor within an inch of its lino-ed life before the new carpet went down. There was nothing to see anyway.'

'I know. It's just the thought...' He gave a dramatic shiver. 'You're not *really* going to work in here are you?'

'Why not?' Ena carried two mugs of steaming coffee into the office and put them on the windowsill. Side-stepping the middle of the room, Artie joined her. Ena laughed again. 'So,' she said, taking a sip of her coffee, 'to what do I owe the pleasure?'

Artie dropped his gaze and then looked up at her shyly. 'I'm looking for a job and I can't think of anyone I'd rather work with than you, Ena. Since you're the Dudley, and Henry is the Green, I was hoping I could be the Associate.'

'Henry's only a sleeping partner and it would be fun to work with you again—'

'So I've got the job?'

'No, Artie, I'm sorry. If I could afford an associate, you'd be the first person I'd ask, but I just don't have the money to employ anyone at the moment.'

Artie sighed heavily. 'I understand.'

'I don't think you do,' Ena replied. 'Every penny the Home Office gave me when –' Ena put up her hands and made quotation signs with her forefingers – 'I was made redundant, and most of Henry's golden handshake when he left MI5, has gone into buying this place and the flat above. I don't have a bean left. I couldn't pay you a salary, Artie. Not at the moment, anyway. Stick it out at GCHQ for a little while longer and as soon as I get some work – and I'm paid for it – we'll talk again. Just give me six months to get on my feet.'

Artie's mouth fell open. 'Six months? I'd be a shadow of myself by then. That is if I don't die of exhaustion first.'

Ena put her hand on her old colleague's arm. 'Is Highsmith that bad?'

'Ye-es! Rupert doesn't need an assistant, he needs an errand boy,' Artie said. 'He treats me like he's the Head Boy of a public school and I'm his Fag. Character building, he calls it. A way of getting to know each other. Huh! I told him, I said, Rupert, I am thirty-eight years old! I am not an eleven-year-old child living away from home for the first time.'

'You're talking in the past tense. Artie, have you resigned?'

'I would have, but he got in first and let me go. He got accounts to pay me until the end of the month though.'

'That was good of him.'

'I've earned every penny and more.'

Ena laughed. She knew Rupert Highsmith well. She had crossed swords with him on several occasions in the past. 'I'm sure you have.'

'He insists we remain friends. No hard feelings and all that,' Artie scoffed. 'I'm not sure Highsmith knows the meaning of the word, 'friend'. Still, whatever we are, we're meeting for a drink tonight.'

'Is there any chance Highsmith will give you your job back?'

'No.' Artie grinned. 'I kind of implied I was coming to work with you.'

Ena blew out her cheeks. 'Oh, Artie! It would be lovely, but...'

'We worked well together before. And, you said on the day Highsmith offered me the job at GCHQ that if I changed my mind —'

'I did, and I meant it.' Artie's face lit up. 'But, as I said, I can't afford to take you on at the moment. Not you, not anyone.' Artie looked downcast and absent-mindedly stirred his cooling coffee. 'As soon as I can afford an associate, I'll let you know, I promise you, Artie.'

Her old colleague sighed. 'I suppose I'd better let you get on,' he said, making no attempt to leave.

Banging in the flat above the office resumed. 'I tell you what. I've done enough cleaning for one day.' Ena looked at her watch. 'It's half-past eleven. Let's get out of here. I need to show my face upstairs and say hello to the builders. Why don't you come up with me and tell me what you think of the work they've done so far. The office furniture's being delivered this afternoon, sometime after one, which gives us plenty of time to go to Café Romano at the top of Mercer Street and have a coffee and a sandwich. Fancy something to eat?'

'I am hungry...'

'It's a date then. Give me five minutes to get changed.' Ena pulled off the scarf she had tied around her head like a turban to keep her hair clean and out of her eyes and shook her hair out.

'It's good you've had a window put in this wall,' Artie said, peering out. 'Can't see much, there's a wall and the building next door is too close. At least it lets in some daylight.'

'Apparently there was a window there originally. It was only a matter of knocking a few bricks out and putting a frame and windows in again.' Ena picked up the coffee cups and took them into the kitchen.

'I wonder why it was blocked up. All seems very odd,' Artie mused.

'The Home Office had it bricked up to make the Cold Case department more secure.' Ena said.

Walking around the edge of the room to the door, he said, 'Isn't it a bit... spooky being here, where Helen Crowther killed herself?'

'Not at all.' Ena took off her pinafore and draped it over the door of the cupboard she'd been cleaning. 'I'll finish in here when we get back,' she said, skipping down the step from the kitchen and locking the office door behind her. 'So,' she said, catching up with Artie in the foyer. 'What do you think of the inside courtyard now it's an entrance lobby?'

'Much better. And,' he said, opening a door on his left, 'it's good that you've made use of the old utility room?'

'It'll be a second office; somewhere where clients can speak confidentially. The big old store room is now a waiting room with a washroom and toilet.' Ena pushed open the door between the main office and the second office, entered, and combed her hair in the mirror above the hand basin. Returning, she took her jacket from a coat stand by the door and put it on.

'It's looking good.'

'Thank you, I think so too, and there isn't much left to do down here. I know the work should have been finished before we advertised and by rights it would have been but the buildings along here are Listed buildings, which meant red tape. What with the HO causing endless delays, the work got put back and because I couldn't afford to pay the builders to sit around drinking tea all day, they had to take another job. It wasn't their fault they didn't start work here on time. Anyway, they'll be back tomorrow to finish down here and then they'll go upstairs to help the chaps up there. By the time they've finished and the furniture's in, it won't look anything like it did when it was the Home Office's Cold Case department.'

'If you say so.'

'I do! Besides, Henry and I got it for a song. No one wants to buy a property with sitting tenants, so we made the HO an offer thinking we'd wait for the couple upstairs to leave and in the meantime, I'd set up the investigation agency down here. But by the time the newspapers had finished making up ghoulish stories about the spy who was murdered at No, 8 Mercer Street and *according to several eye witnesses who didn't want to be named*, had seen an apparition in white leave the building and walk the streets of Covent Garden—'

Artie gasped.

'Which wasn't true! Oh, Artie...' Ena punched him playfully on the top of his arm. 'But it put the wind up the young couple who lived upstairs and they did a moonlight flit.' Ena laughed. 'By then the Home Office, as owners of the property, had begun to attract a lot of attention and couldn't wait to get rid of the place.'

'There's a rumour going around GCHQ that our old boss, Director Bentley, had a personal property portfolio paid for with Home Office money.'

'That's why the new director almost bit my hand off when I offered him half the amount the property was worth. I had to sign a disclaimer document to say I wouldn't speak to the newspapers about the previous owners or its history – the spy who was the director of the Home Office or the mole at MI5, which I had no intention of doing anyway – so here I am.'

'And you're going to live in the flat upstairs?'

'Eventually. There's a lot of work to do yet, but 8a Mercer Street will one day in the near future be mine and Henry's new home. The flat in Stockwell has been broken into so many times that I'm not comfortable there anymore.' Ena kicked off her old tennis pumps and slipped her feet into a pair of court shoes. 'It has bad memories for me.'

'And this place hasn't?' Artie said with irony.

'No, it hasn't. I don't feel the same way about Helen Crowther's death as I do about Frieda Voight's. I don't care about Crowther, but Frieda... She'd been my work colleague and friend during the war. You know she came to see me at the flat in Stockwell on the night she committed suicide. I've often wondered whether if I'd done things differently that night, said something, perhaps I might have saved her.' Ena picked up her handbag and left the cloakroom. 'The flat in Stockwell isn't home anymore,' she said, thoughtfully. 'I just don't feel safe there.'

'And you feel safe here with the ghost of Helen Crowther walking the corridors?'

Ena laughed and pushed him playfully towards the door. 'I'm not superstitious and I don't believe in ghosts. Besides, there aren't any corridors.'

Artie made an O of his mouth and pulled a ghoulish face.

'For goodness sake,' she said, shaking her head in fun. 'It isn't the dead you have to worry about, it's the living,' she added, crossing the newly decorated lobby.

Artie pulled open the street door and screamed with fright.

CHAPTER THREE

'I'm sorry. I didn't mean to startle you. I wanted to speak to Mrs Green, but I'll come back another time.'

'Mrs Hardy?' Ena recognised the voice. She looked past Artie and seeing the worried expression on the woman's face, said, 'What on earth's the matter?'

Doreen Hardy was pale, her usually bright eyes were dull with dark rings under them and she looked thinner than when Ena had last seen her.

'I'm sorry to trouble you, but Inspector Powell at Bow Street said you might be able to help me.'

'If I can, of course I will.' Ena turned to Artie, 'It was the testimonies of Mrs Hardy's sons that led to Henry being cleared of Helen Crowther's murder last year.' She stood back and motioned to the mother of the three boys to come in.

Ena led the way across to the small lobby. As she unlocked the door to her office the sound of banging grew louder. 'Sorry about the noise, we've got the builders in upstairs.' She pushed open the door. 'The office isn't furnished yet. I'm expecting the furniture to arrive this afternoon,' she said, pronouncing each word clearly so she didn't have to shout. She looked across the empty room. 'There isn't even a chair for you to sit on. Would you mind if we talked in the café at the top of the street? At least we'll be able to hear each other speak in there,' Ena said, as the dull thud of a mallet thumping against wood joined the orchestral sounds of an electric drill and a hammer hitting nails.

Before Mrs Hardy had time to reply, the telephone rang. Ena handed Artie the keys to the outer door. 'Would you answer that, Artie? There's a notepad on the windowsill if you don't mind taking a message.

Oh, and would you hang on until the furniture arrives?'

'Er... sure...' Artie turned immediately and walked briskly into the office.

'Thank you. Lunch is on me, later,' Ena shouted after him. She didn't know whether Artie had heard her, and smiled. Lunch had always been on her.

Ena led Mrs Hardy into Café Romano and to a secluded table between the door and a potted plant. When they were seated, Ena ordered a corned beef and tomato sandwich and a pot of tea, while Mrs Hardy requested a cup of tea.

Seated with their drinks, Ena asked Mrs Hardy how she could help her.

'Nothing I can say will make what I'm about to tell you sound any better, so I'll just say it as it happened, Mrs Green.' Mrs Hardy took a deep breath. 'I've been accused of stealing and the money, twenty-pounds, was in my coat pocket. I don't know how it got there. I swear I don't. I wouldn't do such a thing. With my husband Arnold being away...' She paused and cleared her throat. Ena nodded, giving her a sympathetic smile. 'I'm all the boys have got. If the hotel manager's fancy piece goes to the Police as she threatened to do, and they charge me, I don't know what will happen to my boys. As God is my witness, I didn't steal that money,' Doreen sniffed, bursting into tears.

'It was good that you went to see Inspector Powell. The woman's threatening behaviour is now on record.'

Mrs Hardy's eyes widened with fear. 'So is her accusation that I've been stealing.'

Ena passed the distraught woman her handkerchief. 'Don't worry about that. It's best he heard what really happened from you, just in case this woman does go to the Police, which,' Ena added, 'I'm sure she won't. The woman has an agenda of her own.

She either took the money herself, or she wants you out of the way.' When Doreen had calmed down, Ena pushed her cup of tea towards her. 'Drink it while it's hot, Mrs Hardy. Then I want you to tell me everything that happened, starting at the beginning.'

Doreen Hardy wiped her face with Ena's hankie and took a sip of the tea. 'It started when the manager of the Duke of Wellington Hotel, who I clean for, got friendly with one of the customers. I say 'friendly', the woman all but threw herself at him.'

'Is this the woman you called his fancy piece?'

'Yes. Mr Walters, the manager, took her out a few times. It didn't make any difference to me. Me and Mr Walters have always been on good terms, friendly terms you might say, and nothing changed. Except Dolly, that's the woman's name, didn't like him being friendly with me. She didn't even like him talking to me.'

'There hadn't been anything between you and your employer before he met Dolly, had there?' Ena enquired.

'No!' Mrs Hardy sounded horrified that Ena could even think such a thing. 'And, there isn't now, even though he seems cooler with Dolly. I think he's seen her for the flighty Miss she is. No,' she emphasised, 'Mr Walters is a gentleman. He's always been kind to me, gives me nice bits of meat to take home at the end of my shift – if there's any left after the lunches – and he sometimes sends a couple of bottles of lemonade or Vimto for the boys, but nothing like you're suggesting, Mrs Green.'

'I'm sorry, Mrs Hardy, I wasn't suggesting there was anything inappropriate going on between you and your boss.' Ena had offended Mrs Hardy, which hadn't been her intention. 'I just wondered if he was perhaps a little too fond of you.'

Mrs Hardy's face changed from frowning to thoughtful. 'Come to think of it he is very friendly. But he knows I've got Arnold...'

Who is in prison, Ena thought, but didn't say. 'And then what happened?'

'Well, Mr Walters told me the takings had been short on the days I'd worked.'

'You don't work every day then?'

'No, I share the hours with my sister-in-law, Maisie. I do three days one week and she does four, then we swap and the following week I do four days and she does three. We clean before the bar opens in the morning so it's ready for lunchtime, and again in the afternoon so it's clean for opening at night.'

'And Mr Walters said money only went missing on the days you were there?'

'Yes.'

'How many people work at the hotel altogether?'

'Mr Walters, of course, then there's the barman.' Mrs Hardy's cheeks coloured. 'He's been off a couple of times lately and Mr Walters got me to stay on and work behind the bar at lunchtime. Washing glasses mostly, but he said he'd teach me how to serve drinks.'

'Would you like that?'

'Yes. The pay would be better. I'm good with money,' Mrs Hardy said, confidently. With a thief for a husband who spent more time in prison than he did out of it, she'd need to be, Ena reflected. 'I can do sums in my head. The till's easy, you add up the prices of the drinks, put the money the customer gives you on top of the till's drawer, ring up the price and take the change out of the till before you put the customer's money in it.'

Ena was impressed by Mrs Hardy's knowledge, as

well as her confidence. 'Who else works there?'

'There must be staff on the hotel side but I've never met any of them. The hotel and the public bar are quite separate. So besides me and Maisie, Mr Walters and Fred, the barman, there's only the kitchen staff. There's Ida who does the cooking and Dolly who waits on the tables.'

'Dolly? Mr Walter's lady friend works in the kitchen?'

'Yes. She said she needed a job and Mr Walters couldn't really say no. She says she's a barmaid, but I don't think Mr Walters wants her working behind the bar because she likes a drink, if you know what I mean. Food is ordered at the bar and whoever takes the order tells the kitchen and when the food's ready Dolly brings it out to the customer.'

'And, she's there every time you're there?'

'She's there every day. Morning and night – opening hours.'

'It's only a thought, but it's possible that Dolly the waitress is jealous of your friendship with the manager and wants you out of the way.'

'Do you think Dolly took the money?'

'She could have. She may not only be jealous of your friendship with the landlord, but if she knows he's promised to teach you the barmaid's role when she's already told him that's her profession, she probably feels he's passing her over for you.'

'Poor Dolly.'

Ena raised her eyes, 'I wouldn't feel too sorry for her. If it was her who planted the money in your coat pocket, she had all but succeeded in getting you the sack, as well as threatened you with the Police. Dolly doesn't deserve your pity, Mrs Hardy.' Ena finished her tea. 'How did you leave it with the manager?'

'He said he didn't believe I'd taken the money, but I wasn't to go back to work until he'd found out who had. For the time being Maisie's doing my shifts as well as her own and I'm looking after her children. I don't mind, they're good kids – and with Maisie being a widow, she needs the money.' Doreen Hardy sighed. 'I liked going out to work. I liked the company and I liked earning a bit of money. To be honest, Mrs Green, I need that money.'

'Don't worry, Mrs Hardy, I'll find out who the culprit is and I'll do my best to get you your job back.' The café door opened, attracting Ena's attention. 'Artie?' She raised her hand and beckoned him over to join them.

'The furniture's here.' Artie put the office keys on the table. 'I thought I'd come and get something to eat now it's arrived.'

'Good idea. Who was the telephone call from?'

'An old friend of Margot's. George Derby-Bloom, or Brown. She sounded upset. Anyway, I've written her name on your notepad. It's on your desk.'

'I know the name,' Ena said, thoughtfully. 'I think she worked with Margot at The Prince Albert Theatre in the war.'

'She did. She said she was going to the Prince Albert to see Natalie Goldman this afternoon and she'd telephone you later today, or tomorrow.'

'I'll be in the office all day tomorrow. I'll sort the furniture out then.' Artie raised his eyebrows. 'I'll call into the Prince Albert after I've been to the Duke of Wellington Hotel.' Ena gave Mrs Hardy a reassuring smile. 'Someone has accused Mrs Hardy of stealing from her employer. She didn't, of course, so I'm going to see him. Dudley Green Associates' first investigation.'

Ena smiled sweetly at Artie. 'I was wondering... Well, hoping really, that you'd go back to the office and man the telephone while I go to the hotel? I know I've got a cheek to ask, but I'll pay you. I'd go later but the bar will be open and the manager will probably be busy then. Ignore the furniture, I'll deal with that tomorrow. Alright!'

Artie flicked his head back and tutted. 'I don't suppose I've got anything better to do.'

'You're the best, Artie Mallory. I owe you.' Ena turned to Mrs Hardy, 'Could you come into the office on Friday morning?' She took a card from her handbag and gave it to the maligned woman. 'My telephone number, in case you need to speak to me before then.' Ena got to her feet and picked up her handbag. 'Mrs Hardy, if your sister-in-law tells you anything, or if you hear from either the manager or Dolly, would you telephone me?' Mrs Hardy nodded.

Ena took a couple of pound notes from her purse and laid them on the table. 'That's for my sandwich and pot of tea and Mrs Hardy's tea. Do you have any money on you, Artie?' He nodded. 'Good. Get Mrs Hardy something to eat and have something yourself – and if it comes to any more than that, take the money out of petty-cash when you get back to the office.' She didn't wait for him to reply, but prepared to leave. 'Oh,' she said, turning back to Artie. 'Don't forget to put the receipt in the tin. It's in the kitchen, in the cupboard under the sink. I'll see you on Friday morning, Mrs Hardy, and Artie, thank you.' She blew him a kiss. 'I'll see you later.'

Ena found the Duke of Wellington Hotel car park on Cornwall Road, just off The Cut. She jumped out of the car and knocked on a door marked Private. A woman answered, her hair, piled high on top of her head, was the colour of corn at the roots, her topknot was bleached much lighter. The neckline of her blouse was low and her skirt tight and far too short for a woman of her age. Ena suspected this was Dolly. She ignored the belligerent look, smiled and asked to speak to Mr Walters. Dolly, if it *was* Dolly, crossed her arms over her chest and told her in an off-hand manner that Mr Walters was unavailable, saying he was at the wholesalers and, as she didn't expect him back until opening time, it would be best if Ena called back some other time.

Tomorrow morning first thing, Ena thought, thanked the woman and drove up to Maiden Lane to see Margot's dancer friend, George, who had told Artie when she phoned the office that she'd be with Natalie Goldman at the Prince Albert Theatre.

CHAPTER FOUR

As she entered the stage door of the Prince Albert Theatre, Ena was greeted by Stan, the stage doorman, who shook her hand for so long she thought it would drop off. 'Good to see you, Ena, it's been too long.' Stan took a step back, opened his arms and looked Ena up and down. 'You look a picture. Now,' he said, patting her hand, 'what can I do for you?'

'I'd like to see Natalie and George Derby-Bloom, if she's still here.'

'I'll ring through and tell Mrs Goldman you're here. Take a seat, I won't be a jiffy.' Ena sat on the familiar bench opposite the glass hatch of Stan's office. She didn't have to wait long before Stan was back by her side again. 'Mrs Goldman said they're both in her office.'

Ena thanked the doorman and went through the door marked, 'No Entrance'. She followed the green fluorescent dots on the floor of the winding corridor at the back of the stage that her sister Margot had called the 'rabbit warren' until she came to Natalie Goldman's office.

The door was already open. 'Come in, Ena,' Natalie called, as Ena lifted her hand to knock. 'Ena, I don't think you know George.'

'We haven't actually met, but I've heard a lot about you, George. Pleased to meet you,' Ena said, shaking George's hand.

'Hello, Ena. I've heard a lot about you too from Natalie.' Ena pulled a worried face. 'All of it good,' George added.

Ena gave Natalie, their mutual friend, a warm smile. 'You were here at the Prince Albert in the shows with my sister Margot, in the war.'

'That's right, and then Margot, Betsy and I joined the ENSA concert parties.'

'I remember Margot telling me.'

'The three musketeers,' George grinned, attempting to laugh.

Natalie fetched a chair from the other side of the office and placed it next to George.

'Coffee?'

'Please.'

After pouring three cups of coffee, Natalie took her seat behind her desk as Ena asked George how she could help her.

George took a shaky breath. 'My father's in a private nursing home called The Willows. At least he was until today. He was convalescing after an operation on his knee. This morning, Mrs Sharp, the manageress of the nursing home, telephoned and told me that Dad had been taken ill after breakfast and that I should get there as soon as possible.' George wiped tears from the corners of her eyes. 'I'm sorry.'

'Take your time,' Ena said, sympathetically.

George nodded and, giving Ena a grateful smile, continued. 'When I got there, Dad was dead. I know he was getting on in years, but apart from his knee he was in good health. He had a good appetite and he kept himself fit. Until the problem with his knee, he walked several miles every day. He liked the occasional port and a glass of wine in the evening with his dinner.' George put her hand up to her mouth and stifled a sob. She took a couple of calming breaths and when she had recovered, said, 'My father wasn't ill, Ena. He only went into the nursing home to recover from the operation. Unless he had underlying health problems which neither he nor I knew about, he shouldn't have died.'

'Did the manageress of the nursing home give you any explanation?'

George shook her head. 'No, except the nurse who took Dad back to his room said he closed his eyes as if he was asleep and the next thing he had gone. She told Mrs Sharp that he didn't appear to be in distress, nor was he in any pain.'

'And that's all she said?'

'Yes. The manageress said I could go over tomorrow and collect Dad's belongings.'

'I don't mean to alarm you, George, but tomorrow might be too late. If a mistake has been made, and it sounds to me as if it has, we need to go to the nursing home today, before anyone has time to clean the room. I'd also like to speak to the nurse who attended to your father this morning.'

George nodded. 'Alright. Are you free to go now?'

Before Ena could answer, Natalie said, 'Are you sure you're up to going back today, George?'

'Yes!' George said with determination. 'I need to get this sorted out as soon as possible so I can bury Dad.' She looked tired. Her eyes were red-rimmed. 'If Ena has the time…?'

'I do.' Ena said goodbye to Natalie, hugging her and kissing her on both cheeks as was Natalie's custom.

'I'll see you later, Natalie.' George kissed her friend goodbye in the same continental manner.

George took her jacket and shoulder bag from the coat stand behind the door and followed Ena out of Natalie's office, along the labyrinth of backstage corridors and through the stage door.

CHAPTER FIVE

The Willows Nursing Home was set in several acres of countryside. Gardens surrounded by tailored lawns with benches at regular intervals faced brightly coloured flower beds. On the left of the three-storey 19th Century, gabled, country house was a small lake, and on the right hand side, two strikingly white willow trees – one either side of a stream – gave the nursing home its name.

'A beautiful setting,' Ena remarked. 'I can see why the house and grounds would be ideal for anyone recuperating after an operation.'

'There are permanent residents here too, I believe,' George replied.

The door was opened by a nurse who George didn't recognise. She led them along a corridor to George's father's room. 'If you'd like to go in, I'll let Mrs Sharp know you're here and she'll arrange for someone to pack up your father's belongings.'

'Don't worry, Nurse,' Ena said, looking at her wristwatch. 'It's lunchtime, and I'm sure everyone's busy. I'll help George pack her father's things.' Ena made a mental note of everything in the room before opening the wardrobe door. 'Oh,' she said, turning back to the nurse, 'Do you know who was with Mr Derby-Bloom when he died?'

'Yes. Nurse McKinlay.'

'Is she here?'

'She should have gone home by now. She's on the early shift this week; six till twelve, but after Mr Derby-Bloom … she was upset. She said she didn't want to go home and offered to help in the dining room. Would you like me to see if she's still here?'

'If you wouldn't mind,' Ena said, looking at George for reassurance. George nodded and the nurse left.

George took her father's suit from the wardrobe and laid it on the bed while Ena emptied the chest of drawers of shirt, vest, socks and underpants, putting them all on the bed next to the suit.

'Anything else?'

'Dad didn't bring much.' George took her father's clothes, folded them and placed them in his suitcase. 'I'll get his toiletries.' She disappeared into the small en suite bathroom and reappeared with a leather shaving bag. 'What else?' she asked.

'A handkerchief, a book and a pair of spectacles,' Ena said, taking them out of the drawer in the bedside cabinet. 'And –' the toe of her shoe caught on something under the bed – 'what's this?' Taking the handkerchief so she didn't add her fingerprints to those she hoped belonged to the last person to see Mr Derby-Bloom alive, she carefully picked up a glass from the floor and held it at eye level. White sediment had settled in the bottom of the glass. Holding it by its base, she put it to her nose and sniffed. It smelt sweet and slightly fruity. She sniffed again. Lemon cordial she thought, or perhaps lime. Hearing someone outside the door, Ena wrapped the handkerchief around the glass, stood it upright in her handbag and turned round.

A stout woman in her late-fifties with dyed black hair, wearing a smart navy-blue two-piece, plain white blouse and flat serviceable shoes, entered the room. She gave George a concerned smile. 'I'm afraid the nurse who was with your father this morning, Nurse McKinlay, has left for the day. Is there anything I can do, Miss Derby-Bloom?'

'Yes, Mrs Sharp. My father was doing really well

after he came out of hospital. I don't understand why he suddenly died. Did something go wrong with the operation that no one knew about, did he have other health issues, or perhaps it was his medication?'

'I'm sorry, Miss Derby-Bloom, the truth is we won't know until the doctor has examined your father, Until then, I can't say.'

'How long will that take?' George asked. 'I need to bury Dad within twenty-four hours, forty-eight hours at the most.'

'I don't think that will be possible, George,' Ena said. 'There should be a post-mortem to establish exactly how your father died.'

George looked horrified. 'Autopsies and post-mortems are forbidden. They are considered to be a desecration of the body. There must be some other way.'

'I'm sorry, I didn't realise. George?' Ena chose her words carefully, 'You need to know why your father died and it may take longer than forty-eight hours.'

'If I can get permission from Dad's rabbi to delay the funeral, the doctor could examine him, but not cut him open and only if the rabbi is there.'

George's request rendered Mrs Sharp speechless. She then looked at Ena and scowled. 'Personally, I don't think a post-mortem is necessary.' She turned to George. 'The operation your father had on his knee could have put a strain on his heart – and at his age—'

Ena was losing her patience. For George's sake she needed to keep herself in check. 'I'm sorry, Mrs Sharp, but as Mr Derby-Bloom was in good health apart from his knee, I think it's necessary by whatever method, to find out why he died. However, it's up to George…'

'Dad was coming home at the end of the week,'

George said as if she were a million miles away. She looked at Ena. 'There has to be a reason why Dad died so suddenly, doesn't there?'

Ena nodded sympathetically.

'Then I'll speak to the rabbi and ask him to liaise with you,' George said, turning to Mrs Sharp. 'If that's alright?'

'Of course. And I shall speak to the doctor and explain the situation to him.'

Ena looked at her watch. It was almost one o'clock. 'Will the nurse who was with Mr Derby-Bloom when he died be here tomorrow?'

A worried look appeared on the manageress' face. She cleared her throat. 'Nurse McKinlay is very experienced. She is also a very caring young woman.'

'I'm sure she is, but we'd like to speak to her because she was the last person to see Mr Derby-Bloom.'

The manageress turned to George. 'Nurse McKinlay would not have been neglectful in any way, Miss Derby-Bloom...'

'That isn't why we want to speak to her,' Ena said, cutting in. 'We would just like to ask her a couple of questions.' Ena crossed the room to the door and George followed. 'We'll see you tomorrow.'

***

While they waited for Natalie to join them, as well as to take George's mind off the death of her father, Ena asked her about her time at the Prince Albert Theatre in the war, when she was in the shows with Margot.

'I wasn't what you'd call *a natural dancer*. I wasn't overweight,' George said, thoughtfully, 'I had big-bones. And I was tall. I was too tall for a chorus line, but the right height for a showgirl. I was cast as every female warrior from Sekhmet in Egyptian mythology to Zeus the Greek God of sky and thunder. I was able to stand in a dramatic pose without moving for ages.' She grimaced. 'Some of the dancers wobbled like jellies after a few seconds. Margot could hold a pose without moving too.' George rolled her eyes in fun. 'Margot could do anything and everything; she could sing, dance, was a terrific actress – and she could hold a dramatic freeze.'

'Margot told me if it hadn't been for you and Betsy pushing her onto the stage of a nightclub to sing, she may never have had the confidence to be in the show.'

George laughed. 'Margot didn't tell you everything. Singing in front of an audience might have given her the push she needed, but she had learned every step to every dance and every word to every song long before that night. It's why she wanted a job as an usherette. As soon as she had shown people to their seats and the curtains had been drawn across the exits, Margot went to the back of the auditorium and practised the moves and steps that the dancers on stage were performing. Margot's ambition was to be a professional dancer and she achieved it. She was a natural, unlike me. Not that I wanted to dance, but I needed to…' George brushed the air sending the reason why she needed to dance into the ether.

'I had the traditional pantomime wicked stepmother from an early age who, when I was sixteen, tried to marry me off. She introduced me to the sons of all her well-to-do friends; boys who had good prospects but were as dull as dishwater. "He's good husband material," she would say. I had no interest in boys and, even at the tender age of sixteen, I knew I didn't want to get married – not then, not ever. When I told my stepmother, she packed me off to a finishing school in Switzerland.'

'Switzerland? I was in Austria last year. Flew over the Swiss Alps... But that's another story.'

'I spent my winter holidays in the Alps, skiing. I loved Geneva, but I loathed finishing school. It was full of the daughters of wealthy socialites. It would have been perfect for the daughter of my stepmother if she'd had one, but not for me. I didn't fit in. Most of the girls were there to bag a wealthy husband when they *came out*.

'It was good in the respect that I learned deportment and dance, how to dress my hair and apply make-up – and how to act in the way society thinks a young lady should act – perish the thought. And I made some friends. But,' she said, 'working here during the war was where I made real friends. It was here that I learned how to be myself. The Prince Albert Theatre changed my life.'

'And you changed the lives of many other people,' Natalie said, coming into the office. As she passed George, she gave her shoulder a gentle squeeze. 'How did you get on?'

'Alright.' George caught her breath. 'I'm glad I wasn't on my own today,' she said, smiling at Ena, and picking up the suitcase containing her father's clothes. 'I have to make arrangements with the rabbi to be with Dad when the doctor at the nursing home examines him.' George looked from Natalie to Ena. 'Would you think it rude if I left? I'd like to see the rabbi and give him the telephone number of the nursing home before I pick Betsy up from her parents' house.'

'Is there anything else I can do?' Ena asked.

'No, you've done enough. I'm sorry to dash off.'

'I'll see you tomorrow. We need to get to the

nursing home before the nurse who was with your father today finishes her shift. Would ten-thirty be alright for you?'

'Yes, that's fine. Shall I come to your office?'

'No, I have an appointment in the morning. I'll pick you up here on the way back.'

CHAPTER SIX

Natalie saw George out of the theatre and returned to her office where Ena was waiting. 'It's so unfair George's father dying so suddenly. He was a wonderful man. Anton respected him greatly.' Natalie smiled at the memory and poured Ena a cup of coffee.

Ena felt Natalie wanted to talk about George's father and her late husband, Anton – and she was happy to listen.

'In the war, George and her father helped Jewish students escape the Nazis. George was at finishing school in Switzerland and got to know people in a Jewish organisation who smuggled students across the German border into Switzerland and then across the Channel to England. George persuaded her father to finance getting the students out of Germany to America, and she asked Anton if he would hide them when they got to England.'

'I remember when I was at your house last year, Margot mentioned dressing rooms eight and nine?'

'Yes, that's where we hid the students. After the children, their nanny and nurse had been evacuated to Foxden, lights on in an empty house would have been noticed. So, as there were only two or three students at a time we brought them to stay at the theatre. Young people came and went all the time unnoticed. With young women being called up on a regular basis there were always cast changes. No one noticed that there were more chorus girls one week and fewer the next.'

'What happened to the students? Where did they go?'

'First to Ireland and from there to America. Another wonderful network of people in New York found homes for them.'

'Margot told me about Goldie, the dancer who she took over from when she was beaten up by her Nazi boyfriend, Dave Sutherland. She said Goldie was smuggled out of London.'

'She was. We got her to Ireland with the Jewish students, but then, instead of travelling on to America, members of the escape network took her from the ship to her aunt where she had her baby.' Natalie's voice became abrasive. 'And where Goldie died soon after giving birth. It's a miracle the poor child lived long enough to give birth, the injuries she sustained at the hands of that monster. But she did live. Goldie was determined to see her baby and she named her Nancy after Nancy Diamond, the Albert Theatre's beautiful leading lady who was killed when a bomb fell on the taxi she was in. If she had arrived at the theatre earlier... Two minutes, and she'd have been in the backstage area when the bomb fell.' Natalie wiped tears from her eyes.

'In different ways, the war took both Nancy Diamond and Goldie.'

'Goldie would be happy that Bess and Frank adopted her daughter.'

'I didn't know Goldie, but, yes, I think she would have,' Ena said thoughtfully. She laughed. 'When Nancy first came to Foxden Hotel with her aunt Maeve, she took a shine to Bess' husband Frank. Frank kept laying hens, pigs and a few other animals, and Nancy loved helping him to feed them.' Ena laughed again. 'Bess said she followed Frank around like a puppy. He loved her from the very beginning. Bess did too. Nancy knew she was adopted from the start. Bess had always talked about her real mother. When her aunt Maeve went back to Ireland, she knew she wouldn't be able to nurse her dying mother and bring up Nancy. She told Bess that to expect Nancy to live with constant sickness wouldn't be right, or fair, on a young girl. She also wanted Nancy to have a better education than she'd have got in the village school, make friends with other children, and to have the freedom that she never had.'

'So she left her small ward in England and went to look after her sick mother. That was an unselfish thing to do. She must have been heartbroken,' Natalie said. 'And is Maeve still in Ireland?'

'Yes. Bess and Nancy go over and visit her every year. She's in a convent.' Natalie's eyed widened with surprise. 'She's a nun. She sold the house and, apart from a few pieces of family jewellery that had belonged to her mother and to Goldie which she gave Nancy, all her possessions were sold and the money given to the convent for her board and lodging.

'Nancy was old enough to understand and settled down at Foxden with her new mummy and daddy, and my mother, her new grandma. She loves Bess and Frank, devoted to them. She loves her aunt Maeve too, but understands why Maeve had to go back to Ireland. And, she loves Goldie. Nancy has enough love in her for her biological mother and for her adopted mother and father.'

'What about her father? Does she know about him?'

'Dave Sutherland?' A shudder as cold as ice ran through her. Ena shook her head vehemently. 'No! And she never will. Maeve told Bess that when Nancy was five and started school, she noticed that all the other children in her class had mummies and daddies. When she asked her aunt Maeve where her mummy and daddy were, Maeve told her that her father had been a brave airman in the RAF and had died when his plane was shot down.'

'I hope she never finds out her real father was actually a fascist bully who killed her mother.'

'There's no reason why she should. His name isn't on her birth certificate.'

'What did her aunt tell her when she asked her about her mother?'

'The truth, with a little elaboration. She told her that her mother had loved her very much and she didn't want to leave her, but she was very poorly, so, once she knew Nancy was safe and would be loved by her aunt Maeve, she went to heaven.'

Natalie looked questioningly at Ena.

'At the time Nancy's aunt Maeve was telling her about her father. Bess' fiancé, James Foxden, was missing after his aeroplane was shot down over Germany. It's uncanny that Bess became Nancy's mother.'

'Bess' fiancé was a brave man. Sutherland was a coward.'

Ena nodded in agreement.

'Sutherland almost killed Goldie. He would have too, if Margot hadn't found her, brought her to the theatre, and took her place on the stage that night. Until we received word that Goldie was safe in Ireland, Margot went on stage in her place. She wore her costumes, sang her songs and took her curtain call every night. Even after she had been followed, threatened and sent a bunch of dying arum lilies, she did the show as Goldie. Margot was very brave.'

It was Ena's turn to wipe away the tears. Thinking about the constant pain her sister Margot was in, and how she rarely complained, she said, 'Margot is still brave.'

CHAPTER SEVEN

On her way back to Mercer Street Ena called into Bow Street Police Station and asked to speak to Inspector Powell. She was told by the jovial desk sergeant that the inspector was in his office. The sergeant picked up the telephone to inform his boss that Ena was there and motioned for her to go through the door marked Private. A short buzz told Ena the door was unlocked. She thanked the sergeant and pushed the door open.

Inspector Powell met Ena as he always did, at the door of his office. 'It's good to see you, Ena. I hear you're working out of the cold case office in Mercer Street.'

'I am, but you wouldn't recognise the place.' Ena took a business card from her wallet and gave it to the inspector. 'If you need help with an investigation, I am discretion personified – and my terms are very reasonable,' Ena said, laughing.

DI Powell looked at the card. 'Very professional. I'll be in touch if I need you,' he said laughing with her. 'Though, with the Met's resources, it may not be often.'

'Well, I am at your disposal should you ever need me,' Ena replied.

'And I am at yours,' Inspector Powell said.

'That's good because I have a favour to ask.'

The inspector laughed at Ena as she had laughed at him earlier. 'Go on,' he said, shaking his head.

'Is the lovely pathologist, Sandy Berman, still at St. Thomas' Hospital?'

'He is. What have you got for him?'

'This.' Ena carefully lifted the half-pint glass with the remains of the lemon cordial she'd taken from Mr

Derby-Bloom's room from her handbag and unwrapped the handkerchief from around it.

'Looks interesting.' Inspector Powell lifted it to his nose and sniffed. 'Lemon and not a lot of anything else.'

'No, but if it was analysed properly by Sandy Berman in his lab at St. Thomas'.' Ena said, 'I think you'll find the liquid contains more than lemon.'

'I'll get it to him.'

'I need it doing quickly,' Ena pulled an overly emphasised apologetic face. 'I wouldn't ask, but my friend's father is Jewish. She needs to bury him as soon as possible, but I'm certain he died in suspicious circumstances. Oh, and the other thing,' Inspector Powell raised his eyebrows. 'I need the glass back, now. I was wondering if you could transfer the contents to another glass. I wouldn't ask, but I forgot to tell the woman who runs the place I'd taken it. If I sneak it into his room tomorrow, she'll be none the wiser.'

Inspector Powell picked up the telephone on his desk and dialled one digit. 'WPC Jarvis, could you find an evidence jar and bring it to my office?'

***

Ena dug deep into her handbag before remembering she'd given Artie the keys to the office when she'd taken Mrs Hardy to Café Romano. She didn't have a spare set and rang the bell.

Artie was flushed and perspiring when he opened the door. 'Thank God you're back, Mrs Hardy has had me charring.'

Distracted by the sight of a long padded seat standing flush against the wall in the entrance hall, Ena hadn't taken in what Artie had said. 'That's a nice piece of furniture,' she remarked, running her fingers along the top of it. She followed Artie to her office and stood in the doorway open-mouthed. 'I've come to the wrong office,' she said, 'I could have sworn the plaque outside said, Dudley Green Associates.' Laughing Ena walked around the room. 'Good Lord. How on earth-'

'Mrs Hardy insisted on coming back with me to help with the furniture and she's had me... She and I have been arranging it and cleaning all afternoon.'

'Mrs Hardy, thank you. And you, Artie. Thank you both so much.' Ena looked around the office in amazement.

'Mrs Hardy vacuumed while I polished. I found a piece of paper in the kitchen with a hand drawn plan on it and I assumed it was how you wanted the layout of the room, so, ta-dah!'

'I don't know what to say. I left an empty room and now. Well, it looks like a real office; an office that says, "ready for business".' Ena walked from desk to desk, stopping when she came to the filing cabinet. 'Good Lord. This is the filing cabinet from the visitors' room in the Albert Theatre.'

'A couple of stagehands dropped it off.'

'I've just seen Natalie at the theatre. She didn't say anything.'

Artie handed her a note.

'*Ena dear, I thought this might come in handy. If there's anything I can do, or if there's anything else you need from the visitors' room let me know. Good luck, Natalie.*'

Ena smiled. 'It locks, which is good,' she said, pulling open the top drawer. She turned and looked around the room. Taking everything in, she saw something on the windowsill. 'What...? An African violet house plant?' She went to it and touched the soil. It was damp. Emotion rose in her throat. 'Thank you.'

'I was dispatched at a jog to get that from Covent Garden market before you got back,' Artie said, pulling a comical face at Mrs Hardy.

'It's lovely. Mrs Hardy, you shouldn't have, but thank you. Thank you, both. I can't believe how much work you've done in such a short time.' She opened the door to the small kitchen and caught her breath. 'You could eat your lunch off this worktop,' she said, running her hand along its smooth surface. 'I think we should celebrate with a cup of tea, don't you?'

She tiptoed across the clean linoleum, filled the kettle and took three mugs from the cupboard above the sink. 'It's so clean, I hardly dare put the tea in the pot for fear of spilling the leaves and making a mess.'

'Risk it!' Artie shouted, 'I'm parched.'

Ena carried their drinks into the office on a tray. 'Milk and sugar,' she said, taking both off the tray, 'help yourselves.' Going back to the kitchen she returned with a half-bottle of whisky.

'That's more like it,' Artie said, as Ena poured a measure into his tea.

'Not for me.' Mrs Hardy put her hand over the top of her cup. 'I don't drink spirits.'

'Come on, Doreen,' Artie said, 'we've worked hard and we deserve a tot to celebrate.'

'If *Mrs Hardy*,' Ena said, addressing Doreen by her surname and glaring at Artie for using her Christian name, 'doesn't drink whisky, don't force her.'

Ena lifted her cup. 'Thank you, both of you.'

When they had finished their tea, Ena told Mrs Hardy and Artie about her fruitless trip to the Duke of Wellington Hotel.

'The blonde was Dolly,' Mrs Hardy said. 'I'm sorry she was rude to you.'

'Not rude, just a bit brash. Don't worry about Dolly, Mrs Hardy, if I find out it's her who has been stealing money, she won't be so smug.'

Ena saw Doreen Hardy out of the office and returned to find Artie in the kitchen washing up. She laughed. 'Mrs Hardy has made a good impression on you.'

'Doreen and I are colleagues in grime.'

Ena pulled a face and groaned at Artie's joke. 'That's as maybe, but she's also a client, so best to call her Mrs Hardy.'

'She told me to call her Doreen and, as I've called her Doreen all afternoon, I can hardly go back to calling her Mrs Hardy now. Besides, she isn't really a client, is she?'

'Not a paying client, no, but...' Ena took the tea towel from the worktop and began to dry the crockery that Artie had washed up. 'The investigation into the theft of money at the Duke of Wellington Hotel, which Doreen Hardy has been accused of, means we have our first investigation. The death of George's father could well be our second.' Ena couldn't help feeling excited, rolled up the tea towel and bowled it at Artie.

Artie caught it and hung it on the hook where it belonged. As he put the cups and saucers in the cupboard, Ena put the milk in the small refrigerator. 'Come on, let's get out of here, it's been a long day.'

CHAPTER EIGHT

The following morning Ena went to the Duke of Wellington Hotel. It was hardly a hotel at all. It might have been in its day, but that day had long gone. It now looked like a guest house for travelling salesmen selling corsets and encyclopaedias and everything in between. From the outside it looked like an old Victorian London pub – three storeys, large bay windows downstairs at the front, a grey façade which once had been white, but was now soot-stained by smoke from the many trains that came in and out of Waterloo station.

Ena drove past the public entrance on Waterloo Road and turned left opposite the Old Vic Theatre to The Cut and left again down Cornwall Road that took her to the car park at the rear of the hotel. She parked and walked along the side of the building, turning into a courtyard that would have been large enough for several horse and carts in Victorian times. Now the yard, like many since the invention of the motorcar, was used by delivery lorries rather than dray horses and carts. Beneath the first-floor windows were large barn doors where horses would once have been stabled. Like most of the mews houses in London the Duke of Wellington's stables had been converted into garages. Ena knocked on the door marked Private.

After several minutes she heard a key turn in the lock and a bolt slide back with a clunk.

'Mr Walters?' Ena enquired.

A ruddy-faced, rotund figure of a man wearing a cellarman's apron rubbed the sleep from his eyes. 'Yes, what can I do for you, Miss?'

'Mrs Green.' Ena gave Mr Walters her card.

He held it at arm's length before moving it nearer to his face. 'Need my reading glasses,' he said, pointing his thumb over his shoulder in the direction of the hotel's interior.

'I'm representing Mrs Hardy. I believe, until yesterday, she was an employee of yours.'

'Doreen was, yes...' He lifted the card up to his face and squinted. 'Who did you say you were?'

'Ena Green, Dudley Green Associates, Private Investigators. Mrs Hardy is my client.'

'Then you'd better come in,' Mr Walters said, holding the door open for Ena to enter first. She stood to one side and when Mr Walters had closed and locked the door, followed him into an untidy room cluttered with old newspapers. 'You'll have to excuse the mess.' He picked up a teacup and an ashtray from an occasional table next to a well-used settee, which he cleared of several newspapers. Ena sat down. Mr Walters removed more newspapers from the armchair before lowering himself into it.

'I'll get straight to the point, Mr Walters. Mrs Hardy told me that she has been falsely accused of theft. She swears she did not steal your money and, as I know her to be an honest woman of good character, I believe her.'

Mr Walters nodded. 'I didn't think she'd stolen the money, but it was in her coat pocket and—'

'You assumed she had taken it?'

He nodded again.

'Would you show me where the money is usually kept?'

Mr Walters crossed the room to a walnut bureau, took a watchchain with a brass key on it from the breast pocket of his waistcoat, unlocked the bureau and pulled down the lid, turning the piece of furniture into a writing desk. He pulled a black and red metal cash box the size of a large writing pad from the back of the bureau and placed it on the top. 'I put the morning's takings and the night's takings in here.' He opened the box using a small key that he took from beneath a red cash book in a drawer in the middle of the bureau. 'I count it, make a note of how much I put in the tin,' he lifted a bank deposit book, 'and then lock it.' Ena watched him put the key back in the drawer and the cash book on top of it.

'And you do the same every day?'

'And night.'

'When do you bank the money?'

'Usually Monday morning, first thing. But because it's been so warm at night these last few weeks I've taken a stroll and deposited it in the bank's night safe. I didn't know money was missing until the bank telephoned to inform me the amount written on the bank deposit slip didn't tally with the money banked. I'd been adding the money up and writing down how many tens, fivers, pound and ten-shilling notes there were, then bagging up the silver and coppers and writing it in the bank book. I do that every night and then there's only Sunday's takings to put in. As I said, if it's a nice night and I finish early, I walk it round to Barclays myself.'

'If you don't mind me asking, how much money do you have in your bureau at the moment?'

He consulted the bank deposit book. 'Fifty-three pounds.'

'And that would be what, twenty, thirty notes?'

Mr Walters nodded. 'Give or take.'

'Has there been more than fifty pounds stolen in any one week?'

'No. Last week the bank said there was a

difference of twenty pounds, the week before, fifteen.'

'Good. Then I suggest you mark twenty pounds of the money you have in the bureau. Make a small hole in each note with a pin. Prick the plume on Britannia's helmet or make a tiny hole on the end of George's spear. Vary it, so it isn't easy to see, but keep a record. A different place on ten-shilling notes, pound notes and five-pound notes. A small hole in the eye of St. George's dragon wouldn't be seen unless the thief held the note up to the light. But why would they? Put the marked notes back in the bureau and whatever you take from now until you go to the bank, put underneath the marked money. You never know, some of the notes might turn up in the till in the public bar within a couple of days. If they do, keep a list of how many come back, the value of them and the date.'

'You don't think it's someone I know?'

'You thought it was Mrs Hardy and you know her.'

'No, I didn't think it was Doreen. Dolly said she'd seen her put some money in her pocket and when I asked Doreen about it, she went to her coat, put her hand in the pocket and there were four five-pound notes in it. Doreen looked as shocked as I was. She stood and stared at the money for some time before pushing it into my hands. She swore she hadn't taken it. She said someone must have put it in her coat pocket because she didn't.'

'No, Mr Walters, she didn't.'

'I shouldn't have listened to Dolly.'

'Perhaps not, but you did and it's too late now. There's a chance that whoever is stealing your money is being overly generous with it. Have any of the staff been into the bar at night with friends, buying rounds for them?' Walters shook his head. 'Has anyone brought friends here to eat?'

Mr Walters cast his eyes down thoughtfully and shook his head again. 'No.'

'Don't worry. We'll soon know who is stealing from you,' Ena said, standing up and preparing to leave. 'So, mark the notes as I suggested and let's catch this thief.'

With a broad smile on his face, Mr Walters said, 'Thank you, Mrs Green.'

'No need to thank me, Mr Walters, I'm doing this for Mrs Hardy, to whom I owe a great deal.'

***

Ena took the glass that George's father had been drinking from out of her handbag and put it on the floor where she'd found it. A second later, there was a tap on the door and a young nurse entered. She looked nervous.

'I understand you want to see me, Miss Derby-Bloom?'

'Yes, thank you for coming, Nurse McKinlay. This is my friend, Ena Green. She'd like to ask you some questions.'

The nurse looked at Ena and nodded.

'Hello, Nurse McKinlay,' Ena said with a smile. She picked the glass up from the floor and put it on the bedside cabinet. 'Can you tell me what was in this glass?'

'Lemon and barley cordial – and water, of course. Mr Derby-Bloom enjoyed a glass at breakfast. It helped his digestion. Several patients drink it as a tonic. Some of our patients don't have much of an appetite, so lemon and barley water is a source of nourishment.'

'How did Mr Derby-Bloom's cordial end up in his bedroom?'

'After breakfast, he took it through to the resident's lounge as he always did. When he asked to go back to his room, he asked me to bring his cordial.'

'He *asked* to go back to his room? Do patients need permission to go to their rooms?'

'No, but Mr Derby-Bloom said he wanted to lie down. When I helped him out of his chair, he was fine and walked back to his room unaided. I picked up the cordial from the table and carried it for him.'

'So had he already drunk some of the cordial before he went to his room?'

'Yes, about half. Some with breakfast and some afterwards, but it couldn't have been the cordial that made your father ill,' the nurse said, turning to George, 'I poured it myself. One-part lemon barley and three parts water. Mrs Thornton had the same and she was fine.' Nurse McKinlay's eyes filled. 'It couldn't have been the cordial,' she said again, wiping her tears.

'I'm sure it wasn't the cordial that made him ill,' Ena said, 'not if Mrs —?'

'Mrs Thornton and Mr Derby-Bloom got on really well. They sat together at mealtimes.'

'And Mrs Thornton was with him in the lounge when he began to feel unwell?'

'For a short time, yes. Her granddaughter came to visit her. She wanted to talk to Mrs Thornton about a private matter she said, so they went to her room. When her granddaughter left, I popped in to see if Mrs Thornton wanted anything. She said she didn't, but she was tired and was going to rest.'

'She was tired. She didn't feel ill after drinking the cordial?'

'No. At least she didn't say she felt ill.'

'Have you seen her today?'

'At breakfast and again at lunch.'

'She didn't suffer any ill effects after drinking the lemon barley water?'

'None.' The nurse's eyes sparkled with tears and she wiped them again with the back of her hand. 'She was devastated when I told her Mr Derby-Bloom had died. They had become good friends.'

Ena put her hand on the nurse's forearm. 'What happened to Mr Derby-Bloom was not your fault. Do you understand?' Ena looked at George, who nodded in agreement.

Nurse McKinlay sniffed and nodded. 'Yes,' she whispered.

'Thank you for looking after my father,' George added.

'It was a pleasure.' Nurse McKinlay looked from Ena to George, and, appearing to take George's thanks as a cue to leave, left the room.

CHAPTER NINE

'Inspector?'

Ena leapt from her chair and ran across the room. 'Inspector Powell. How lovely to see you,' she said, shaking his hand. 'I've been meaning to telephone and ask you to come over and see the office. Sit down, sit down. Artie's making a cup of coffee. Artie?' Ena called, 'we have a visitor.'

Artie poked his head around the kitchen door and grinned. 'Hello, Inspector. You're not here to see me, are you?'

'Not today, Artie.'

Artie raised the back of his hand up to his brow. 'In that case, I'll make you a cup of coffee.'

'The old place has certainly changed.' Inspector Powell said.

'It needed to. The cold case office was very ... sterile,' Ena said.

'Dowdy,' Artie corrected, carrying in a tray of tea cups and a plate of biscuits which he put down on Ena's desk.

'Good to see you and Ena working together again,' the inspector said, putting out his hand.

Before shaking the inspector's hand, Artie whispered, loudly, 'We're working together, alright, but she won't actually give me a job. I'm only, what did you call it yesterday and again today?' he asked Ena. 'Oh yes, holding the fort!' Artie put his hand up to the side of his mouth and whispered, 'Put a good word in for me, will you, Inspector?'

'Help yourself to sugar,' Ena said, pretending she hadn't heard Artie's aside and pushed the bowl of sugar towards the DI.

The telephone began to ring. Artie jumped up. 'I'll get it.'

'He's worth his weight in coffee, but I don't have the money to pay him,' Ena whispered. She took a drink of her coffee with one ear on the telephone call.'

'That was Doreen,' Artie said, replacing the telephone receiver on its base. 'She hasn't heard anything and will be here in the morning as arranged.' Having passed on the message, Artie went into the kitchen.

'Thank you for referring Mrs Hardy to me, Inspector.'

'I'd have been happy to help her, but she didn't want the Met officially involved.'

'And as you're a DI in the Met...' The rest of the sentence Inspector Powell was aware of and she let it trail off.

'She told me that she'd been accused of theft where she worked and that the stolen money was in her coat pocket. I believed her when she said she hadn't stolen it.' The inspector laughed. 'She wanted my advice because she said I'd been good about the mischief her boys got up to last year.'

'She meant you'd ignored the fact that they'd taken money from Helen Crowther to say they'd seen Henry's car outside the office when Crowther killed herself?'

'That's about the size of it.'

'I'm glad you sent her to me. I'm hoping that by looking into the theft – and clearing her name – it will go some way to thanking her for what she and her boys did for Henry. If Doreen hadn't brought the boys to Bow Street and made them confess that they hadn't seen Henry's car, he'd have hanged for a murder he didn't commit. Henry owes Doreen Hardy his life.'

The inspector took a drink of his coffee. 'Is it a lot of money that's missing?'

'Not really. Thirty-five pounds, as far as I know.'

'Suspects?'

'A waitress named Dolly is jealous of the friendship between the hotel manager and Mrs Hardy. There's nothing in it of course. The manager's just a nice man as far as I can tell. The waitress had her nose put out of joint when the manager offered to train Mrs Hardy to be a barmaid, a job the waitress had been coveting. I'm going back to the hotel later this afternoon to see if any marked notes have come into the till of the public bar since I was last there. According to Mrs Hardy, Dolly frequents the hotel bar when she isn't working.' Ena gave DI Powell a quirky grin. 'I met her the day I came to see you. I haven't decided yet whether she's a hard case or whether she felt threatened by me and was being defensive. Either way, she's a feisty madam.'

'She might have been drinking.'

'According to Doreen, she does drink.'

'Let me know if I can do anything to help. Doreen's a decent woman. I wish there were more like her.'

'Have you had the result of the cordial I gave you; the supposed lemon and barley from the nursing home?'

'Not yet. I'll chase it up and let you know as soon as I get it.'

'So, is this is a social call?'

'Not exactly.'

'Then what can I do for you?'

'I have a job for you, but with thieves and poisoners to investigate, you may not have the time.'

'For you, I'll make time. Is it a personal matter? I

mean, with you coming to me instead of using the Met's resources.'

'It isn't personal to me, but it is personal to a friend who I trust and respect. Do you need to know the name of the person before you take the job?'

'No.' Ena shook her head. 'If you trust the person that's good enough for me.'

'Thank you, Ena. I've been asked to make private enquiries into an art gallery. The gallery owner, Giselle Aubrey, is the goddaughter of my friend, which is why I'd like you to investigate the setup, unofficially. Depending on your findings, I may have to make it official, but for now, I just want you to go to the gallery and have a look round, meet a few people. I'd go myself, but Giselle knows me. I don't want to alarm her by telling her I think someone involved with the gallery could be an art thief. Let me explain. There's been a spate of art thefts, mainly from offices in and around Covent Garden. Recently two paintings were stolen from private individuals and one was stolen from the German Embassy. All three were replaced by forgeries. Neither of the house owners knew their paintings had been stolen. One was in storage because the owners were moving home, and the other couple had been away on holiday. They didn't realise for some weeks after they got back because the painting had been replaced by a forgery. The same with the painting that came out of storage, that had also been replaced by a forgery.

'The MO's aren't the same. Someone with a German accent told the guy on the front desk at the German Embassy that the painting was being taken away to be cleaned. It was wrapped in thick brown paper and carried out of the building in the middle of the afternoon. Two weeks later the same man took it back to the Embassy and hung it in its original place. He'd have got away with it too, but for the guy whose office door is opposite the painting. He noticed there was something different about it, argued that it was not because it had been recently cleaned, and got an expert in. By the time the painting was confirmed as a forgery, several weeks had passed and any trail that there might have been, had gone cold.'

'If the man on the desk at the German Embassy remembered the man taking the painting to be cleaned had a German accent, did he remember anything else about him? Could he describe him or remember what he was wearing?'

'No. He only remembered the thief's accent,' Inspector Powell said, shaking his head.

Ena sat back in her seat. 'You don't think the forgeries could be anything to do with Horst Villiers? Do you remember me telling you about the phoney uncle of Frieda and Walter Voight who Henry knew when he shared a cottage with Walter while they were at university, and again when he worked undercover and went on the run with Walter at the end of the war?'

'No. Villiers has been off the radar since '46. He'd have hightailed it back to Germany.' The inspector's brow furrowed. 'No...' he said again.

'Do I detect the smallest degree of doubt in your voice?'

'Anything is possible, but why would Villiers risk coming back to England where he's wanted by military intelligence?'

'You're right, he wouldn't. I don't think he'd be that stupid. Sorry, I interrupted you. What have thefts in a private house and at the German Embassy got to do with the goddaughter of your friend's art gallery?'

'An oil painting, one of a set of four, by the 18th

Century artist, William Hogarth, was mislaid while being transported from The Savoy to the art gallery. The gallery is exhibiting paintings and antique jewellery in advance of an auction later in the month. Until last week the four paintings – called the Four Times Of Day – had hung in The Savoy. The ground floor of the hotel is being decorated and the paintings had hung in the private office of the outgoing manager. The new manager, a young chap, wants to put his mark on the place and likes modern works of art. No one realised the value of the paintings until the manager took an art dealer who was a guest at the hotel to see them.'

'Was the art dealer German?'

'No, American.'

Ena exhaled. 'Private houses, hotels, embassies – I wonder what the common denominator is here. There must be one. German and American accents?' she mused. 'It isn't difficult to put on a German accent or an American one for that matter. However,' Ena shook her head, 'there has to be more than one thief. If all the thefts were carried out by the same person, he'd have to be Houdini. No, there are at least two people involved in the thefts, if not more.'

'I suspect the American and German – if they are different people – are part of a bigger gang.'

'I agree. Whoever is pulling the strings may not even be in London. Or England for that matter.'

'Can the manager of The Savoy describe the American art dealer he showed the paintings to?'

'Yes, but his description is sketchy. The receptionist on duty the day the American left The Savoy remembered him.' Ena put her cup down to concentrate. 'Average height and she thinks he had brown hair. He wore a lightweight, stone coloured raincoat and a grey trilby. She said he didn't have a strong American accent and at first thought he was Canadian.'

'Or he's an American who has lived in London a long time.'

'It was impossible to tell his nationality from the hotel register. His name was Bartholomew Hudson.'

Ena laughed. 'If that's his real name, I'll eat my hat. And if it is, he could be from anywhere. Bartholomew shortened to Bart, sounds American. Hudson on the other hand is very English. Either way he's no fool. German for one sting and American for another.'

'And I don't think he's finished. He's got away with several thefts that we know of, but there could be others that haven't yet been reported.'

'They may never be reported, if the forgeries are good.'

'He's clever, but if he carries on stealing there's every chance we'll get him. Thieves don't usually give up when they're on a roll as lucrative as this one. Anyway, the security guard from the gallery boxed up four paintings.'

'And only three arrived?'

'Good guess. But the missing painting turned up. It was brought into Bow Street the following day and left by the desk sergeant's hatch.'

'Anyone see who left it?'

'The desk sergeant. But, like the German at the Embassy and the American at The Savoy, there was nothing memorable about him. Again, average height, brown hair. He was wearing a lightweight mackintosh and a brown trilby. The only thing the sergeant was sure about was the man spoke with an American accent. Apparently, he pushed in front of a woman the sergeant was dealing with, saying he'd found a painting in the alley at the back of The Savoy.'

'He said a *painting*?'

'Yes.'

'Wasn't it wrapped up?'

'Yes, in the same thick brown paper the other three were wrapped in and then in a wooden crate.'

'Then how did he know it was a painting?'

'He couldn't know. Unless he'd seen it.'

'Exactly. So,' Ena said, her eyes sparkling with interest, 'what do you want me to do?'

'The Hogarth was stolen en route from The Savoy Hotel to La Galerie Unique, the gallery that was commissioned to exhibit it before taking it to be auctioned. Therefore, the responsibility lies with the gallery owner. The young woman who owns the gallery knows if word got out that a painting had gone missing while it was in her care, she would lose a lot of business. The art world generates a great deal of money – and some of it is under the counter, if you get my meaning? Documentation confirming a painting's authenticity – its previous owners' history – goes with the artwork to prove it's genuine. If a painting is stolen and there's no documentation, it means its provenance isn't known, and the painting plummets in price.'

'A collector wouldn't spend thousands on something that wasn't the real thing, surely? Unless the document proving its provenance is also a forgery.'

'That's right. Some art collectors would still have a painting authenticated by an expert. Don't quote me, but I'm told that some collectors in the Middle East will buy works of art for their private collections – no questions asked. They don't require a receipt of purchase. As long as there's a certificate of provenance, that's all that matters.'

'I don't see the point of that. Why own a painting you can't show anyone?'

'Apparently, it's very exciting to own a piece of art that no one but yourself can look at.'

'Not exciting for the people who have had their painting stolen.'

'For them, depending on the value of the painting, it can be a huge financial loss. It's even worse for an art gallery. If the Hogarth that was brought into us is found to be a forgery, La Galerie Unique, who was responsible for the painting when it was stolen would have to make an insurance claim, which means their insurance premium would go up to an unaffordable price; that's if the insurance company pays out of course. If they don't, the gallery would be sued for the amount the stolen painting was worth, plus the insurance company's time and several other inconveniences. In this young woman's case, it would mean the gallery would have to close. Even if the insurance company paid up, it would still mean a huge financial loss.'

'As well as the loss of trust and respect. Do you know who she's insured with?'

'Galbraith. They're a big insurance company. They specialise in insuring the contents of museums and art galleries in London.'

Ena had heard of Galbraith. 'You said *if* the insurance company paid up? Why wouldn't they?'

'Security, or the lack of it, is one of the main reasons. They won't pay out if the gallery's security isn't good enough – and that covers transporting paintings as well as in-house security. If everything is secure and the insurance investigators can't find anything wrong, they pay out. Then, as I said, the premiums go up sky high.'

'Either way, a small gallery can't win.'

DI Powell shook his head. 'La Galerie Unique has an exhibition of 18th Century masters, as well as modern paintings and jewellery on Saturday night. It's invitation only and the owner has given me two tickets.'

'And you'd like me to accompany you?'

'What I'd like is immaterial. What I need comes from the top.' Ena looked quizzically at the inspector. 'I need you and Henry to go to the exhibition.'

Ena laughed. 'And here's me thinking you'd gone all arty on me.'

'I'd be a fish out of water in an art gallery. Henry, on the other hand, having been an artist, wouldn't. I was hoping he'd have a look at the paintings exhibited – and in particular, the Hogarth that went missing overnight. Giselle Aubrey is certain it's authentic, but to put her godfather's mind at rest, I suggested she had it authenticated by a professional before it went to auction. She'll have to do that, but she's adamant that she wouldn't have it authenticated before the exhibition on Saturday night because word would get around and other sellers might pull out. Eventually, I persuaded her not to exhibit the Hogarth until Henry had looked at it.'

'I can see why she's worried.' Ena frowned. 'I'm sure Henry would enjoy the exhibition but it's been a while since he was an artist. I don't think he has painted seriously since before the war. But, you know Henry, he'll do what he can.'

'Thank him for me,' Inspector Powell said. 'You'll like Giselle Aubrey, she's a bit highly strung, but she's a clever young woman. I hope for the sake of my friend that she isn't mixed up in the thefts. I came away wondering whether she might know more about the Hogarth than she was letting on.'

Inspector Powell took two tickets for the Saturday night's exhibition at the La Galerie Unique from his inside pocket and gave them to Ena. 'I'm hoping that while Henry is looking at the paintings, you'll have a look at the potential buyers for me.'

'What am I looking for?'

'I don't know. It's an alien world to me. Art lovers are not the type of people I socialise with.'

'And I socialise in the art world all the time,' Ena said laughing. 'Seriously though, if the gallery owner, who is an art dealer, can't tell if it's a forgery, how is Henry supposed to tell.'

'I can see that would be a problem, if...'

'What aren't you telling me, Inspector?'

The DI looked sheepish. 'Because the gallery owner isn't an expert, she's just starting out – and like I said, she's adamant that she won't have an accredited art expert in to authenticate the paintings before the opening on Saturday night, I might have led her to believe that before the war *my friend* Henry was something of an art expert and he would be able to tell if the painting was a forgery.'

Ena laughed. 'Not much pressure on Henry then.'

'It might be best not to tell him too much. On the other hand...'

'Leave Henry to me. He'll enjoy an evening at an art gallery, I know I will. And for me, it'll be a chance to get dressed up,' Ena said, waving the tickets in the air.

***

'How do you fancy going out on Saturday night?' Ena asked Henry. 'We could have something to eat in

Leicester Square or Soho and go to a preview night of a new exhibition at an art gallery.' Ena fanned herself with the tickets Inspector Powell had given her.

'Art gallery? Since when have you been interested in art?'

'Since I was given free *invitation only* tickets to a viewing of art in a swish new gallery called La Galerie Unique in Covent Garden.' Henry laughed. 'I like art!' Ena said, pretending to be offended. 'I enjoyed the exhibition at The National Gallery last year. I was fascinated by the different kinds of paintings.'

'You couldn't wait to get out of the place and find a café.'

'That was because it was in the middle of the afternoon on a very hot day and my feet were killing me. I needed to take the weight off them for a while, that's all. Saturday there'll be different works of art. As well as paintings there'll be jewellery, and, it will be the first time this particular exhibition will be open to the public. Well, not the public, buyers and collectors. It's in the evening so it'll be cooler and I'll wear comfortable shoes.'

Henry laughed again. 'So, why exactly do you want to go on Saturday night?'

'Inspector Powell wants you to look at the paintings to see if you can spot any forgeries, but the painting he really wants you to look at is a Hogarth that went missing for twenty-four hours. The gallery owner needs to know if it's authentic before it's added to the collection that's going to be auctioned. It's one of four paintings called Four Times Of The Day that's being sold by The Savoy.'

'Why authenticate only one. If it's part of Four Times Of The Day, why not authenticate them all?'

'Because three arrived at the gallery safely, but

one went missing and turned up at the back of the hotel by the dustbins. A passer-by, or a member of an art theft gang, who knows – he didn't stick around long enough to be questioned – took it to Bow Street Police Station. He said he'd found it.'

Henry put down his knife and fork. 'Go on.'

'Well, a number of paintings have been reported stolen in the past few months. The problem is, the owners didn't know their paintings had been stolen because they'd been replaced by forgeries.'

Henry leaned back in his chair. 'Good God!'

'One painting was stolen from a private house while the owners were away on holiday, and another was stolen while it was in storage. The owners of that painting didn't know until they moved into their new home.'

'And that too was replaced by a forgery?'

'Yes. And a painting was carried out of the German Embassy without anyone turning a hair. It was also replaced by a forgery which, Inspector Powell said, was also very good.'

'And Powell wants me to take a look at the Hogarth that went missing?'

'Yes. Would you be able to tell?'

'He isn't asking for much, your friend Inspector Powell.' Ena tutted. 'But, forged oils are quite easy to spot. There should be slight bumps or paint waves on a canvas. And if there's a significant amount of texture, there's a good chance the painting is authentic. A flat surface probably means it's a forgery. The colours are often different too. Forgeries are a combination of new colours mixed together to make the paintings appear old. Also, old frames have an X or a H shape in the back, modern frames don't. I won't be able to see the back of the frames if they're already being exhibited but then the back isn't that difficult to reproduce anyway.' Henry exhaled loudly. 'Okay, we'll go to the exhibition. Whether I'll be able to tell if any of the paintings are forgeries is another matter.'

'Inspector Powell said it was him or you, and you know a heck of a lot more about art than he does.'

Henry left the table and went out of the room. 'I have a book on Hogarth. I'll fish it out.'

Ena cleared the dishes and took them into the kitchen. By the time she'd washed up and returned to the sitting room, Henry had poured them both a glass of whisky and was flicking through the pages of a book about Hogarth.

'I'm looking forward to going to the art exhibition,' Ena said, picking up her glass and holding it at arms-length before sweeping the air with it and taking a drink. 'It'll make a change to get dressed up and mingle with the arty set of Covent Garden.' She gasped. 'I don't have anything to wear.' Henry looked at her over the top of his glass. 'What? I don't have anything suitable! I'll just have to buy something,' she said, to which Henry laughed.

CHAPTER TEN

'I'm nipping down to Oxford Street. I need something to wear to go to the art gallery tomorrow night, I won't be long.'

'I'll come with you. It's been quiet all morning. Besides, I don't want you buying something your mother would wear.'

'Cheeky b!' Ena swiped Artie's cup from his desk and took it and her own into the kitchen. 'There's really no need.'

'Au contraire,' Artie said, 'there is every need.'

'Alright, but no bullying me into buying something I'd look ridiculous in – and nothing too short.'

It was fun shopping with Artie. Apart from anything else, he loved shopping. Ena, on the other hand hated it, especially clothes shopping.

'Ooo, look at this,' Artie said, steering Ena past John Lewis to a small shop called a boutique. 'This is new. And look at that fab frock in the window.'

'I'm not wearing that!' said, Ena, commenting on the orange, yellow and black striped mini-dress, white patent boots and boater. 'Too short, I'm not a teenager.' She wrinkled her nose. 'I'd look like a bumblebee in it. A fat bumblebee too. Stripes going round the body makes anyone look bigger.' She took a step back and viewed the outfit from a distance. 'Or a Rugby player. If I looked down they'd think I was going into a scrum, not view paintings at an art gallery.'

'That is only one dress. There'll be dozens inside.' Artie left Ena standing on the pavement and swanned into the shop. 'What about this?' he said when Ena joined him. He took a black and white check dress from the rack. 'This is just you. Well, a younger version of you.'

'I like it. The checks are a bit loud, but I could wear a little black jacket with it to calm it down.'

'Black jacket, with white patent boots and hat,' Artie said. 'You'll look wonderful. You must try it on.'

'I will. Hang onto it. I like this dress.' Ena took down an orangey-red and cream dress. Cream at the top, red at the bottom. 'I like the colour and it's A-line, it's a bit short but at least I won't have to breathe in all night.' She gave it to Artie to hold. 'What about this one?'

'Noooooooo... gathered skirts went out with the last decade. Box pleats are okay,' he said, taking a darker red dress down. 'Not my favourite, but worth a try.'

Ena looked at her watch. 'We've been ages, I'd better try them on,' she said, leading the way to the changing rooms. She took the dresses from Artie, giving him her handbag. 'Hang onto this. I'll put each dress on and you tell me what you think.'

The first dress, the black and white check, was very short. Ena came out of the changing rooms and into the shop. 'What do you think?' She turned around.

'It fits. But,' Artie said, putting his hand up to his chin, 'There's something about it that doesn't look quite right. He levelled the shoulders. 'No, it isn't right. Try the next one.'

Ena was secretly pleased that Artie didn't like the dress. It was far too short. Maybe if she was in her early twenties, she thought, pulling the dress over her head. She put it back on its hanger and looked at it again. No, not even then. 'What about this,' she said, strutting out into the shop like a model.

'I love it. It's just you. I love the colours; the cream at the top shows off your hair, and I love the way the collar sits away from your neck. Yes! that's the one.'

'I like it the best too. I like the other red dress, but not as much as this one, so I won't bother trying it on. This,' she said, catching sight of herself in a full-length mirror on the wall and twirling, 'is the one.'

'Boots?'

'In this weather? No. I have a pair of cream kitten heels at home. They'll go perfectly with it, and, because it has short sleeves there's no need for a jacket.'

Having paid for the dress, Ena left the shop. She turned to Artie to again tell him how much she loved the dress, but he wasn't with her. Squinting in the bright sunshine, she could just make out his frame against a mirror.

'Artie?'

'Ena, you have to try this on. It's just right for the gallery viewing.'

'What, trousers?'

'Don't be so provincial. It's an evening trouser suit. Very arty, very fashionable, and it could be very you.'

'Artie I don't have time to try it now. We've been out of the office for an hour and a half.'

'Stop making excuses. Put it on, it'll take two minutes.' Artie pushed the trouser suit into Ena's arms.

'Alright,' she agreed, returning to the changing room. When she had slipped the outfit on and looked in the mirror, Ena fell in love with it. 'Well?' she said, dancing out of the changing room onto the shop floor.

'I love it. It's just you.'

Ena looked at the price and swallowed. 'Thirty-four pounds ten shillings?' she said, unable to keep the shock out of her voice. I can't afford that. I can hear Henry sighing now.'

'Will he disapprove?'

'No. It's just that we've spent a lot of money getting the office renovated and decorated and now we're spending on the flat upstairs.' She chewed on her bottom lip. 'But I do love it.'

'Then have it!' Artie said, sighing.

Ena gave the assistant thirty-five pounds and held out a shaking hand for the ten shillings change.

'Keep the receipt, madam, in case you need to bring the garment back,' the assistant said.

'She won't be bringing it back,' Artie replied, taking the paper carrier bag from the assistant.

***

Raised voices attracted Ena's attention. She looked over her shoulder to where two men; one slightly built, medium height, in his mid-thirties and sounding American was arguing with an older man in his late forties, early fifties; a Londoner by the sound of his accent. Taller and much bigger, the older man was backing away from the younger one, who was jabbing his finger at him threateningly. Ena strained to hear what the men were saying but only caught the words of the American, "own" and "buddy".

'Ena, you have the tickets. Ena?' Henry said again, 'the tickets.'

'What? Oh, I'm sorry, I…' Ena fished the tickets that DI Powell had given her out of her handbag and handed them to a giant of a man of about thirty with broad square shoulders that appeared to be horizontal from his thick neck. He had the type of build Ena imagined a heavyweight boxer to have.

'Welcome to La Galerie Unique, Madam, Sir,' he said holding the door open for Ena and Henry to pass through.

'Did you hear that barney the two men outside were having?' Ena whispered, when they were inside the gallery.

'No, I was keeping our place in the queue.' Henry tutted. 'It's none of our business.'

'I know, but one of the men was American and Inspector Powell said the man who found the missing Hogarth and took it to Bow Street was an American. That's why I was listening. I wasn't being nosy.'

Henry turned to Ena and raised his eyebrows. 'Of course you weren't, darling.'

Standing in line behind a dozen or more art lovers – buyers and collectors – the men in black ties, the women in long flowing arty designer dresses, Ena and Henry shuffled slowly into a large square room. 'So, this is preview night?' Ena said as the cluster of excited people immediately in front of them dispersed in every direction to view paintings in the gallery's other rooms.

'It certainly is,' Henry agreed. 'This is the night the seriously rich get to view the art that's for sale and make private offers before it goes to auction. The place reeks of money.'

'And expensive perfume.' Ena laughed. 'There's so much of both, you'd have a hard time distinguishing one smell from the other.' Ena took a glass of champagne for herself and one for Henry from a waitress weaving in and out of the crowd, thanked her and kept moving forward until she was able to break ranks and find a space without someone exclaiming with amazement at the paintings they were viewing.

'Good Lord,' Ena said, looking at a price tag of twenty thousand pounds alongside a painting that to her looked as if someone had carelessly splashed brightly coloured paint over a large canvas.

'Collecting works of art is an expensive game. For some people, it's the love of beautiful things, for other's a hobby and for some, it's a business. Some people spend their lives going to galleries on preview night in the hopes of finding a valuable masterpiece at a low price, then they match the price hoping it won't increase at the auction.' Henry scanned the walls. 'Nothing like that here tonight, I'm afraid.'

Ena put her empty glass on the tray of a passing waitress, was offered another glass of bubbly and took it. 'Are you going to start with the oil paintings in here while I mingle?'

Henry declined a second drink. 'Why not?'

Before they'd had time to separate, a distinguished looking woman of around thirty with short black hair cut in a stark bob with a fringe that stopped short of thinly shaped eyebrows, was making her way towards them. 'Hello, you must be Ena and Henry, Giselle Aubrey,' she said, shaking Ena's hand and then Henry's. 'And this,' she announced, waving at a man who was entering the gallery, 'is my mentor, sponsor – and dear friend – Louis Mantel, without whom I would not have my beautiful La Galerie Unique.'

CHAPTER ELEVEN

Ena could hardly believe what Giselle Aubrey was saying. Louis Mantel, her mentor and the gallery's sponsor was one of the men she'd seen outside arguing when she and Henry arrived. She gave Henry a quick sideways look. He lowered his gaze and shook his head very slightly before looking up at Mantel. Ena brought her attention back to what the American was saying.

'You flatter me, Giselle darling.' He took Ena's hand, kissed it and gave Henry a courteous nod. 'It is Giselle who is the art connoisseur. I, alas,' Mantel said, opening his arms, hands palms upward, 'am only the money guy.'

'You are much more than that, darling.' Giselle smiled excitedly into Mantel's eyes. Then turning to Ena, said, 'He is very modest. But the truth is, if it wasn't for Louis there simply wouldn't be a La Gallery Unique.'

'And it is lovely.'

'Thank you, Ena. Now, if I can steal your husband, I have something I'd like him to see.'

'Of course. I shall enjoy looking round without a teacher.' Ena winked at Henry as Giselle put her arm through his and guided him through the crowd.

Louis Mantel offered Ena his arm. 'Shall we?' Ena put her arm through his in the same way that Giselle had to Henry. She smiled nervously as Mantel led her across the crowded room, stopping now and then to say hello, or reply to someone who had spoken to him.

'Your husband is an artist, Giselle tells me?'

'Yes, and a good one, although he hasn't painted for some time. I expect it's because he's busy at work.'

'Perhaps coming here tonight will stir his artistic loins and he will pick up his brush again,' Louis said with a dramatic sweep of his left arm. When they had reached the other side of the room and were no longer hindered by people standing around, Louis turned and faced Ena. Looking into her eyes, he said, 'You have a perfect face, Ena, are you Henry's muse?'

Ena hid her embarrassment by laughing.

'What's funny? I'm not trying to flatter you. I'm not saying you're cute or anything. I'm saying your features are in perfect proportion. You have good bone structure, your eyes are wide, your nose is aquiline and you have good cheekbones. A perfect face for a muse. Are you Henry's muse?' He didn't give Ena time to answer before saying, 'If you're not, you damn well ought to be.'

'I'll tell him what you said, it might encourage him.'

'Or make him jealous.' Louis had become animated. His long hair had flopped forward onto his forehead. 'Okay, Ena, what kind of paintings do you like? Do you like a particular style? Oils or watercolours? Maybe you have a favourite artist.'

She had neither and knew very little about art so there was no point in pretending she did. 'No, Louis. Either I like a painting, or I don't. If I do like something it's usually because of the combination of colours used. To be honest, I know nothing about art, though I admire those who do.'

'I ought to go to the office, see what the verdict is on the Hogarth. Will you be okay on your own, Ena?'

'Of course. And by the time I've been in every room and looked at every painting, I'll know which style of painting, or artist I like best.'

Louis laughed raucously and kissed Ena on both

cheeks. 'I'll see you later and I'll ask you again which painting you like the best, okay?'

'Okay.'

Ena didn't like people who talked about money. In her experience, it often meant they didn't have any. Louis Mantel, however, was probably the person to prove Ena's theory wrong. To finance a set up like La Galerie Unique he had to have money – and a lot of it.

Ena couldn't get Mantel out of her mind. He was charming and he had made her laugh, but the man who took the painting that had gone missing between The Savoy and the gallery into Bow Street was also an American? But then there were a lot of Americans in London. A lot had gone home to the States when the war ended, and later when they closed the peace-keeping aerodromes like Bruntingthorpe near Foxden, where she was brought up, some had come back to England to marry girls they'd fallen for while they were based in England. Ena dismissed the thought as a coincidence. Louis was a complex character, charming to her, but angry and threatening to the man he was earlier arguing with outside.

She wandered around on her own quite happily, mingling, chatting about art and when others talked about paintings she appeared interested. She listened openly when being included in conversations and eavesdropped when she wasn't – all the time hoping one of them would say something suspicious, although because of the artistic language they used – and Ena's lack of knowledge – everything sounded suspicious.

She ventured into other rooms. One, an oblong shape, was wall-to-wall with modern paintings. Most of the artists were unknown to Ena. Some names were French, others looked like Dutch, but most were English.

'I love giving unknown artists wall space to show their work,' Giselle said, suddenly at Ena's side. 'And, if one or two paintings have offers made on them in advance of the auction, I shall be delighted for the artists.'

'From what I've seen you have a wide variety of the highest standard of work by new artists. It's most impressive,' Ena said, repeating what she'd heard someone say a minute or two earlier.

'Thank you for saying so, Ena. But,' her dark eyes twinkling with excitement, 'my plan – and it's a long way off – is to exhibit the works of Cezanne, Braque, Matisse and Picasso.' Giselle sighed. 'And to own one of the new Pop Art paintings.'

Ena felt the heat of a blush rise from her neck to her cheeks. 'I'm afraid you'll have to forgive me. Although I enjoy looking at paintings and I appreciate the talent, the time and effort that goes into creating a beautiful piece of art, I only recognise the work of more popular artists like Monet and Picasso,' Ena said, surprising herself by plucking the names of two famous artists out of thin air. 'Henry, as you know, is the artist in our family. I don't know what Pop Art is.'

'And why should you?' Giselle was being generous, Ena thought. 'Although Pop Art has been around for the last two hundred years – portraying the popular culture of the time – it wasn't until the beginning of the 1950s that it was revived. In simple terms, it is the integration of high and low art, a mix of fine art and popular culture. One day I shall own a Demuth or a Paolozzi!' Neither names meant anything to Ena. Giselle raised her glass in a toast to the idea. 'But, I have my feet firmly on the ground. I know that day is in the distant future. For now, this,' she said, swaying from left to right and holding her glass aloft before draining it, 'is a dream come true.'

Ena liked Giselle. She was taken with the young woman's enthusiasm. She watched her weave in and out of friends and fellow art lovers, smiling and chatting, and beckoning waitresses to fill up the glasses of her guests with a smile that lit up the room. Ena felt a pang of sadness for the goddaughter of Inspector Powell's friend. Sadness that whether she was involved with the art thefts or not – and Ena was sure she was not – her dream would end if anyone at the gallery were involved.

Casting her gaze around the room, Ena noticed a middle-aged woman lift the glass lid of a display cabinet and take out a brooch. She then looked around and, unaware that Ena was watching her, unclipped the fastener on her evening bag and dropped the brooch in.

Ena couldn't believe anyone would be so brazen as to steal a valuable piece of jewellery in front of dozens of people. She stood open-mouthed looking at the woman when she realised she herself was being watched by an elderly man with silver hair. He smiled at her, creating soft creases at the corners of startling blue eyes.

The man's smile made Ena feel awkward. She felt as if she had witnessed something very private – had been a fly on the wall of someone's bedroom – instead of the theft of an item of jewellery. She turned away from the man's gaze and, feigning interest in the paintings on the wall nearest to her, made her way across the room to Giselle.

As she approached the gallery owner, she heard Henry assuring her that the painting left at The Savoy and taken to Bow Street Police Station, was a genuine Hogarth.

Giselle threw her arms around Henry's neck. 'So,

can I display it?' Henry nodded. 'Thank you,' she gushed.

The Hogarth being genuine didn't make sense to Ena. Had whoever stole the painting got cold feet and purposely left it at the back of The Savoy, hoping it would be found? Was it a bungled theft, or a genuine oversight? She didn't believe for a second that the men transporting the painting from The Savoy to the gallery had left it behind by mistake. What then?

'Ena?' Giselle gave her a broad smile. 'Did you want me or your wonderful husband?'

'Well done, wonderful husband,' Ena said with a twinkle in her eye. Henry lifted his glass to her. 'It was you who I wanted to speak to.' Ena wished she'd been able to tell Henry what she'd seen before speaking to Giselle. It was too late now; both her husband and the gallery owner were looking at her expectantly.

'I'm sorry to have to tell you, Giselle, but I've just seen a woman in a turquoise dress – early fifties, plump with a pretty face and short fair curly hair – steal a brooch from one of the display cabinets.'

'Did you see which brooch she took?'

'I wasn't close, but I could see it was a coral stone and there were other stones around it.'

'I know the brooch you mean. It's one of the most expensive pieces in the gallery. It was made by the French designer, Gilou Donat.' Giselle looked past Ena. 'If the woman you described wants the brooch, her husband will buy it for her. I assure you she has no need to steal anything. He is very wealthy. And,' Giselle said, 'he is besotted with her.'

He must be, Ena thought. His wife did steal the brooch, both she and the woman's husband saw her. Ena was fascinated to know why someone would steal something that they could so easily have bought, or asked for as a gift.

Giselle moved deftly among clusters of people standing around admiring the paintings, sculptures and jewellery on show. 'Charles,' she said, kissing the distinguished looking man with silver hair and the kind of tan you get from spending long periods in the South of France, not south London.

'This is my friend, Ena. Ena, these lovely people are Priscilla and Charles. Can I help you with anything?'

'Priscilla has taken a shine to the coral and pearl brooch.'

'As always, you have impeccable taste, Priscilla. It is the only one of its kind. There have been no bids made on it, so it's all yours. Would you like to take it with you tonight, or shall I have it sent to you tomorrow?'

The woman's husband looked at her, a smile on his face and love in his eyes.

'I'll take it tonight, please, darling.'

Giselle looked around the gallery, put up her hand and the man who had met Ena and Henry at the door and checked their tickets, made his way across the room to her.

'Victor, would you take the Donat brooch from the showcase and put it in a presentation box.'

'I'd like to wear it now,' Priscilla said.

'Even better. It will look beautiful on your dress,' Giselle turned to Priscilla's husband. 'I'll have Victor bring the box to your office tomorrow with the invoice.'

'Thank you,' he said.

Certain that the case was already unlocked, Ena watched as Victor took a small key from his waistcoat pocket. He inserted the key in the lock, turned it and the case opened. As big as he was, Victor skilfully lifted up the brooch and gave it to the woman who passed it to her husband. He lovingly pinned the brooch of coral and pearls onto her turquoise dress and stepped back. He exclaimed how beautiful she looked and she giggled like an excited child.

Victor, his job done, locked the cabinet. After returning the key to his waistcoat pocket, he straightened his jacket, gave a short nod to his boss and went back to his post by the door.

'I'm going to powder my nose, darling,' Pricilla said to her husband, 'I won't be long.'

I need to spend a penny too, Ena thought and followed her.

Ena was washing her hands when Priscilla exited the toilet. A mirror behind the hand basins ran the length of the wall with a full-length mirror at the end by the door. Ena patted her hair, which had so much setting lotion on it that it hadn't moved. She applied lipstick – she had eaten the first layer, or she'd left it on the champagne glass.

'The brooch is lovely,' Ena said, as Priscilla washed her hands.

'Pretty isn't it?'

'It is. The turquoise of your dress sets off the pink of the coral and the cream of the pearls, perfectly.'

Priscilla dried her hands and moved to look at herself in the full-length mirror as Ena dropped her lipstick into her handbag and headed for the door.

'Have you seen any paintings you like?' Priscilla asked.

'Not yet. To be honest it's my husband who has an eye for art. We'll be moving into a new apartment as soon as it has been renovated and decorated. I'll wait until it's finished, see what wall space there is.'

'How exciting. You'll have a blank canvas to work with, as they say.'

'Yes. I think that will be the time to buy a painting. What about you?'

'I haven't seen anything that takes my fancy, except my brooch,' Priscilla said, stroking the beautiful smooth oval coral. 'I know a good piece of jewellery when I see it, but paintings? Apart from liking or disliking what I see, I know nothing about them. Like your husband, mine also knows about art. I leave anything that hangs on the wall to him. I like what hangs around my neck, can be pinned to my dress or...' She lifted her hands and wiggled her fingers as if she was playing the piano to show Ena a large heart-shaped diamond engagement ring. 'I'm a magpie.' Laughing Priscilla turned her back on the mirror. 'Come on, let's find the men and see what's in the other rooms.'

As they left the Ladies' the two women almost collided with a smiling Louis Mantel who seemed oblivious to everyone in the room. Ena put out her arm to save Priscilla from being knocked over as Louis flew past them and disappeared into the room Giselle had taken Henry to when he looked at the Hogarth.

Giselle followed the excited American into the room and Victor followed her. Some minutes later Louis carried out the two by two and a half feet Hogarth called Night that until fifteen minutes ago was thought to be a forgery, and hung it in the main room beneath Noon and next to Evening. Louis made a meal of standing back and directing Victor to move it a little to the left and then to the right. Ena heard Priscilla sigh. When the American was finally satisfied that the painting was level, he put up his thumb and Priscilla hissed. 'Silly little man.'

CHAPTER TWELVE

A gold plaque on the wall of the Chambers at No 15 Old Bailey listed the names of the barristers who had offices in the building. Sir John Hillary QC was top of the list. Faced with a large black door knocker or a push-bell, Ena chose the bell.

'Mrs Green?' A man in his mid-fifties wearing a smart grey suit, pristine white shirt, plain black tie and highly polished black shoes greeted her with a professional smile as he opened the door. 'Jack Martin,' he said, 'Sir John's clerk.'

'Good morning, Mr Martin.'

'If you'd like to follow me,' the clerk said, in a strong London accent. He led her across a black and white tiled hall to the office of the prosecution barrister in the trial of Shaun O'Shaughnessy. Gold leaf gilded lettering across the frosted glass in the top half of the door read, Sir John Hillary QC, Barrister At Law. Mr Martin gave the door a sharp rap, didn't wait to be asked in but opened it and said, 'Mrs Green, Sir.'

A distinguished looking man, tall and lean, with a head of thick black hair giving way to silver strands at the temples, got to his feet and rounding his desk, approached her. 'How do you do, Mrs Green?'

'How do you do, Sir?' Ena replied, shaking the prosecuting barrister's outstretched hand.

With a swoop of his left arm, Sir John Hillary motioned for Ena to sit in a high-backed maroon leather chair at his desk. Mr Martin followed Ena across the room and sat in a matching chair on Sir John's right. While Sir John settled himself into his chair, his clerk took a notebook and pen from his briefcase, placed them neatly on the corner of his boss' large dark wood desk and clasped his hands on his lap.

'Thank you for coming in so promptly, Mrs Green.' The prosecuting councillor leaned his elbows on the ornate desk and gave Ena a searching, but pleasant, smile. He then looked at his clerk who picked up the pen and pad. 'Before I call you as a prosecution witness in the case of the Crown versus Shaun O'Shaughnessy, tomorrow, I'd like to go through a few things with you.'

Tomorrow? Mr Martin hadn't said anything about her being called as soon as tomorrow when he telephoned. Still, Ena was aware of court procedure and could remember everything that had happened when she met O'Shaughnessy.

'Before we begin, however, is there anything you would like to ask me?'

'Yes, Sir, there is. Why wasn't O'Shaughnessy convicted of treason?'

Sir John took his elbows from the desk and leaned back on the leather backrest of his chair. 'Because he's a German national – a citizen of Berlin to be precise with a German passport, who said he was working for the fatherland – he was found not guilty of treason.'

'Damn the man! He had three passports hidden in the house in Brighton. One was English, one Irish and one German. I should have taken the German one when I had the chance.' Ena was careful not to say it was her sister Claire who had seen the passports and not her. 'O'Shaughnessy had covered every eventuality.'

'That he had.'

'My late colleague Sid Parfitt, who was murdered on Waterloo Bridge two years ago by O'Shaughnessy or Crowther, or both of them, was in Berlin in 1936 covering The Olympics for The Times. He was also working for the intelligence services. He left me clues to find a key and a ticket to retrieve a suitcase that he had deposited in the left-luggage office at Waterloo Station. There were documents in the case that proved Helen Crowther was German. Her real name was Krueger. There were newspaper cuttings of O'Shaughnessy and Crowther, one of O'Shaughnessy on a Hitler Youth march in Berlin and another on a Nazi rally with Helen Crowther. Beneath that photograph were the names, Frau Krueger and Herr Krueger.'

'Could Helen Crowther have been O'Shaughnessy's mother?'

'No. O'Shaughnessy was in his teens. Crowther was older than him, but not old enough to be his mother.'

Ena dropped her gaze. She wondered whether to tell Sir John about Nick Miller. Nick had given her a great deal of help. He'd provided names, dates and places. She chewed her lip thoughtfully and came to the conclusion that, if she was going to tell Sir John about O'Shaughnessy, she needed to tell him about Nick. She looked up at the clerk. His pen was poised.

'Nick Miller, the owner of the Minchin Club in Brighton, an ex-spy, born in Berlin of Austrian parents, told me that Crowther was the wife of his old university lecturer. According to Nick, Professor Martin Krueger had been a high-ranking military man. He was a lot older than Helen. Nick told me Crowther, or Frau Krueger, had an affair with one of her husband's students and bore him a child. Her husband had been a Nazi supporter and close confidant of Hitler's so, fearing for her life, when she found she was pregnant she disappeared. When the child was born, she gave it up for adoption which, Nick said, she had regretted ever since. It was after that Frau Krueger came to England as the spy, Helen Crowther.'

'Could O'Shaughnessy have been the father of her child?'

'No. Nick Miller would have said if he was. Anyway, twenty years later Crowther learned that her illegitimate daughter was also in England.'

'And by then she was the Personal Assistant to the Director of MI5.' Sir John blew out his cheeks and shook his head. 'And you believed this, Nick Miller-?'

'Yes. Her daughter's name was Freida Voight.'

Sir John's eyes widened. 'The double agent your husband handled at MI5?'

'The same,' Ena said, doing her level best to keep her voice even. How did Sir John know Henry had been Frieda's handler? Aware that he was waiting for her to continue, she said, 'Frieda Voight committed suicide and Helen Crowther blamed Henry. She later convinced herself that Henry had killed Frieda.'

'So, in her mind your husband had got away with murder.'

'Which is why Crowther went to inordinate lengths to make her own suicide look as if Henry had killed her. She almost got away with it too.'

A thoughtful silence followed. Then Sir John asked, 'Do you think O'Shaughnessy was involved in Helen Crowther's death?'

'Undoubtedly. They weren't related, but there had been a strong bond between them since 1936.'

'Love?'

'Yes, for the fatherland,' she spat in disgust.

'His cover as an Irish actor was a good one.'

Ena inhaled deeply, swallowing the emotion that threatened to erupt in the form of tears. 'I'd like to see O'Shaughnessy swing for killing my associate Artie

Mallory's friend, Hugh Middleton. Hugh's only crime was being in the wrong place at the wrong time. My friend Sid Parfitt and Mac Robinson too. I don't suppose we'll ever know to what extent O'Shaughnessy was involved with their deaths, but Nick Miller told me he was.'

Sir John shrugged his shoulders. 'I can't promise you we'll get him for the deaths of Parfitt or Robinson, but we'll get him for the murder of Hugh Middleton and the attempted murder of Mrs Robinson. As for treason, because of his German passport there's nothing we can do about that. He swore on oath that the passport in the name of O'Shaughnessy was given to him in Berlin before he came to England, the one in the name of Crowther was given to him by Helen Crowther when he arrived in England – both of them forgeries, but he insisted the German passport was authentic. The Sussex Police had it examined and agreed. O'Shaughnessy may be a murderer, a liar and cheat, but in the eyes of the law he owed the King of England no allegiance. He said he was an honourable man, a patriot who was loyal to his country as McKenzie Robinson was to his.'

'How dare he liken himself to Mac Robinson, the director of MI5. Good God, the man has some nerve. Ena told Sir John Hillary everything she knew about Shaun O'Shaughnessy. She remembered every detail about their first meeting in the house of Helen Crowther, when he appeared out of the blue. A planned meeting by him and Crowther that she now knew was a set up to find out what Ena knew about the murder of her colleague, Sidney Parfitt – and if Sid had left anything that would incriminate either of them.

'At the time of his death, Sid was about to share with me the network of spies and agents he'd unearthed. At Crowther's house, while she was out of the room, O'Shaughnessy tried to intimidate me. He began to flirt with me.' Ena shuddered at the memory. 'As I said, he was intimidating and asked me about someone named Collins. I told him nothing. Later, however, when Crowther and I were at the station before I boarded the train to London, I warned her about him. What a fool I was.'

Sir John changed the subject quickly. 'How did you meet Helen Crowther?'

'I met her after McKenzie Robinson's funeral. I knew of her before then because Henry worked for Mac Robinson. Crowther had been Mac's private secretary before becoming his personal assistant. She worked for Mac for decades. Everyone at MI5 trusted her completely. Her cover was rock solid. She had lived a lie for so long that no one suspected her of being a spy. She even befriended Mac's wife, Eve,' Ena said with distaste. 'She confided in me that she and Mac had been having an affair. She said she had loved him from the day she started working for him and was heartbroken when he died.' Ena looked at Sir John, her eyes sparkling with loathing. 'McKenzie Robinson didn't die from a stroke, as the newspapers reported, Sir John. Mac was murdered. At the time they thought by Frieda Voight, but it was his lover, Helen Crowther who murdered him.'

Sir John Hillary pushed himself out of his chair, strolled over to the window and looked out. 'What I don't understand is, O'Shaughnessy got away with treason because he was a German citizen with a German passport. Why didn't Helen Crowther do the same? Why kill herself?'

'She wouldn't have needed her German passport. She was so high up the food chain if she'd have wanted to get out, Berlin would have got her out. No, Sir John, Helen Crowther didn't kill herself to escape the noose. She was consumed by hate. She took her own life and made it look as if my husband had killed her because she believed he had killed the only person she had ever loved, her daughter.'

'Revenge!' Sir John sighed. 'I've read the case. Even so,' he looked perplexed. 'She would have known that there's nothing personal between a foreign agent and their handler.'

'Frieda Voight, Crowther's daughter, jumped from a church roof. Crowther convinced herself that my husband had killed her.' Tears stung the back of Ena's eyes and she swallowed to rid the sadness she felt. 'I'm sorry, I knew Frieda Voight and I feel partly to blame for her death.'

'Could you elaborate?'

'We had worked together in the war. We worked for an engineering company in the Midlands, making components for a secret communications facility...'

Sir John looked sideways at Mr Martin and after the slightest shake of the head, his clerk stopped writing.

'I exposed her as a spy in '45. Thirteen years later I exposed her again. The night she committed suicide she came to my home and ever since then I've felt that I could have done more to help her.'

'Good God. Is any of this on record?'

'I don't think so. I saw the woman thirteen years after she'd been caught as a spy. I thought she was dead. I went to her funeral, but her death was a cover.'

'The best!'

'It was until I saw her in Oxford Street. But to answer your question, no, there is no record. I searched the Home Office and MI5's archives trying to find her.

I even went up to the engineering factory where we were employed. There was no record of her anywhere. Every trace of her had been removed. It was as if she had never existed.'

Sir John picked up a four-page document from his desk. 'I've thoroughly read your account of Shaun O'Shaughnessy, but I must tell you, however, that there are holes in it. There are times and dates missing.'

'When I knew O'Shaughnessy, I worked for the Home Office. I was head of the Cold Case department and as such, I signed the Official Secrets Act. Some things I was not, nor am, at liberty to disclose. Not even under oath at the Old Bailey.'

'O'Shaughnessy's lawyer will take advantage of that.'

'If he does, there is nothing I can do about it. I'll tell the truth, but I will not break the Official Secrets Act.'

CHAPTER THIRTEEN

Ena slammed the office door shut and marched across the room to her desk. She took a quarter bottle of whisky and two glasses from the bottom drawer, poured three fingers of scotch into each glass and motioned to Artie that one was for him.

'It was that bad, was it?'

'Worse,' Ena spat.

Artie left his seat, pulled out the chair on the other side of Ena's desk, sat down and took a drink of his scotch. 'What happened?'

'As you know, Sir John Hillary, QC has called me as a prosecution witness in the case against O'Shaughnessy.'

'Which is why you had a meeting with him today.'

'Yes, but I'm called tomorrow. It doesn't give me much time to prepare.' Ena took a swig of her whisky. 'And, Sir John Hillary said O'Shaughnessy's brief will be hard on me when he cross-examines me, so I'll need to be on the ball. Damn!' Ena said again and poured herself another shot of whisky. 'How has it been here?'

'In between taking calls, which there have been many,' Artie said, jumping up and retrieving Ena's diary from his desk and placing it in front of her, 'I've been checking the files, making sure dates are correct and putting them in alphabetical order.' He grinned. 'A bit like old times.' He knocked his whisky back. 'But without Sid.'

Ena poured him another drink. 'You're a star, Artie Mallory, I don't know what I'd do without you?'

Artie took drink of his scotch. 'I'm sure you don't,' he said, with a touch of sarcasm in his voice, 'but you'll soon find out.'

Ena lifted her head from the diary. 'What do you mean? You can't leave. Not with all the work we've got on.'

'Ena, I need a job with a salary. I've loved working with you for the last couple of weeks, but I need to pay the rent and the bills.' Artie looked around the room. 'I've even got used to being here again, but I need to eat.'

Ena laughed, 'I thought you did eat, on me. Sorry, that was a stupid thing to say.' But seriously, Artie, I need you. With Doreen Hardy's case, the art theft and the death of George's father, which by the way was murder, I was going to offer you a job.'

Artie almost choked on his drink. 'You were?'

'Of course. I was hoping you'd do the surveillance work on the Hardy case anyway, but now I've been called into the Old Bailey tomorrow, I need you to be a full-time investigator.' Ena leaned back in her chair and smiled cheekily at her old colleague.

'With a proper salary?'

'And a payslip, tax, National Insurance stamp – everything done properly. I'll ring the accountant the first opportunity I get and tell him to put the new investigator at Dudley Green on the books. What do you say?'

Artie squealed with delight. 'Yes! I say yes!'

Ena topped up their glasses. 'Here's to the new investigating agent at Dudley Green Associates.'

Artie raised his glass. 'Thank you, Ena.'

Ena lifted her glass and clinked his. 'Artie, you've earned it.'

***

Ena was beginning to feel hungry. Sir John Hillary's

clerk, Mr Martin, had shown her into the waiting room at nine o'clock that morning and she had been twiddling her thumbs for more than three hours. She looked around the room. It was typical of most waiting rooms, chairs with high backs and hard seats, small windows that were too high to let in much light and plain painted walls – in this case, light green. Ena stood up and stretched. Three black and white framed prints hung on the walls. She looked at the nearest one. It was by William Hogarth. 'He gets around,' she said aloud. The first print was called Beer Street. Ena turned up her nose at the drunken men and women – fat presumably from consuming too much beer. The next was called Gin Street. 'Ugh!' Her eyes fixed on a baby falling through the air upside down, dropped by its drunken mother. She didn't look at the third print, but walked over to the window.

From the little she could see of the sky, it was azure blue with candyfloss clouds. White clouds were unusual in London. Standing on tiptoe she could see the bell tower and four spires of The Church Of The Holy Sepulchre. The Sepulchre-without-Newgate, as it was called locally. The Sepulchre always reminded her of the nursery rhyme, Oranges and Lemons. 'When will you pay me said the bells of Old Bailey.'

Ena had walked past the church that morning on her way to the Central Criminal Courts. Eerie to think the Old Bailey had been built on the site of the old Newgate Prison. Parallel to the court, the road followed the line of the city's wall and beneath it, it's said, runs the Fleet River. Ena was fascinated by history and decided to buy a book about the City of London.

The room was hot and airless. She tried to force open the window, but it wouldn't budge. She flopped down on the chair and exhaled with frustration. She was beginning to feel irritable. The porcelain face of the big clock on the wall above the fireplace said five minutes to one. She had now been sitting in the claustrophobic little waiting room for four hours.

She was humming Oranges and Lemons when the door opened. 'Sir John sends his apologies, Mrs Green. They have broken for lunch, so perhaps you'd like to get something to eat?'

'Thank you. It's fresh air I need more than anything. And a telephone.'

'There's a bank of telephones in the main entrance, but at this time of day, they are usually occupied. If they are, turn left out of the main entrance and cross the road. You'll see several telephone boxes on the corner of Old Bailey and Limeburner Lane.' Sir John's clerk held the door open for her. 'The case will resume at two o'clock,' he said as she passed.

There was one free telephone in the main entrance. As she headed towards it a man pushed past her. 'Press!' he shouted and took the telephone. With his head in the booth, the man lit a cigarette before lifting the receiver. Ena stood at the side of the booth and strained her ears hoping to hear what the reporter had to say about the O'Shaughnessy case that morning, but she was unable to hear above the frantic reports of half a dozen journalists shouting at the same time.

Ena made her way out of the building. She needed a telephone. She needed to know if Artie had any success at Wandsworth Prison where Mrs Hardy's husband was doing time for armed robbery.

She crossed Old Bailey and as she neared Limeburner Lane saw two red telephone boxes. They were both empty, she stepped into the first and dialled the number for the office in Mercer Street.

'Dudley Green Associates. How can I help you?'

'Artie, it's me, Ena. What did you find out this morning?'

'Visiting is this afternoon from three o'clock until four. I had to part with a fiver, but it was worth it. The screw on the gate rang through to his mate in the office who said Hardy was having a visitor this afternoon. A visiting order was sent to Mrs Hardy.'

'He's getting out in a few weeks. What's his game?'

'Money? A job? And I don't mean work.'

'I knew what you meant, Artie. Do you think you can get back to the prison before visiting time?'

'If I leave now.'

'Tell Mrs Hardy not to let her husband know she has money saved. Bloody man will take her for all she's got again.'

'I'll get over there now. Tell me about O'Shaughnessy tonight.'

'Court finishes at five.'

'Shall we meet back at the office at, say, five-thirty?'

'Say six in case Hillary needs to speak to me. But not at the office. Let's meet at the Lamb and Flag. I'll need a large drink by the end of today.'

Ena found a café along Limeburner Lane and bought a sandwich.

CHAPTER FOURTEEN

Waiting outside Court No 1 at the Old Bailey, Ena listened to Sir John Hillary's address.

"My Lord, the prosecution's case is that Shaun O'Shaughnessy did murder in cold blood, Mr Hugh Middleton on February 27th 1959." There was a short pause. "The prisoner is also accused of orchestrating the murders of Sidney Parfitt, an investigating officer with the Home Office in September 1958, and the director of MI5, Mr McKenzie Robinson, in September 1958. There is also evidence that he assisted in the suicide of Helen Crowther on December 23rd, 1958. What I know for a fact is that Shaun O'Shaughnessy murdered one man and was complicit in the murder of two others." Another silence, this time longer. Ena made a fist of her hand and punched the air. Sir John was giving the jury time to digest the severity of O'Shaughnessy's crimes.

"My Lord, the prisoner was apprehended by the East Sussex Police while attempting to strangle Mrs Evelyn Robinson, the widow of McKenzie Robinson, in her home at 15 Victoria Crescent, Hove, on March 3rd, 1959. There is no doubt in my mind that if the Police had not arrived at Mrs Robinson's house when they did, she too would have perished at the hands of Shaun O'Shaughnessy – and today the prisoner would have four counts of murder to answer for, not three. My Lord, I would like to call my first witness, Mrs Ena Green."

"Call Mrs Ena Green!"

Mr Martin opened the door and as Ena entered Court No 1 a sea of faces turned to look at her. Her heart began to thud, but refusing to let her nerves get the better of her, she held her head up and took a steadying breath. Court No 1, the most famous of England's criminal courts, was smaller than she imagined. Wood-panelled walls and stained oak desks and tables made the room appear dark. The only colourful image was that of the judge, Justice Hubert Peckham who, in a red robe trimmed with white fur, sat on what looked to Ena like a throne directly above the clerk of the court. The desk of Sir John Hillary as the prosecution barrister was nearest the jury. The desk of the defence lawyer, Mr Theodor Anderson, was near the prisoner in the dock. An icy shiver ran down Ena's spine as she caught sight of Shaun O'Shaughnessy standing in what looked like an ornate wooden fortress. The dock dominated the room and dwarfed O'Shaughnessy, as it must have done William Joyce. The infamous Lord Haw-Haw appeared three times in Court No 1 in 1945 before being convicted of treason and hanged in January 1946. Abhorrent as hanging was to Ena, she hoped the same fate awaited Shaun O'Shaughnessy for murdering Hugh Middleton and for the part he played in the murders of her friends, Sid Parfitt and McKenzie Robinson.

She was met by the court usher who led her to the front of the court. The usher held up the Bible, Ena placed her right hand on it and was sworn in. Having given her name and occupation as a private investigator at Dudley Green Investigations, 8 Mercer Street – her current job and address – Ena stepped into the witness box and Sir John Hillary, QC, rose from his seat.

'Mrs Green,' Sir John said, walking towards her with a reassuring smile, 'would you tell the court your occupation before you became an independent private investigator?'

'I was Head of the Cold Cases department at the Home Office.'

'An investigating department?'

'Yes, sir.'

'Thank you. And it was while you were working for the Home Office that you met the prisoner?'

'Yes.'

'When was it that you met, Shaun O'Shaughnessy?'

'October 1958.'

'And where did you meet him?'

'In Brighton, at the home of a woman named Helen Crowther.'

'And when did you first meet Helen Crowther?'

'September 1958, after the funeral of the Director of MI5, McKenzie Robinson.'

'Would you tell the court how you came to be at staying at the house of Helen Crowther and the circumstances that led to you meeting the prisoner?'

'Helen Crowther had been the late McKenzie Robinson's personal assistant for many years. After his funeral she invited me to visit her in Brighton. She said if I ever wanted to get away from London, have a break and get some fresh air, I'd be welcome to stay with her.'

Sir John nodded. 'And when did you take up Helen Crowther's invitation to visit her?'

'Six weeks later, after several attempts had been made on my life – the last being a hit and run in which I was almost killed – my husband suggested I left London for a while. I didn't want to stay with my family in the Midlands in case whoever was trying to kill me knew where they lived, so I took Helen Crowther up on her offer and I went to Brighton.'

'You went to Brighton to stay with Helen

Crowther who, as PA to the late Director of MI5, you believed you could trust and who you thought would understand the danger you were in?'

'Yes. I thought, as no one knew I'd met Helen Crowther, I wouldn't be putting her life in danger by staying with her. I also thought I'd be safe.'

'And were you?'

'I thought so at first, but later I don't believe I was safe.'

'Would you explain why you later believed you were not safe?'

'I thought Helen's house would be quiet, a... sanctuary. I thought there was only going to be the two of us. But that night, Shaun O'Shaughnessy arrived. I heard him say he'd called on the off chance, which I thought nothing of at the time. Later Helen told me that O'Shaughnessy was an old friend who she had worked with many years before at MI5.'

'Which you accepted as the truth?'

'Of course, I had no reason to think the PA to the Director of MI5 would lie.'

'Did you later think they were lying about not having seen each other—?'

'My Lord!' Mr Anderson jumped up from his seat. 'My learned friend is putting words into the witness's mouth.'

Sir John turned to the judge and put up his hands. 'Apologies, My Lord, I will rephrase…'

Judge Peckham gave Sir John a surly nod.

Sir John turned back to Ena. 'Mrs Green, did you later have any concerns about the relationship between Miss Crowther and the prisoner?'

'Yes. When I went to the dining room to join Miss Crowther she was looking up into the man's face and he was smiling down at her. It was clear to me that they were enjoying an intimate conversation. I turned to leave, but Helen had seen me. They quickly parted but I had already noticed an intimacy in their body language.'

'But they had worked together?'

'Yes, and for the rest of the evening they were friendly and polite to each other, as you'd expect two people who hadn't seen each other for many years to be. But when I came into the room, unannounced, I felt as if I was imposing.'

'Was there anything else that happened that weekend that made you suspicious of the prisoner?'

'Yes. He said he was an old friend of my work colleague, Sidney Parfitt, who had been murdered on Waterloo Bridge two months previously, and he asked me if I knew someone called Collins. It was then that I realised something was very wrong. I didn't believe O'Shaughnessy when he said he was a friend of Sid's.'

'Would you elaborate?'

Ena took a deep breath. 'Sid was a quiet man, reserved. In the ten years we worked together, he had never mentioned Shaun O'Shaughnessy. Apart from which, no one outside the department – other than the Director of the Home Office – knew that Sid had left the name Collins as a clue to discovering a major spy ring connected to the cold case that he and I were working on – the case that led to his death. Until O'Shaughnessy said the name Collins, I thought he was just a show-off and a braggart.'

'How long did you stay with Helen Crowther?'

'Three days. I cut my visit short because of O'Shaughnessy. I would have left sooner, but I didn't want to offend Helen. At the time I believed she was my friend.'

'Did you see Helen Crowther again?'

'No.'

'Did you see the prisoner again?'

'Yes. In the street three months later. However, I learned from my associate, Mr Mallory, that O'Shaughnessy had befriended him in a pub, bought him a drink and drugged him. Mr Mallory also said he had seen a woman fitting the description of Helen Crowther with O'Shaughnessy that night.' Ena looked over at the dock. 'That was the first time the prisoner said he was a friend of our dead colleague, Sid Parfitt.' She looked back at Sir John. 'Mr Mallory told me that O'Shaughnessy said he knew Collins had killed Sid and, while he was under the influence of drugs, O'Shaughnessy pumped Mr Mallory for information. Fortunately, I hadn't had time to tell my colleague before I went to Brighton that Collins was not the name of a man. Collins was the first clue to cracking the code to expose the spy ring to which Helen Crowther and Shaun O'Shaughnessy belonged.'

Again, the defence barrister stood up. 'My Lord, we only have the witness's word that my client drugged her friend.'

'Sir John...' Judge Peckham sounded bored.

'Apologies, My Lord.' Sir John took a few steps away from Ena then spun round. 'Mrs Green *do you now know* who told the prisoner the name, Collins?'

'Director Richard Bentley of the Home Office.'

'Thank you, Mrs Green.' Sir John looked pleased. He then changed his expression to one of sympathy. 'Did you know Hugh Middleton?'

'I knew of him. He worked at GCHQ and was an old school friend of my colleague, Mr Mallory.'

'Did you see him with the prisoner?'

'Yes, when I next saw the prisoner three months later in February 1959.'

'Was he to your knowledge a member of the spy ring?'

'No, he was not. Shaun O'Shaughnessy befriended him as he had my colleague, Mr Mallory.' For a long time, Ena had kept the feeling that she was in some way to blame for Hugh Middleton's murder at bay. That feeling now threatened to rise up and choke her. 'Mr Middleton was not as lucky as my colleague. Artie Mallory was only drugged by the prisoner, Hugh was killed—'

Mr Anderson sprang to his feet again. 'My Lord, hearsay! How can the witness possibly know how lucky or unlucky Mr Middleton was!'

The judge looked from Sir John to Ena and then to the defence lawyer. 'Sit down, Mr Anderson.' Anderson blew out his cheeks and dropped onto his seat. 'Mrs Green, for the jury, would you explain what you mean?'

'Mr Mallory was drugged and pumped for information by the prisoner. It was lucky for him that it was in a public bar in London's West End. Mr Middleton's life ended in a private house. The house in which Shaun O'Shaughnessy lived, in Brighton.'

'My Lord. Mrs Green cannot know—'

The Judge put up his hand and the defence lawyer remained seated.

'I have no more questions for Mrs Green at this time, My Lord. May I reserve the right to question her further, if necessary.' Judge Peckham nodded and Sir John Hillary said, 'Thank you, Mrs Green.' He looked briefly at the defence lawyer before returning to his seat.

CHAPTER FIFTEEN

'Your witness, Mr Anderson.'

'My Lord.' O'Shaughnessy's defence lawyer stood up. His eyebrows met in the middle as he consulted his notebook. He walked over to Ena and with a patronising smile said, 'Mrs Green, Miss Crowther was a mutual friend of both you and Mr O'Shaughnessy, was she not?'

'No! She was not. She was a friend of O'Shaughnessy, yes, but she was not a friend of mine. I hardly knew her. I didn't know O'Shaughnessy at all.'

'I find that strange,' he said, his brow furrowing theatrically, 'and I'm sure the jury does—'

'My Lord?' Sir John said angrily. 'My learned friend is telling the jury what to think.'

'Mr Anderson...?'

'Apologies, My Lord.' The defence lawyer turned back to Ena. 'You stayed with Mrs Crowther in Brighton as her guest for three days, you said, and you dined with Mr O'Shaughnessy, yet you didn't consider either of them to be your friend?'

'I thought Miss Crowther would become a friend, but it was the first time I'd met O'Shaughnessy. As far as I was concerned, he had turned up without an invitation. I didn't know him, so I didn't consider him a friend.'

'Had you stayed with your friend Helen Crowther in Brighton before that night?'

'No! And she was not my friend. As I said earlier, I hardly knew her.'

'Oh!' Mr Anderson feigned a look of shock, walked back to his desk and studied his notes. 'Are you in the habit of spending holidays with people who you *hardly know*?'

'No. And it wasn't—'

'Would you tell the court the circumstances in which you met Miss Crowther?'

'As I have already said, we met after the funeral of her late boss, Mackenzie Robinson.'

'Ah, yes. That was when his widow accused you of killing her husband?'

Ena's mouth was suddenly dry. She looked at Sir John Hillary for help.

'Answer the question, Mrs Green,' the judge instructed.

Ena ran her tongue over her lips and found her voice. 'Mrs Robinson only accused me because—'

'And that was when your friend Helen Crowther came to your defence?' Anderson said, cutting Ena off.

'Yes, but Helen Crowther was not my friend. I had never met her before McKenzie Robinson's funeral.' Ena shook her head. 'You're taking what happened out of context.' She turned to the judge. 'Mrs Robinson was upset because her husband was going to help me with a case I was working on and she thought that was the reason why he was killed.'

With a vacant expression on his face, the defence lawyer folded his arms and looked around the room. When Ena turned away from the judge, he looked at his watch. 'If you've finished, Mrs Green, I should like to get back to the business in hand?'

Embarrassed, Ena dropped her gaze.

Sir John stood up. 'My Lord? My learned friend is intimidating the witness.'

Judge Peckham leaned forwards and looked over the top of his glasses. 'No need for theatrics, Mr Anderson.'

'My Lord.' Anderson bowed his head by way of an apology. 'Mrs Green, you said you had gone to Miss Crowther's house in Brighton because you needed sanctuary?'

'Yes!'

Turning his back on Ena, the defence lawyer again walked to his desk and glanced at his notes. 'You told the court that when you first met my client, you didn't like him. Why was that?'

'As I said, he was loud and arrogant – a show-off. I had hoped to have a quiet weekend.'

'*You had hoped to have a quiet weekend* and yet when my client invited you to a nightclub in Brighton, you accepted.'

Ena felt the heat of embarrassment rise from her neck to her cheeks and her stomach churned. 'I went because Helen wanted to go.'

Mr Anderson looked at the jury, lifted his shoulders and shook his head as if he was confused. Walking back to Ena he said, 'Are you in the habit of going to nightclubs and drinking and dancing with men you don't like, *Mrs* Green?'

Ena wanted to scream. The defence lawyer was twisting everything she said. 'Helen Crowther wanted to go to the club. It would have been rude of me not to go too. Besides, I could hardly stay in her house on my own.'

'And after your night out with my client, you kissed him—'

'I did not kiss him! He tried to kiss me and I pushed him away.'

'My client mistook your body language perhaps?' Anderson said, raising his eyebrows.

'I gave him no encouragement at all. I was, and still am, a married woman.'

'Of course.' Anderson paused thoughtfully. 'Let me ask you about your boss at the Home Office, Director Richard Bentley who last year was tried for treason and hanged.'

Ena's stomach lurched. She felt sick at the thought of Dick Bentley's betrayal. The defence lawyer was making a statement which did not require her to answer.

'I believe you worked closely with Director Bentley at the Home Office?'

'Yes.'

'How many years had you worked with him?'

'Thirteen.'

'Thirteen years!' the defence lawyer exclaimed. He looked at the jury. 'Thirteen years,' he said again. 'And you would have us believe that in all that time you never once suspected he was a spy?'

'No.'

'What changed your mind, suddenly?'

'I had reason to question Richard Bentley's motives in a certain matter.'

Anderson swung from left to right, his black gown flaring theatrically as he looked around the court. 'Reason to question? Motives? A certain matter? It all sounds very Machiavellian.' He put his hand up to his face, his fingers on his lips. 'And who was it that gave you *reason to question* the Director of The Home Office?'

Ena had been waiting throughout the cross-examination for a question like this. 'I am not at liberty to say.'

'Was it the same person who fed you lies about my client and his lover, Hugh Middleton? The truth is, Mrs Green, Hugh Middleton was not the victim in the relationship. The victim was my client. Mr Middleton cheated on him, lied to him and stole from him. My client regrets the outcome of their relationship and wishes there had been some other way. Alas,' O'Shaughnessy's lawyer looked down and sighed, his voice growing deeper and softer as if with emotion, 'there was no other way.' The defence lawyer then turned to the jury, cleared his throat, and in a matter-of-fact way, said, 'During one of Middleton's aggressive outbursts he attacked my client who, fearing for his life, struck out in self-defence, accidentally killing Mr Middleton.'

Ena looked across at the dock for the first time. She held O'Shaughnessy with a cold stare. As arrogant as ever, he grinned at her. Still looking at O'Shaughnessy, Ena said, 'Hugh Middleton did not lie, cheat or attack your client. On the contrary—'

'And how would you know, Mrs Green!'

Ena looked back at the defence lawyer. 'I am not at liberty to say,' she said again.

'Whether you tell the court or not is of no consequence,' Anderson said, 'because, Mrs Green, the information that you received came from Nick Miller, a man of dubious character who owned the Minchin Club, a nightclub that my client and his lover frequented in Brighton.' Anderson looked at the jury, leaned his elbow on the edge of the witness box and crossed his legs as if he was at a bar waiting for a drink. Then, as if something had that second come into his mind, he turned and faced Ena. 'Perhaps you know Nick Miller better by his real name, Nicolaus Müller – a German spy who became a south London gangster whom you accompanied to Austria. Is that not so, Mrs Green?'

'I—'

'I know!' Anderson spat, shutting Ena down, 'You

are not at liberty to tell us what information Müller gave you for his freedom.'

Before Ena could retaliate, Anderson turned to the judge. 'No more questions, My Lord.'

Ena looked up at the judge in disbelief. She then looked pleadingly at Sir John.

The judge waved his left hand. Sir John was already on his feet.

'If I may, My Lord.'

The Judge nodded.

'Mrs Green,' Sir John said with a reassuring smile, 'would you tell the court why you were not at liberty to answer some of the questions asked you by my learned friend?'

'I have signed the Official Secrets Act. The work I did at the Home Office was... highly sensitive.'

'Top Secret?'

'Yes.'

'Thank you. You were also asked questions that you were not given time to answer. I apologise in advance if the questions I shall ask you now are repetitious.' Ena nodded. 'On the day of McKenzie Robinson's funeral, did Mrs Robinson accuse you of killing her husband?'

'No. Mrs Robinson said it was my fault that her husband had been killed, *not* that I had killed him.'

'Your fault? Why?'

'Director McKenzie was going to help me with an investigation I was working on before he was murdered. He gave his wife a folder to give to me, which she gave me on the day of his funeral.' Tears filled Ena's eyes as Mac's last words came into her mind. "*Make sure Ena Green gets this.*"

'No,' Ena said, wiping her eyes with the back of her hand, 'Eve Robinson did not accuse me of killing her husband. 'Her exact words were, "I hope what you find in there was worth my husband's life. If you hadn't come to the hospital to see him, he would still be alive."'

'Thank you for clearing that up, Mrs Green.' With a sympathetic smile, Sir John said, 'Are you happy to continue?' Ena nodded. 'I think the court has been misled about your association with Mr Nick Miller. Would you describe the relationship between yourself and Mr Miller and tell the jury why you travelled with him to Austria?'

'There was no relationship. Nick Miller had been taken into Police custody for questioning. He had valuable information that the security services – my department in particular – and the Police needed in order to expose a large and deep-rooted spy ring. As you know, the Director of the Home Office was the head of the cell, Helen Crowther and Shaun O'Shaughnessy were members. Nick Miller said he would release the information once he had arrived safely in Austria. I didn't choose to go with him, he insisted I went as insurance.'

Ena looked at the jury. 'But I did have a personal reason for accompanying Nick Miller to Austria. Nick had proof that Helen Crowther, who was found dead on December 23rd, 1958 in my office, had killed herself. Crowther went to extraordinary lengths to make her suicide look as if my husband had murdered her. I flew to Austria with Nick Miller to save my husband from being hanged for a murder he did not commit.'

'Thank you, Mrs Green.' Sir John turned to the judge. 'No more questions, My Lord.'

CHAPTER SIXTEEN

Ena joined Artie at the bar of the Lamb and Flag. 'I've got you a scotch.' He passed the whisky to her and she took a drink.

Ena glanced around the bar. 'There's a vacant table by the door.'

Artie followed Ena to the table. 'So, how did it go?' he asked when they were seated.

'It was a nightmare. O'Shaughnessy's lawyer twisted everything I said. He made me out to be a liar and didn't give me a chance to answer some of the questions.' Ena took another drink of her whisky. 'Out of context some things did sound....'

'Dodgy?'

'Questionable is a better word. He made me sound as if I was the guilty party.'

'Did you tell John Hillary what O'Shaughnessy did to me?'

'Yes, and the defence lawyer shouted hearsay.'

'Tell Hillary I'll go to court if necessary.'

'I will. Sir John countered the defence lawyer's cross-examination and asked me questions which allowed me to put the record straight. What about your day? Did you get to Wandsworth Prison in time to speak to Doreen?'

'Yes and no. I got there in plenty of time but she didn't turn up.'

'That's odd. Why would she accept a visiting order and not use it? I'm pleased of course, but I'm curious to know why she didn't visit him?'

'Perhaps she's realised at last that her excuse for a husband is a waste of time. Let's hope she gives him his marching orders when he gets out.'

'I don't think she'll do that. She'll have him back for the sake of the boys.'

'In that case, why didn't she visit him today?'

'You could ask her. She hasn't got a telephone so in the morning, when you've been to the office and checked the post, drive over to her house. I'll phone you when we break for lunch.'

***

Ena arrived at the Old Bailey just before nine o'clock. She was about to enter the waiting room when she heard someone calling her.

Stopping short of entering the room, she turned to see Mr Martin, ruddy-cheeked, at her side. 'I'm sorry, Mrs Green, but you won't be required to give evidence today,' he said out of breath and sounding flustered. He took the handkerchief from the top pocket of his black suit jacket and mopped his brow. 'Mrs Robinson is giving evidence today.'

'I thought Eve Robinson had already given evidence.'

'She had. Well, she began to give evidence last week, but she was taken ill. I think going over how the defendant had almost killed her was too much for her. She collapsed. A doctor was sent for and she was diagnosed with exhaustion. He ordered complete rest. She telephoned the Chambers yesterday and said she was better.'

'I hope she's up to being cross-examined by O'Shaughnessy's lawyer.' Mr Martin nodded in agreement. 'I should like to hear Mrs Robinson give evidence.'

'Come with me, I'll find you a seat in the public gallery.'

Entering the gallery they were met by loud chatter. Mr Martin whispered in the ear of a large man who had spread himself across two seats. Glaring at the clerk and looking Ena up and down, the man reluctantly shuffled along to allow her to sit.

It seemed to Ena that half the spectators were so theatrically dressed they might have been auditioning for pantomime at the end of Brighton Pier. Probably friends of O'Shaughnessy or they had worked with him at one time or another. The other half with their short-cropped hair and sour faces – looked like relics of Mosley's BUF or the splinter party, the League of Empire Loyalists. Either group of fascists left a nasty taste in the mouths of decent human beings. Ena sat quietly, hoping no one would recognise her from giving evidence against O'Shaughnessy the day before.

'Order!' the clerk of the court called to no effect. He called again, this time louder, 'Order!' Not until everyone in the court was silent, did he continue. 'All rise for his honour, Judge Peckham.'

When the judge was seated, Sir John Hillary stood up and addressed him. 'My Lord, I would like to call Mrs Evelyn Robinson.'

Judge Peckham leaned forward 'She is recovered, I hope.'

'Yes, My Lord, Mrs Robinson is quite well.'

The Judge gave a cursory nod. And the clerk of the court shouted, 'Call Mrs Evelyn Robinson.'

Eve Robinson entered the court to an outcry of boos and jeers. The usher met her and led her down the centre aisle to the witness box.

With a face like thunder, Judge Peckham glared at the mob in the public gallery until they stopped heckling.

As Eve Robinson was being sworn in, a woman

shouted, 'Liar! She threw herself at him and when he turned her down she cried wolf.'

'Madam! Hold your tongue in my court!' Judge Peckham looked sternly at the woman who had shouted out and then at the men who Ena assumed were O'Shaughnessy's fascist followers on the front row, 'One more outburst and I shall have you all taken to the cells.' He eyeballed the man sitting next to the woman. 'Do I make myself clear!'

The man and the woman looked down and muttered, 'Yes.'

'Proceed,' Judge Peckham said to the usher.

Eve Robinson gave her name and address and stepped into the witness box.

Sir John Hillary picked up several sheets of paper and walked over to Eve. 'Thank you for coming in today, Mrs Robinson. If you need to take a break at any time, please say so.' Sir John looked up at the judge. He nodded.

Sir John flicked through the pages of the typed manuscript until he had scanned all six pages. 'I do not wish to go over old ground or to ask you to repeat evidence that the jury have already heard; evidence that may be distressing to you, but I must ask you again if the man who tried to strangle you is in this court?'

Eve barely glanced at O'Shaughnessy. 'Yes, Sir, he's in the dock.'

'The defendant?' Eve nodded. 'Mrs Robinson, do you know why the defendant tried to strangle you?'

'My husband's personal assistant, who Shaun O'Shaughnessy lived with, was writing my husband's memoirs. After she killed herself, he, O'Shaughnessy, came to my house and said that he would finish the memoirs. We had a couple of meetings, then one day he arrived at my house drunk. He told me that my husband's PA, Helen Crowther, had been my husband's mistress. He said they'd been having an affair all the time I was married to McKenzie and that they had been lovers right up until the time she...' Eve took a shuddering breath, 'she killed him. O'Shaughnessy laughed. He took pleasure in telling me.'

O'Shaughnessy's lawyer stood up. 'Speculation, My Lord, unless my client told the witness how he felt, she couldn't possibly know.'

'I'll rephrase, My Lord.' The judge nodded. 'Mrs Robinson, what made you think the defendant had taken pleasure in telling you his friend had murdered your husband?'

'He laughed about it, taunted me. He said Helen Crowther was a spy, a German agent, who was married to a military officer in Berlin. He said my husband was besotted with her. He said McKenzie didn't care that she was a spy, or that she was married, and that he'd given her a job to be close to her.' Eve looked pleadingly at Judge Peckham. 'My husband was a good man, a loyal man. He was the Director of MI5,' she continued. 'He didn't know about Helen Crowther's past,' she sobbed, 'I swear he didn't.'

Sir John interrupted. 'Mrs Robinson, would you like a break.' Eve shook her head. 'A drink of water, perhaps?' Sir John looked across the room to the clerk who immediately poured water into a glass from the jug on Sir John's desk and took it to her.

After taking a sip, Eve put the glass down on the ledge at the left of the witness box and whispered, 'Thank you.'

She looked frail. Her hair was greyer than Ena remembered and she had lost weight.

'Mrs Robinson, do you feel well enough to continue?'

'Yes, Sir.'

'If at any time you feel unwell, I'm sure My Lord would allow a recess.'

Eve nodded. 'Thank you, but I'd like to carry on, Sir.'

Sir John gave Eve a sympathetic smile. 'Mrs Robinson, did the defendant tell you anything else?'

'Not then, no. He told me when he was…' Eve lifted her head high and, for the first time since she had entered the witness box, she looked directly at O'Shaughnessy. 'When he was choking me, he said I knew too much. He said, "I'm going to shut you up."'

'And by *shut you up*, you believed the defendant was going to kill you?'

'My Lord!' Mr Anderson leapt from his seat. 'My learned friend is putting words into the witness's mouth.'

'Rephrase your question, Sir John.'

Sir John acknowledged the judge with an apologetic nod. 'Mrs Robinson, what did you understand the words *shut you up* to mean?'

Eve looked at O'Shaughnessy again, 'That he was going to kill me. While he was strangling me, I lost consciousness and collapsed. The doctor said collapsing had saved my life.'

'Hearsay, My Lord!'

Judge Peckham gave the defence lawyer a quizzical look. 'Were you not in court on the day Mrs Robinson's doctor gave his testimony?'

'Yes, My Lord but—'

'Proceed, Sir John.'

'I have no more questions, My Lord. Unless your honour has any questions…?'

Judge Peckham waved the suggestion away and beckoned the clerk of the court.

After a brief exchange, the clerk called, 'All rise!' Judge Peckham stood up, acknowledged the court with a nod and made his exit in a flurry of red – and the clerk called, 'There will be an hour recess for lunch.'

Two guards – one on either side of O'Shaughnessy – took him down to the cells, the court usher helped Eve Robinson out of the witness box and Ena left the public gallery.

CHAPTER SEVENTEEN

Hoping to speak to Eve Robinson, Ena stood among the journalists as if she was waiting to use a telephone. Within minutes, Eve emerged from Court No 1 sandwiched between Sir John and Mr Martin. Sir John took his leave, and Mr Martin whisked her away through the door leading to the waiting rooms. Ena waited for a couple of minutes. When Mr Martin didn't reappear, she left for the café on Limeburner Lane.

As she passed the public telephone boxes she could see people were already queuing outside the café. If she was going to get a sandwich for herself and Eve, she needed to take her place in the queue before anyone else joined it, or the hour would be up.

Ena had no idea what Eve Robinson liked, so to be on the safe side she ordered two cheese and tomato sandwiches.

On her way back to the court, she decided to give Artie a quick call. She took some coins from her purse and dialled the telephone at the office. 'Artie,' she said, before he had time to speak, 'did you see Doreen Hardy?'

'Yes, and she hadn't received a visiting order. She showed me a letter from Arnold telling her not to visit him. He said he didn't want her to remember him in prison. The creep said he was ashamed of his past and promised to change. He went on about how he had paid his debt to society, saying he would have a clean sheet and wanted to start again.'

'I don't believe a word of it.'

'Nor do I, but Doreen does. You should have seen her face. Her cheeks were flushed when she was telling me. She looked positively blooming.'

'I'd like to know what he's up to. Doreen promised me she wouldn't tell Arnold she'd saved some money while she was cleaning at the Duke of Wellington, so what's his game?'

'We won't know until he comes out.'

'Nor will Doreen. That reminds me, will you go to the hotel and ask the manager if he's found any marked notes in the till. Best time to go is between lunchtime closing and evening opening, and don't be put off if Dolly the guard dog answers the door. Insist on speaking to the manager, Mr Walters. Unfortunately, I don't think there'll be any marked notes.'

'Why not?'

'Stealing money and planting it on Doreen has served its purpose. She's out of the picture. Argh! It's the least complicated of our cases but the most difficult to fathom. Before I go, was there any post this morning?'

'A letter from George Derby-Bloom. She's coming to London on Friday and wondered if you had any news about her father's death. I telephoned and told her you were at the Old Bailey and said you'd phone her as soon as you were next in the office.'

'Would you give her another quick call for me? Tell her I need to speak to her father's friend at the nursing home. Tell her I'll be going there on Thursday and I'll talk to her about it on Friday. Right! If there's nothing else, I'd better get back.'

Crossing the entrance hall, Ena saw Mr Martin exit through the door to the waiting rooms. She followed him to the room where she had spent the morning before she was called to give evidence, tapped on the door and Mr Martin answered.

'I'm sorry, Mrs Green, the public aren't allowed

back here.'

'I'm not the public, I'm a witness.'

'You were a witness. You are not one now.'

'Mr Martin, please allow Mrs Green in.'

Flushed, Mr Martin said, 'It is most irregular. But if you are sure, Mrs Robinson.'

'I am.'

'I'll be back at two o'clock to escort you to Court No 1.'

Since Ena had last seen Eve Robinson, she had aged several years. Her face was pale, although Ena could see she had rouge on her cheeks, and her eyes were dull with loose skin and dark rings beneath them.

'How are you holding up, Mrs Robinson?'

'Call me Eve, Ena, please.'

Ena crossed to Eve and sat next to her. 'I don't suppose you feel like eating, but I think you should have something before you go back for the afternoon session.' Ena opened the paper bag containing the sandwiches and took one out. She offered the bag to Eve. 'They're nothing fancy, just plain cheese and tomato.' Eve Robinson stared at the sandwiches. 'I think you'll feel better with something inside you.' Eve nodded and took one.

The two women sat in silence and ate their lunch. When they had finished, Eve said, 'I owe you an apology, Ena. I was led to believe that you were responsible for my husband's death.'

'No apology needed. Helen Crowther was a very convincing liar. You weren't the only one to suffer because of her lies. But, forget about her, she can't hurt you now.'

'No, but O'Shaughnessy could if he got off.'

'He won't get off, Eve,' Ena said, concerned that Eve's resolve to make O'Shaughnessy pay for what he did to her was waning.

'That's what Sir John said.'

'And he's right.' Ena screwed up the empty sandwich bag and lobbed it into the waste paper basket. 'Shaun O'Shaughnessy will hang.'

Eve inhaled sharply and her body trembled. 'During the last few weeks I had begun to feel a little better, you know, after O'Shaughnessy attacked me. I daren't close my eyes for months, I kept seeing his snarling face next to mine, like it was the day he tightened his hands around my neck. Recently I'd started to sleep again. Only an hour here and there, but it was something. Then Sir John Hillary called me into his office and asked me to tell him about O'Shaughnessy and what he had done to me. He knew already of course, but said he needed to hear about the attack from me.' Eve clutched Ena's arm. 'You know, he almost killed me. The doctor told me if I hadn't lost consciousness and fallen to the floor when I did, he'd have killed me.' Eve let out a shuddering sob. 'And she, Helen Crowther, according to O'Shaughnessy, murdered McKenzie. How could she do that? She had worked with him all those years as his personal assistant and she killed him when he was in hospital.'

'I know. I'm so sorry, Eve.'

'Going over it again this morning brought it all back to me.' Eve put her hand up to her mouth. 'Seeing that evil creature standing there smirking at me frightened me to death. And this afternoon I shall have to go through it all again when his lawyer cross-examines me.'

'If it's any consolation, what you said this morning should have been enough to send O'Shaughnessy to the gallows. Witnesses have to undergo cross-examination, it's the law, but I think everyone knows he's guilty – even his lawyer.' Ena took hold of Eve's hands. 'You were very strong this morning.'

'I didn't feel strong.'

'Believe me, you were. And you must be strong this afternoon too. O'Shaughnessy's lawyer will try to confuse you, twist what you say, make you out to be the liar – as he did me – but stick to your guns. Try to stay calm. Don't let him fluster you.'

There was a knock on the door and Mr Martin appeared. 'They're ready for you, Mrs Robinson.'

Eve took a deep breath and stood up. 'Thank you, Ena. Will you be in court this afternoon?'

'Yes, but I'm afraid I won't be able to see you later as I must get back to the office, but...' Ena took a business card from her purse and pressed it into Eve's hand, 'if you ever need anything, telephone me. Good luck and stay strong.'

Eve put her arms around Ena and held her tightly. Mr Martin cleared his throat and Eve broke away. She looked at Ena's card. 'Thank you.'

As the clerk led Eve out of the waiting room, Ena said again, 'Don't forget, be strong.'

'I will,' Eve replied.

CHAPTER EIGHTEEN

Ena listened to the harsh and often unfair cross-examination of Eve Robinson for two hours and not once did Eve lose her nerve. The defence lawyer did his best to twist her words, but she repeated what she had said without losing her composure.

Ena felt a tap on her shoulder and turned to see Mr Martin backing towards the door, beckoning her. She didn't want to leave, but she knew something important must have happened. She left her seat, and because she was sitting on the end of the row at the back of the public gallery, she didn't disturb anyone. Crouching, she made her way out of the door.

'Mrs Green, there has been a telephone call for you from a man who said he is an associate of yours. A Mr Mallory?'

'Yes, he's my colleague.'

'Taking telephone messages is most irregular and fetching someone out of court—'

'I'm sorry, Mr Martin. My associate wouldn't have asked you to fetch me unless it was urgent.'

Mr Martin didn't look happy at being used as a messenger. 'He said there has been a development in the case he is working on, and you must go back to the office at once.'

Ena put her hand up to her mouth and inhaled sharply. 'Thank you. It is of paramount importance.' She thanked Sir John's clerk again, ran down the stairs, out of the building and she hailed the first cab that came along Old Bailey.

Ena spotted Artie walking towards Long Acre as the black cab she was in turned into Mercer Street. She tapped on the glass pane separating the driver from the passengers. 'Would you drop me here, please?'

As the cab pulled into the kerb, Artie ran to the driver's window, gave him a pound note, shouted 'keep the change,' and pulled Ena from the back seat.

'What the hell's going on?' Ena asked as Artie hustled her into Café Romano.

'Mrs Hardy's in the office.'

'Why?'

'She called in and... I asked her to clean the windows.'

'You what?'

The waiter came to take their order. 'Two coffees,' Artie said without asking Ena what she wanted.

'Cleaning the windows was the only thing I could think of to keep her there until you got back. She was telling me how she'd spring cleaned her own house and threatened the boys not to make a mess. She's even made new curtains and matching cushion covers, like the ones in the magazine in the waiting room, she said.'

'Artie, you didn't have me called out of the Old Bailey to tell me about Doreen Hardy's curtains. So, what is it?'

'It's her old man, Arnold. He gets out of Wandsworth nick in a day or two, and the bastard isn't going home to Doreen and the boys.'

'How do you know?'

'Arnold did have a visitor yesterday and she signed the visitor's book as Mrs Hardy. Not Doreen Hardy, but Mrs M Hardy, as in Maisie. As you know, I went to the Duke of Wellington Hotel to see if any of the marked notes had been spent in the bar.'

'And had there been?'

'No, but when I was leaving, I saw a woman who looked familiar. At first, I thought I knew her. I didn't, but I had seen her before.'

'At the prison?'

'How did you know?'

'A lucky guess. Maisie works at the Duke of Wellington and her surname is Hardy. She was married to Arnold's younger brother.'

'Was?'

'Doreen told me Maisie's a widow. Go on.'

'Well, I was sure it was Maisie Hardy that I'd seen waiting to go into the prison yesterday, so when I left the hotel I drove over to Wandsworth and asked to speak to the officer on visitor duty the day before. After the third degree as to why I wanted to see him, they sent for him. It cost us another fiver but it was worth it. The guard said Arnold is playing his missus for a fool, that he'd been bragging to the other lags that she'd saved a good amount of money while he'd been inside.'

'Damn, Doreen must have told him.'

'He wasn't talking about Doreen, he was talking about Maisie. Maisie told Arnold she'd saved money for them to start a new life in Margate. Apparently, Arnold thought that was very funny. He said he'd have her money, but he didn't want her, and would be buggering off and starting again on his own once her money had run out. The guard said Hardy's wife was a regular visitor and that the only time she hadn't been to see him was when Arnold's first wife came asking him for money for her kids.'

'First wife? The lying swine. Doreen's his only wife.' Ena looked questioningly at Artie, 'Isn't she?' He lifted his shoulders, as if to say he didn't know. 'And as for asking that waste of time for money, I don't believe him. Doreen has always worked. She's had to because he's spent most of their married life in jail.'

The waiter brought the coffee and Ena took a sip. 'Did you say anything to Doreen?'

'She knew I'd been to the hotel, so I told her there hadn't been any marked notes in the till. She looked crestfallen so I said, "not this week".'

Ena sipped her coffee. 'She's going to be more than crestfallen when she finds out her sister-in-law, who she thinks is doing her job to keep it open for her, is doing it to save money so she can run away with her husband.' Ena finished her coffee. 'Come on, let's go to the office. We'll sit Doreen down and talk to her together.'

'Doreen isn't here,' Artie said, unlocking the office door and looking around. 'And her coat's gone.'

'She's left a note on your desk.' Ena went to Artie's desk and picked it up. '"I had to leave. I'm picking Maisie's little ones up from school. I'll see you and Mrs Green on Friday."'

Ena blew out her cheeks. 'A reprieve,' she said. 'The worst part of this job is having to give people bad news.' Ena put down Doreen's note. 'I'll go if you don't mind, Artie. I want a long hot soak before Henry gets home. We're meeting Priscilla and her husband, Charles. for dinner, tonight.'

'The two people you met at the gallery on preview night?'

'The very same. And, before you say it, no it isn't a conflict of interest. I know Priscilla is a magpie, but it isn't her or her lovely old husband stealing works of art. Besides, tonight is a social occasion. Strictly *no* shop talk.' Ena grabbed her jacket. 'Tomorrow I'll fill you in with what happened at the Old Bailey, and what Eve Robinson said. See you in the morning. Okay if I take the car?'

Artie pulled a disappointed face. 'Course it is, it's your car. I'll write up the Hardy case before I leave,' he said, taking the car keys from his desk and throwing them to Ena. 'Enjoy tonight.'

CHAPTER NINETEEN

Ena heard a noise. She turned off the hot water tap and listened. It was the front door. Henry had come home early. 'I'm about to have a bath, darling,' she shouted.

Henry poked his head around the bathroom door. 'Want your back scrubbing?'

Ena laughed. 'Is there time?'

'There's always time,' he said, undoing the belt of her bathrobe. Pushing the robe from her shoulders, he kissed the small of her neck and then her breasts. As the robe fell the floor, he picked her up and carried her to the bedroom.

'Henry, don't go to sleep,' Ena said when they had made love.

Henry opened his eyes and reached for his cigarettes and lighter from the bedside cabinet, 'Want one?'

'No, I'd better get up and have a bath while the water's still hot.' Henry lit a cigarette, passed it to Ena and she took a drag. Exhaling, she sat up and swung her legs over the side of the bed. 'There's a couple of sandwiches in the kitchen. You need to eat something before we go out.'

'What about you?'

'I ate when I got home.' She looked at Henry. 'I would take little persuading to come back to bed which,' she said, cutting him off as he began to speak, 'is why I am going to have my bath.' At the door, she looked back at Henry and blew him a kiss.

'I love you, Mrs Green,' Henry said.

'Not as much as I love you, Mr Green,' Ena replied, leaving the bedroom.

Glowing from having made love, Ena added

bubble bath to the warm bathwater and stepped in.

She heard Henry close the bedroom door and walk along the passage. 'Save the water for me,' he called as he drew level with the bathroom.

Ena laughed. The new immersion heater would have heated the water up again during the half-hour they had been making love. Ena relaxed back in the bath and, keeping her hair clear of the water, slid down until the bubbles covered her body.

For the last couple of years Ena and Henry's marriage had been, not exactly on the rocks, but rocky. Owing to the nature of their previous work in the intelligence services there had been too many secrets between them. But now she had left the Home Office and worked for herself, and Henry had left MI5 and worked at GCHQ, they saw more of each other. Henry occasionally had meetings in Cambridge – and sometimes stayed over – but he was now based in an ordinary-looking building in Palmer Street, St. James's Park. Although his work was classified and he wasn't able to talk about it, there were no conflicts of interests between his job and hers and no secrets between them as man and wife. Henry's work at GCHQ was more like the work he did at Bletchley Park in the war. He rarely spoke about his work and Ena didn't ask. She did, however, talk to him about hers. Tonight his experience as an artist was going to be a great help.

'Do I look alright in this, Henry?' Ena asked when they were both dressed.

'You'd look better out of it.'

She bowled the bath towel he'd left on the dressing table stool at him. 'Be serious. Is this dress good enough for dinner at The Savoy?'

'Yes, it's beautiful. You are beautiful.'

'You're not so bad yourself,' Ena said,

straightening Henry's tie and giving him a peck on the cheek. She laughed and rubbed lipstick from where she had kissed him. 'Nice colour, but it looks better on me,' she said, dancing out of the bedroom and into the sitting room to collect her wrap and evening bag.

A car's horn hooted, and Henry switched off the sitting room light.

There was very little traffic south of the river and Ena and Henry arrived at The Savoy early. Henry paid the fare and followed Ena into the foyer. 'The cocktail lounge?' she asked the doorman.

'Across the foyer and right past reception, Madam. You can't miss it.'

The doorman touched his cap as Henry passed him and a moment later they were being greeted by Priscilla and Charles.

Priscilla was wearing a black below the knee cocktail dress that might have been in Vogue magazine, except for the size. She threw her arms around Ena. At the same time, Henry and Charles shook hands.

'Our table is booked for eight, we have time for a drink before we go into the restaurant. What would you like, Ena?' Charles asked.

'Dry Martinis,' Priscilla said before Ena had time to reply. 'And make them very dry, darling.' Priscilla giggled and linking her arm through Ena's, steered her into the swish cocktail bar of The Savoy.

When they were seated with their drinks, Priscilla chatted animatedly. She pointed to the diamond necklace that Charles had bought her earlier that day and giggling, said that her husband had neglected her piteously while pulling off a large business deal and the necklace was because he felt guilty.

Charles looked embarrassed. 'I'm sure Ena and Henry don't want to hear how I neglect you, my love.'

Priscilla laughed and said, 'The truth is, Ena, my darling husband spoils me. I don't know what I've done to deserve such a generous, kind, loving man.' She put her hand on top of her husband's. Looking into his eyes she said, 'Whatever it was, I'm glad I did it.' A perfectly round pink blush coloured Charles' cheeks as he lifted Priscilla's hand and kissed it. Priscilla suddenly stood up. 'Ena and I are going to powder our noses before we eat.' Slightly taken aback, but trying not to show it, Ena got to her feet. 'I want to show you the gilt mirrors. And you must smell the divine soaps. Won't be long,' she called to the men, leading the way across the cocktail bar and through a door that said Ladies Powder Room. It was an oblong room, brightly lit with floor to ceiling mirrors, dressing tables on three walls with chairs under them. A door in the wall opposite led to toilets and hand basins – and more mirrors. While they washed their hands, Priscilla said, 'Try this.' She passed Ena a round lilac coloured soap. 'Mmmm... I love lavender. Oh,' she exclaimed, 'this is new.' She sniffed a cream soap. 'Lovely.' She reached across two basins, took two lavender scented soaps and a cream one – all three still in their packaging – and dropped them into her handbag.

Having seen Priscilla steal a brooch that was worth hundreds of pounds, Ena wasn't surprised that she took soap home from The Savoy. She washed her hands in lavender scented soap and dried them on a soft white towel. When she had finished, she went into the powder room. Priscilla was spraying perfume on her wrists.

'Chanel No 5,' she said, 'put out your arms.' Ena did and Priscilla sprayed far too much perfume on her wrists.

She put the small square glass bottle into her handbag. 'They don't have Chanel in the restaurant's toilet,' she giggled, 'and we don't want to use another fragrance, do we? How's my hair?' she asked, catching sight of herself in the mirror.

'Perfect,' Ena said, winding a stray curl around her finger that had been set free when she took off her wrap.

Humming a lively tune, Priscilla sashayed across the room to the door. She turned back and looked at Ena. 'Your hair looks lovely. Come on, I'm starving.'

'There's an anniversary ball next week. On August the sixth, it will be seventy years since Richard D'Oyly Carte built The Savoy. He didn't build it personally of course, he had it built with the profits from his Gilbert and Sullivan opera productions.' Priscilla laughed. 'It was either cheap to build, or D'Oyly Carte put on an awful lot of shows. You will come, won't you?'

'I doubt there'll be any seats left in the restaurant on that night.'

'Charles has already booked. It isn't only D'Oyly Carte we're celebrating. It's Charles' birthday that day.'

'We'll see,' Ena said.

When the women arrived back at the table, Charles stood up and pulled out Priscilla's chair. Ena was too quick for Henry and was already seated by the time he stood up.

'I don't need a menu,' Priscilla said, 'I know what I'm having. The chef is French, Ena. I recommend steak de filet with champignons and pomme puree, and stuffed squid to start.'

'That sounds good. I'll have the steak, too,' Henry said, 'and to start...' he looked down the list of hors d'oeuvres, 'salmon rillettes.'

'And,' Ena said, 'I shall have chicken liver pate followed by sole meunière with green beans and pomme puree.'

No sooner had the party put down their menus than a waiter collected them and bowed to Charles who gave him everyone's order, adding fish soup and a pork chop with asparagus for himself. As the waiter left, Charles lifted his right hand and a wine waiter brought over two bottles of wine.

'Henry and I took the liberty of ordering the wine while you were powdering your nose, darling,' he said to Priscilla. Charles thanked the waiter, who poured a small quantity of red wine into a glass and handed it to him. He breathed in the wine's aroma before tasting it. 'Thank you,' he said again. The waiter put down the red wine and took a bottle of white from a wine bucket. 'Ena, as you're having fish, would you like to taste the white wine?'

Ena knew nothing about wines, other than she liked the taste of most wines that she had tried, and passed the buck. 'I'm having pate to start. Henry is having salmon. Darling, why don't you taste the white wine?'

Henry did and declared that it was crisp and dry, but not sharp. 'Just right.'

The food was delicious. The wine, Henry and Ena agreed, although neither were connoisseurs, was the best they'd tasted but what made the evening was the vibrant, often cheeky, anecdotes told by their hostess. Priscilla was fun and Charles was an interesting man who, like Henry, could speak on any subject. Ena was sure Priscilla exaggerated to make the tales she told funnier, but that was part of her charm. Ena liked her. She liked her sense of humour and the fact that she didn't take herself seriously, which most women with wealthy husbands did. Priscilla was fun and entertaining throughout the meal.

Over brandy and coffee, Priscilla said, 'We must do this again. What about next week on The Savoy's seventieth anniversary? We have a table booked, don't we, darling?'

Charles looked from Ena to Henry and back to Priscilla. 'I am sorry, my dear, it's a table for two. It was the only table they had left. If I'd known…'

'Then Ena and I shall go out to lunch. I shall take you to Chez Maurice. Ena, when would be best for you?'

'I have client meetings the rest of this week and early next week.' She needed to go to The Willows Nursing Home before meeting George. If her suspicions were correct, she would expose the killer of George's father. On the other hand, she wanted to learn more about the gallery owner and her American sponsor. 'Wednesday would be good for me.'

Outside, waiting on the pavement while the men hailed cabs, Ena said, 'Priscilla, may I ask you something?'

Priscilla's eyes lit up. 'Of course.'

'I'm about to close an investigation. It's an adultery case involving two women who work at the same hotel. One woman stole money from the hotel and planted it on the other one. The money was kept in a bureau, which hadn't been left unlocked nor had it been broken into.'

Priscilla gave Ena a sideways look and laughed. A cab pulled up and her husband called her. 'The money had been left in a writing bureau?' Ena nodded. 'My dear, almost any small key will unlock a writing bureau. The key to my china cabinet and the drinks cabinet fits Charles' bureau. Writing bureaux are not safes.'

'Thank you.' As Priscilla joined her husband in the back of the black cab, Ena gave her a card. 'Telephone me to arrange where to meet.'

A second cab pulled up behind the first. Henry held the door open and Ena jumped in.

CHAPTER TWENTY

Ena was late getting to the office. She parked the Sunbeam in one of the two spaces designated to Dudley Green Associates, ran across Mercer Street and into the office, taking off her coat as she entered. 'Doreen not here?'

'No. There's been no sign of her.'

'It's unlike her to be late.'

'Unlike you to be late too. Had a boozy night, did we?'

'We didn't. I did. And, my head's throbbing. I had far too much to drink, I need coffee.' Ena went into the kitchen and picked up the kettle. There was plenty of water in it so she switched it on.

Artie put coffee into three cups and Ena poured boiling water into two of them. She took milk from the small refrigerator, added some and while she put the milk back, Artie took their coffees through to the office.

'When Doreen has gone, we need to sit down and work out what we should do about the art theft case.'

They drank their coffee in silence. When they had finished Artie said, 'It's ten o'clock, Doreen's now an hour late.'

Ena looked up at the office clock and then at Artie. Chewing his bottom lip, his brow creased with worry, he was staring into his empty cup. 'Something's wrong. You think so too, don't you?' Ena asked.

'Yes, I do.'

'She doesn't have a telephone, so we'll have to drive over to her house.' Ena picked up the car keys. 'Lock up Artie, and I'll turn the car around.' By the time Artie had locked the office, and the outer doors,

Ena was in the car and facing up Mercer Street to Acre Lane. Artie jumped into the passenger seat and Ena put her foot down on the accelerator. 'I don't want Arnold Hardy to get home and blurt it out that he's leaving her for Maisie. I want to break it to her gently, it's the least I can do.'

'Do you want me to come in with you?'

'Since it was you who solved the case, yes. I'll tell her that we have evidence that Arnold and Maisie are more than friends. If she asks how we know, you can explain how you found out. Don't go into detail. Just say you saw Maisie in the visitor's queue at Wandsworth Prison waiting to visit Arnold.'

As they passed the Duke of Wellington, Ena said, 'By the way, I think I know how Maisie stole the money from Mr Walter's bureau. But it can wait. I need to check something first.'

Ena turned into Rutland Road. Most of the houses looked dilapidated with curtains or nets that hadn't been washed in an age. The gardens on either side of the paths leading to the front doors of Doreen's neighbours were earth with tufts of grass. One had a broken hand basin in it, another a car without wheels. Doreen's garden was neat and tidy with a small square of lawn surrounded by flowers.

Ena knocked on the door. She turned to Artie. 'I'm not looking forward to this.'

'Nor am I.'

'She's a long time answering.' Ena took a couple of steps to the right and peered through what she assumed was the front room window. 'I can't see anything because of the nets.' She tapped the window, lightly at first and then louder.

'No sign of life. I hope she isn't on her way to the office.'

'So do I.' Ena made a fist and knocked again. 'She might be upstairs or in the back.'

'I'll have a look,' Artie said, already halfway down the path at the side of the house. 'Ena,' he shouted, 'Ena, she's here.'

Ena heard the urgency in Artie's voice and ran like a hare to the back of the house.

'She's in the kitchen on the floor. She must have fallen.' He turned the doorknob. 'The door's locked.' He pushed the window. It didn't open.

Ena grabbed a towel from the washing line, wrapped it around her fist and punched the glass panel in the door nearest the lock. The glass shattered leaving a hole big enough for Ena to put her hand in. She crouched down and found the key, turned it, and recoiled. 'Gas. I can smell gas.' She dropped the towel, pulled open the door and, with her hand over her mouth and nose, ran into the kitchen and turned off the gas in the oven and on the top of the cooker while Artie opened the window.

'Help me get her outside,' Ena gasped, choking from the fumes.

Coughing, Artie took hold of Doreen's shoulders and Ena her feet and together they carried the unconscious woman out of the kitchen and laid her on the concrete slabs in the back yard. Artie took off his jacket and put it under her head.

'Doreen?' Ena laid the flat of her hand on Doreen's chest and put her ear to Doreen's mouth. 'She's breathing,' Ena said with relief. 'Doreen, can you hear me?' Ena pushed her hair away from her face. 'Doreen, it's Ena. Wake up for me, Doreen. Come on, love, wake up.'

A sharp rasping sound escaped Doreen's lips. Her thin body convulsed and she gulped air. Thrashing from side to side, she struggled for breath.

Ena took hold of her arms. 'Be careful, Doreen, you'll hurt yourself.'

From kneeling at her head, Artie moved to Doreen's side and the next time she rolled to the left, he put out his arms and held onto her. Coughing and choking she pushed him away and tried to sit up but she had no strength. Artie helped her into a sitting position holding her hands in front of her while Ena put her arms around her shoulders to comfort her.

'What happened?' she whispered in a hoarse voice.

Artie looked at Ena and raised his eyebrows as if to say, 'what do we tell her?'

Doreen obviously didn't remember and Ena didn't want to frighten her. 'You fell in the kitchen.'

'Did I? Oh…' Doreen lifted her hand to the back of her head, touched it and winced. 'I must have hit the floor hard.'

Ena parted Doreen's hair where her hand had been. 'You've cut your head and it's swollen. Do you feel dizzy?' Doreen shook her head.

Ena lifted her hand level with Doreen's face and put up her forefinger. 'How many fingers can you see?'

'One.'

'And now?' Ena said, putting up three fingers of her right hand.

'Three.'

Ena looked at Artie and lifter her shoulders. 'Do you feel sick at all, Doreen?'

'No. My head hurts. I must have bumped it on something when I fell.'

'I'm wondering if we should take you to the hospital, get you checked over. You might be concussed.'

'I'm not going to the hospital, Mrs Green. I don't feel dizzy or anything, I'm fine. Besides, they'll ask me all sorts of questions and...' She looked around and took in her surroundings. 'Why am I sitting out here? I thought you said I fell in the kitchen.'

'You did. Artie and I brought you out here for some air.'

Doreen frowned and cleared her throat. 'I should like to go into the house.' Letting go of Artie's hands, she looked up at the bedroom windows of her neighbour. 'I want to go inside before anyone sees me. Goodness knows what they'll make of me sitting out here in the back yard.'

Artie helped Doreen to her feet and Ena took his coat. 'Thank you, Mr Mallory, I can manage now,' she said, with a shy, embarrassed smile. Then, as she turned towards the kitchen door, she lost her balance and reached out to him. 'Perhaps I can't manage as well as I thought,' she whispered.

Artie on one side and Ena on the other, they helped Doreen into her house. Although a table and four chairs stood against the wall opposite the cooker, Ena nodded to the door at the far end of the kitchen. 'You'll be more comfortable in the front room, Doreen. Through here, is it?' Ena pulled open the door.

Doreen, with Artie holding onto her arm, walked dreamlike out of the kitchen and across the hall to a small, neat sitting room at the front of the house. In its day the three-piece-suite would have been fashionable. Faded now, it was still good quality. There were loose cushions in a cotton fabric with a floral design on each chair and two on the settee – one at each end – and cream antimacassars with embroidered roses at the corners on the backs and arms of the settee and armchairs. A wooden lampstand stood in the corner of the room next to the sideboard, which was the same wood as the kitchen table and chairs. By its plain design, Ena could see it was utility furniture made during the war – as was the kitchen table and chairs. On the sideboard small place mats in the same fabric and design as the antimacassars had been placed beneath photographs of Doreen's boys. The carpet by the door was worn, which with three growing lads traipsing in and out was not surprising.

'Sit down,' Artie said, lowering Doreen onto the settee under the window.

'I'll make a cup of tea. You stay with her, Artie,' Ena instructed, returning to the kitchen.

She filled the kettle from the cold water tap and set it down on the draining board. As a precaution, she checked the knobs that turned on the gas in the oven and hob were switched off. She then opened the oven door and sniffed. Burnt fat filled her nostrils but there was no smell of gas. Satisfied that lighting a gas jet to boil the kettle would not blow up the house, she closed the oven door and looked in the drawers for matches. She smiled. Doreen Hardy wouldn't put matches where her boys could reach them. She looked up. There was a box of Swan Vesta on top of the kitchen cabinet.

Doreen was a good mother. So why did she try to kill herself? She would know without her the two youngest boys would be taken to a children's home and Alfred, who must be fourteen now, would be sent to a hostel for young men. Could she have thought the boys would be better off living with their father? 'No!' Ena said aloud. Doreen loved her boys too much to condemn them to a life with him.

CHAPTER TWENTY-ONE

Ena took down the matches, struck one and held her breath. She watched the flame turn from yellow to blue, before turning the knob on the nearest gas jet. Placing the kettle above the gas, she exhaled with relief.

While the kettle boiled, she looked around the spotlessly clean kitchen, opened the cupboard under the sink and took out a brush and pan. She then pulled out what remained of the broken glass in the small square in the door and swept up what had fallen onto the lino. Emptying the shards of glass into the dustbin, Ena spotted a thick cardboard box. She reached in and pulled it out. As a temporary measure, cut into shape it would replace the pane of glass that she had smashed in order to unlock the door. She put the box by the door, and when the kettle boiled made the tea. Milk she took from the thrawl in the pantry and sugar from the highest shelf in the kitchen cabinet. Again, out of the reach of small boys.

'I've come to see if I can help you,' Artie said, loudly from the door. He came into the kitchen, closed the door and whispered, 'I asked Doreen if the boys were at school and she said that because Maisie knew she was coming into the office today, she had taken the two youngest to school and her neighbour had taken Alfred to work with him. He's a painter and decorator and his apprentice is off work sick, so he's given Alfred a few day's work.'

'I wonder what could have happened to stop Doreen coming to the office?' Ena looked from Artie to the oven. 'What happened that was so awful, so terrible, that the poor woman tried to gas herself?'

'Perhaps Maisie told Doreen that Arnold was leaving her?'

'Would she put her head in the gas oven because a useless lump like Arnold Hardy was going to leave her?'

'Maybe if Maisie told her that Arnold was going to start a new life with her.'

Ena considered both possibilities. 'I don't think either of those scenarios would make her want to kill herself. Not with the boys to look after. She loves those boys. I think she only put up with Arnold for their sake. And Maisie couldn't have told her. Doreen wouldn't have let her take the boys to school if she had.'

'Well, something made Doreen put her head in the gas oven.'

'Yes, but what? We need to find out what Maisie said to her, how far she pushed her.'

Artie opened the door. 'One of us should be in the office. If I go back when I've had my tea, she might confide in you.'

'She might,' Ena agreed. Putting the sugar bowl and milk on the tray with the teapot, cups and saucers she followed Artie out of the kitchen.

When they had finished their tea, Ena suggested Artie returned to the office. 'Ask one of the builders to come over and replace the pane of glass in the back door.'

Artie, in agreement, jumped up and crossed the room to Doreen. Crouching down beside her, he looked into her face. 'Now, you take it easy,' he said, giving her shoulder a gentle squeeze.

'I shall, Mr Mallory.' She put her hand to her mouth and stifled a sob. 'Goodness knows how long I'd have laid there if you and Mrs Green hadn't found me.'

Probably until your sons came home from school and found you dead from carbon monoxide poison, Ena thought but didn't say. Now was not the time to tell Doreen.

'I'll be back for you at about two, Ena,' Artie said as he left.

'Oh, there's something I want Artie to do at the office. Artie?' she called. He didn't reply, nor did he return. Ena jumped up. 'I'll try to catch him. I won't be a minute, Doreen.'

When she entered the kitchen, Artie was waiting for her. 'Get whoever's coming to replace the glass to call at a hardware store and buy two locks – one for the back.' She pulled open the kitchen door. 'I expect they're standard for this type of semi-detached council house – and one for the front door. Have a look at it as you pass so you can describe it to the builder and give him the money out of petty cash.'

The car keys were on the kitchen windowsill. Artie picked them up, looked again at the lock, nodded and said, 'I'll be back for you later,' before disappearing around the corner of the house.

Returning to the sitting room, Ena picked up the tray of dirty cups and saucers. 'Would you like another cup of tea, Doreen?' She shook her head. 'I'll pop these into the kitchen and put the milk in the larder before it goes off.'

After returning the milk and sugar to their respective places, Ena put the cups and saucers in the washing-up bowl alongside two that were already there. She had noticed them when she and Artie first entered the house and had wondered then if Doreen had had a visitor that morning. She must have made Maisie a cup of tea. Ena quickly washed up, put the crockery in the cupboard and returned to the sitting room.

'That didn't take long,' she said. Seeing tears in Doreen's eyes, Ena went over to her and sat next to her. 'Have you remembered something about this morning? What was it that made you—?'

Doreen's face was ashen, her eyes staring across the room as if she had seen a ghost. 'Maisie!' was all she said.

'Maisie? What did Maisie say or do that made you want to kill yourself, Doreen?'

Doreen recoiled. 'Kill myself?' She began to shake. She looked searchingly into Ena's face. 'I don't want to kill myself! What do you mean?'

Ena reached out and covered Doreen's hands with hers. 'When Artie and I found you, you were lying on the floor.'

'I know. You said I'd fallen.'

'We didn't want to alarm you, so we told you that you'd fallen, but you hadn't, Doreen. You were lying on the floor with your head... next to the gas oven.'

Doreen looked at Ena and shook her head. 'No, that can't be right.' Deep frown lines appeared on her forehead then, as if a light had been switched on in the darkness, she said again, 'Maisie!'

'What about Maisie?' Ena asked in a calm voice.

'Well.' Doreen cast her gaze around the room, finally settling on the door to the hall. 'Alfred had already gone to work with my neighbour by the time Gerald and Billy came down. They'd had their breakfast and were dressed and ready for school when Maisie arrived. She said she'd take my boys to school with hers. They were playing out the front and Maisie said we had time for a quick cup of tea, so we went to the kitchen.'

Doreen got up and Ena followed her out of the sitting room and into the kitchen.

'She was early, you see.' Doreen closed her eyes and exhaled, as if to clear her mind of everything except what had happened next. 'Maisie made us a cup of tea and we sat at the table to drink it. When we'd finished, I put the cups and saucers in the bowl and…'

'And?'

'Nothing. I don't remember anything after that until I woke up in the yard with you and Mr Mallory.'

'So, Maisie didn't give you any bad news, or say anything that made you want to take your own life?'

'Of course not!' Doreen looked outraged by the suggestion. 'Why would she?'

Ena knew that she needed to tell Doreen the truth about finding her. She also knew she needed to be sensitive because what she was about to tell her would break her heart. She cleared her throat, 'Doreen, you know I told you that when Artie and I found you, you were lying on the floor next to the oven.'

'Of course, I know!' she said, her tone a mixture of resentment and exasperation. 'Why do you keep—?' A look of horror swept over her face as the realisation of what Ena was saying registered. 'Are you saying the gas oven was on while I was lying there?'

'Yes, Doreen. I'm sorry, but it was.'

Tears burst from Doreen's eyes. 'I didn't try to kill myself, Mrs Green. Nothing on God's earth could be bad enough to make me want to leave my boys. What would they do without me?' she cried. 'Mrs Green, what made you think I'd do such a wicked thing?' Doreen took her handkerchief from her pocket and wiped her face.

'I thought Maisie had told you that she—'

'She what?'

'Maisie has been visiting Arnold in prison.' Doreen's mouth fell open. 'Artie saw Maisie in the visitor's queue at Wandsworth Prison yesterday. He didn't know it was Maisie at the time, but he went to the Duke of Wellington to ask Mr Walters if he'd had any marked notes in the till and he saw the woman he'd seen at the prison the day before.'

'It couldn't have been our Maisie.'

'I'm sorry, Doreen, but I'm afraid it was. Artie went back to the prison and spoke to the guard on duty the day before. He said Maisie had been writing to Arnold and had often visited him. The earlier dates the guard gave Artie match the days you were working at the hotel.'

'No,' Doreen said, agitated. 'I'm sorry, Mrs Green, Mr Mallory couldn't have seen Maisie. She wouldn't do such a thing. No,' she said, again. 'It's only because Maisie's been doing my shifts and paying me to give her children their tea that I haven't had to spend the money I'd saved for when Arnold got out.' Suddenly, as if she had been struck by something heavy, Doreen cried out, leapt out of her chair and flew across the kitchen.

CHAPTER TWENTY-TWO

Doreen reached up and took a box from on top of the kitchen cabinet, opened it and howled like a wounded animal. Ena got to her as her knees started to buckle. She managed to keep her upright and helped her across the room and back to the chair at the kitchen table.

'All the money I'd saved to take Arnold, the boys and me to the seaside has gone.' Doreen put her head in her hands. 'What am I going to tell my boys? I promised them I'd take them to the seaside. Damn you, Arnold Hardy!' she screamed. 'He was always making the boys promises he couldn't keep and then letting them down. Now I've broken my promise and I'm going to let them down too,' she sobbed.

'Not if I have anything to do with it, you aren't.' Ena got to her feet. 'I'm going to find a phone-box and call the Police.'

'No! No Police.'

'Doreen, Maisie has stolen your money. I wouldn't be surprised if it wasn't her who stole the money from the Duke of Wellington and planted it in your coat pocket so she could do your shifts and earn more money for her and Arnold.'

'I don't care. I am not having the Police here, or my boys will find out that their father was going to abandon them again!'

'Doreen, you can't let her get away with it.'

'I can, and I will. No Police, Mrs Green. My boys have seen enough policemen in their short lives.'

Doreen stared at the oven and tears rolled down her cheeks.

Ena returned to her chair and sat down.

Doreen's thin body began to shake. She put her hand to her mouth and snatched a breath.

'What is it?'

'The last thing I remember before waking up outside was putting the cups and saucers in the bowl to wash up.' Doreen felt the back of her head again. 'No, Mrs Green, I didn't try to kill myself by putting my head in the oven. And, by the size of the lump on the back of my head, I didn't fall by accident.'

Ena knew she hadn't fallen by accident and was grateful that Doreen had realised it. She was about to ask her if she remembered anything else when there was a loud knock.

Doreen spun round. 'What was that?'

'It's alright. It's just someone's at the front door.'

'If it's the Police—'

'It won't be the Police. It'll be a workman from Mercer Street. Artie asked one of the men working on the flat above the office to come over, replace the broken glass in your back door and change the locks. Shall I answer the door?'

Doreen nodded.

By the time the locks had been changed and there was a new pane of glass in the back door it was two o'clock and Artie had returned to pick Ena up.

While showing Doreen the new lock on the front door, Ena noticed that the builder had not only fitted a bolt at the top of the door, he had screwed a metal plate attached to a chain to the door frame and a metal plate with a ring on it to the stile on the door. Ena put her arm around Doreen's shoulders. 'Well, you're safe now. Not only do you have a new lock and a bolt, if you bring this chain across the door and hook it over this fitting here before you open the door...' Ena demonstrated how the security chain worked. 'You can open your door wide enough to see whoever is outside, and if you don't want them to come in, they won't come in.'

'It would take an army to push the door open when the chain's on,' Artie said, pulling on the door.

Ena agreed and leaving the chain in place, closed and locked the front door. 'No one can get into your house now unless you invite them in.'

Artie led the way to the kitchen. He picked up a brown paper bag that the workman had left on the draining board. 'Two keys,' he said, taking one and putting it in the lock. 'Your eldest son will need the other when he's working.'

Doreen looked at Artie and smiled proudly. She didn't touch the key.

'It doesn't matter who's had keys to your house in the past, they haven't got them now,' Ena said. Doreen nodded. 'As an extra precaution, take the key out of the kitchen door when you're in the house. If I can break the glass, put my hand through and unlock the door, anyone can.' Again, Doreen stared at the key.

'Doreen, take the new key out of the door after you've locked it,' Ena repeated, 'then no one will be able to break in. Will you do that, Doreen?'

As if she had only just heard Ena, Doreen took the key and put it on the table. She then unhooked the handles of her handbag from the back of the chair. 'How much do I owe you for the new locks and the man's time?' she asked, taking out her purse.

'I've no idea what locks cost,' Ena said. 'Do you know, Artie?' Artie shook his head. 'Leave it for now. We'll sort it out another time.'

Doreen had tears in her eyes. She looked exhausted and stood for some time without speaking. Then, as if everything Ena had been saying suddenly made sense to her, she pulled herself together. 'I'd better let you and Mr Mallory get back to work,' she said, heading out of the kitchen.

Ena raised her eyes at Artie, he put up his thumb and they followed Doreen to the front door.

As they were leaving, Ena again assured Doreen that she was safe. And again, Doreen thanked her. 'Don't forget to bolt the door and put the chain on,' Ena said, forcing herself to smile cheerily as she and Artie left.

Walking along the path to the car, Ena heard the heavy bolt slide and engage.

'Were there any phone calls while I was at Doreen's?' Ena asked, as she and Artie drove towards Waterloo Bridge.

'One from Inspector Powell and one from a woman called Priscilla?'

Ena laughed. 'Priscilla is my magpie friend. The woman I told you about who stole the expensive brooch from the art gallery when Henry and I went to the opening. By the time I'd told the owner, she or her lovely husband had put the brooch back.'

'She sounds like fun.'

'She is, and yet there's a sadness about her too. I like her,' Ena said, 'she fascinates me. She's like Alice in Through The Looking Glass. What she sees in the looking glass is not what we, or those who don't live in Wonderland, see.'

'She said not to forget that you and her are going out for lunch next week and to telephone her to arrange a day and time.'

'I'll ring her later. Did the inspector leave a message?'

'No, he just said he'd ring another time.'

'It couldn't have been important or he'd have said.

If there's nothing else, you can drop me off at the Duke of Wellington Hotel. I'm going to get Doreen her job back.'

CHAPTER TWENTY-THREE

Both times Ena had been to the Duke of Wellington hotel it had been to the private quarters of the manager, Mr Walters. Today, as it had only just gone two, she decided to enter the hotel from the public side.

Pushing open the door to the bar she was pleasantly surprised. It was a large room, spacious and well laid out with good quality furniture, flock wallpaper – a fleur de Lys pattern in duck egg on petrol blue that gave the room a relaxed warm feel.

As she approached the bar, the barman set down the glass he was drying and met her with a welcoming smile.

'What can I get you, Madam?'

Ena considered having a soft drink, something long and cool, but after the morning she'd had she fancied a real drink. It was a hot day, she was hot, and seeing an ice bucket advertising Teacher's Whisky on the end of the bar, she said, 'Teacher's with ice and soda.'

Acknowledging the order with a nod, the barman turned, took a whisky tumbler from the shelf and pushed it under the Teacher's Whisky optic. He added the same quantity of soda and then picked up the ice tongs. 'One lump or two, Madam?' he asked, taking the top off the ice bucket.

'Just one, thanks.'

The barman placed a drip-mat displaying the hotel's name in front of Ena, put the glass of whisky on it, and the soda syphon next to it. 'That will be two and six, please.'

Ena took the money from her purse and gave it to him.

'Help yourself to more soda.'

She took a drink. It didn't need more soda. The barman put her money in the till and moved along the bar to serve a man who had just arrived. The man asked if it was too late to order lunch. It wasn't, so, after a cursory glance at the menu, he ordered two fish and chips meals. When he had been served his drinks, the man took them across the room to his companion. He looked at the door and then at the window. Ena looked too. Where the couple were sitting they wouldn't be seen by anyone entering the bar or looking through the window. A romantic liaison, she mused. Maybe the boss and his secretary having an affair. Her attention was brought back to the barman who she saw disappearing with the food order through a door at the far end of the bar.

When he returned Ena toyed with the idea of having another drink, but decided against it. 'I'd like to see Mr Walters,' she said. 'Is he in?' The barman's smile turned from being amiable to anxious. He blinked several times, appearing nervous. Ena didn't care why the man suddenly seemed uncomfortable, she needed to speak to the hotel's manager and, unless he had emigrated to Timbuktu, she was determined to see him. 'I'm a friend. Tell him it's Ena Green.'

'I'm not sure he's er, here—'

Ena rolled her eyes. 'Another trip to the wholesaler?' The barman didn't answer. 'You'd better get me another drink, then, I might be here a while.'

At that moment the door from the kitchen opened and Dolly came out carrying a tray with two plates of fish and chips. Seeing Ena, she stopped dead. 'Hello, Mrs Green,' she said, sounding surprised. 'You here to see Mr Walters? He's in the back.'

'Ah, the prodigal manager has returned,' Ena said,

looking at the barman and being intentionally sarcastic.

'Yes, I'll er, tell him you're here, Mrs Green.'

When Dolly had taken the meal to the man and woman in the corner, she beamed Ena a smile. 'Have you seen Doreen? Do you know how she is?'

'Yes, I saw her today. She's very well.'

'That was a terrible thing, her getting blamed for taking that money.'

'Dolly, it will go no further, I promise, but was it you who put the money in Doreen's coat pocket?'

Dolly's eyes sparkled with anger. She was the type of person who, when confronted, went on the attack.

'I give you my word I won't tell Mr Walters, or anyone, but it is important that I know if it was you.'

Dolly looked at the door to the kitchen. 'I shouldn't have, I know, but I could tell that Mr Walters thought highly of Doreen, You see, I wanted the barmaid's job and when Mr Walters said he was going to teach Doreen how to serve drinks, I saw red. I've regretted what I did every day since. When Doreen had gone I asked Mr Walters if I could have the bar job and he said no. He said working behind the bar wouldn't be good for me.' She looked down at her clasped hands and exhaled. 'He said he wasn't giving me the job for my own good. And he was right,' she whispered. 'He's been very kind to me. He has helped me with my problem.'

'So, then you felt you couldn't tell him?'

'Oh no, it wasn't that. Mr Walters knew I'd been having a difficult time. I think he would have understood why I did what I did. No,' Dolly said, shaking her head, 'I was going to tell him alright, get it off my chest so to speak, but Maisie said I wasn't to.'

Ena bristled at the sound of Maisie Hardy's name. What she had done to Doreen made Ena see red. She took a breath and forced herself to smile. 'Go on.'

'Well, Maisie was already doing Doreen's shifts, so when I told her what I'd done she said I wasn't to say anything yet, as Doreen's husband was coming home soon and Doreen wanted to spend some time with him. She said it would work out in Doreen's favour to have time off. She promised me she'd tell Mr Walters it wasn't Doreen who stole the money when she was ready to come back to work. Maisie said she was paying Doreen to look after her children so Doreen wouldn't miss out on her wages.'

The door to the private quarters and the kitchen caught Ena's attention as it opened. Ena assured Dolly that she wouldn't say anything and she returned to the kitchen. Mr Walters held the door for her before lifting the flap at the end of the bar and joining Ena.

'Mrs Green?' Mr Walters put out his hand and Ena shook it. 'I wasn't expecting to see you today. I'm a bit short-staffed.'

'I'm sorry for turning up without an appointment, but I wondered if I could have a word with Maisie Hardy, in private.'

'Maisie isn't here. She came in earlier, but didn't feel well, so I sent her home. She was waiting for her wages in my sitting room, but I hadn't made up the wage packets so she left.' Mr Walters shook his head. 'And, for the first time in a long time, money is missing from the bureau.'

'Was it marked?'

'Yes, I mark it every night. I went to make up the staff wages at the end of the morning shift, opened the bureau and all the five-pound-notes had gone.'

'I think Maisie has gone too.'

'I suspected as much.'

'If it's any consolation, I don't think you'll have to

worry about any more money being stolen.'

Mr Walters inhaled deeply and let out his breath in a sad groan. 'So, it was Maisie Hardy who has been stealing from me. Was it Maisie who put money in Doreen's coat pocket?'

Ena lifted her shoulders as if to say she didn't know. She was not going to break her promise to Dolly. However stupid Dolly had been, Ena believed her when she said she wanted to confess what she had done to Mr Walters. The conniving Maisie had taken advantage of the jealous and probably intoxicated Dolly and manipulated her for her own ends. Ena was determined to keep Dolly's name out of it. 'The real villain of the piece is Maisie Hardy.'

Deep frown lines settled on Mr Walters' forehead and his bushy eyebrows met on the bridge of his nose. 'I think we had better go through to my quarters,' he said, leading the way.

When they were seated in the cluttered sitting room, Ena explained to Mr Walters how Maisie had persuaded Doreen to look after her children while she worked Doreen's shifts, as well as her own. She told him that Maisie had been visiting Doreen's husband in prison, that he intended to leave Doreen and the boys for Maisie, and that she and Artie had discovered Doreen unconscious on the kitchen floor, with her head in the gas oven.

'Maisie was the last person Doreen remembers seeing before we found her. And, if that isn't bad enough, Maisie has stolen all Doreen's savings.'

CHAPTER TWENTY-FOUR

'You said Maisie didn't wait for her wages but went home early because she was ill?'

'Yes, I've got her wages here,' Mr Walters said, hauling himself out of his chair and crossing the room. He took the key from his watchchain, unlocked the bureau and took out a buff coloured wage packet. 'She stole Doreen's money, did she? Then this money belongs to Doreen. Will you be seeing her, or shall I have it sent to her?'

'I'd like nothing more than to see Maisie Hardy's money to go to Doreen, but I was hoping to confront Maisie, persuade her to give back the money she stole from Doreen. The thing is,' Ena said, screwing up her face, 'I need a reason to go to her house.'

Mr Walters lifted the wage packet up. 'If you took her wages to her it would give you the reason?'

'It would.' Not a very believable reason, but as she could not think of a better one at short notice, it would have to do. 'I'll try to do a deal with her. Her wages for the money she stole from Doreen and I won't go to the Police!'

Mr Walters frowned again. 'What Maisie did was attempted murder. Doreen must tell the Police.'

Ena shook her head. 'I tried to persuade her but she won't have the Police involved. She doesn't want the boys to know what a lying, cheating, scumbag their father is – nor that their aunt, who the boys are very fond of, has betrayed them.'

Mr Walters gave Ena Maisie's wage packet. 'Take it to her with pleasure if you think she'll give you Doreen's money. And,' he said, turning back to the bureau, 'you'll need her address.'

Ena stood up and put the envelope in her handbag. Mr Walters scribbled the address down on a piece of paper and handed it to her. Ena looked at the address. Rutland Park Road. A stone's throw from where Doreen lived. 'I know where this is,' Ena said, 'it's the other side of the park from Doreen. Thank you. I'll get a cab from Waterloo Station.'

'I'll show you out the back, it's nearer to the station than going through the bar.'

Mr Walters didn't return to the hotel after showing Ena out, he walked with her to Waterloo Station. 'When you send the bill for the work you've done for me, would you put Doreen's bill in with it?'

'She won't be getting a bill, Mr Walters. Doreen and her sons did my husband and me a great service last year. The investigative work I've been doing for her doesn't begin to repay the debt we owe her. Thank you, anyway, I shall send you a detailed breakdown of my hours and expenses next week.'

They crossed Waterloo Road to the station and the taxi rank. At the first cab, Mr Walters opened the door for Ena to get in before tapping the driver's window. 'Take the lady to 4 Rutland Park Road, wait for her, and then to 27 Rutland Road.' He looked over the driver's shoulder. 'And then to Mercer Street, Mrs Green?' Ena nodded. Mr Walters took a wad of notes from his back pocket, peeled several from it and gave them to the cabby. 'If it's any more, I'll give it to you tonight. Call into The Wellington and have a drink on me.'

Mr Walters moved away from the cab and it pulled out onto Waterloo Road. 'Stop!' he shouted and ran to the back of the vehicle. Ena wound down the window. 'Tell Maisie not to come back to the hotel and tell Doreen her job is waiting for her when she feels up to coming back.' He stepped away from the car again, the driver put up his hand and pulled out into the South London traffic.

As she walked along the narrow concrete path to number 4 Rutland Park Road, Ena noticed the net curtains in the front window twitch. Maisie was in. She knocked on the door and when there was no answer, crouched down, lifted the flap of the letterbox and shouted, 'I've come from the Duke of Wellington hotel with your wages, Maisie.' When there was still no response, Ena turned and began walking back to the taxi. In case Maisie was still looking out of the window and could see her, Ena stopped halfway down the path and opened her handbag. Taking out the distinctive buff wage packet, she held it up and pretended to read what was written on the front. She shrugged and let it fall back into her handbag. Walking away again, Ena heard the front door open and someone call, 'Hello?'

Ena turned to see Maisie Hardy, thief of Doreen's husband as well as her money, leaning against the frame of the front door. With her arms crossed over her chest, she looked ready for battle.

Walking towards her, Ena could see that Maisie had been crying. The remainder of what she suspected had earlier been a fully-made-up face, had been washed off by tears, leaving tramlines of black mascara down her cheeks. One cheek was pink, the other devoid of rouge, and her smudged lipstick looked like a crude red slash across her thin lips. She wore a pale blue costume; the skirt was too short for her thick legs and the jacket too tight for her over-sized breasts. It was a hot day, but Maisie was shivering.

'Can I come in?' Not waiting for a reply, Ena pushed past the snivelling Maisie and took in her surroundings. Cheap ornaments adorned every surface, the glass was cracked in a small china cabinet, the net curtains were yellow from cigarette smoke and unlike Doreen's neat orderly front room, Maisie's was a jumble of uncoordinated colours. Doreen's furniture may have been old, but she had taken care of it a damn sight better than her sister-in-law. The room, like the woman, was a mess.

Maisie took a pack of cigarettes and box of matches from the mantle shelf, lit a cigarette and threw the match into the fireplace, where it landed among a dozen other spent matches and dog-ends in a grate of ash and coal dust. Blowing out a long stream of smoke, she said, 'Well, have you got my wages, or not?'

Ena cringed. What Arnold Hardy saw in Maisie was neither style nor good looks. It was obviously something that was not immediately visible. 'Yes.'

'Can I have them?' she asked, without looking at Ena.

'They're your wages; you earned them.'

Maisie flinched. Her body stiffened, but she didn't move.

Taking the wage packet from her handbag Ena held it out to her. Still Maisie made no attempt to take it. 'If you want it, come and get it,' Ena taunted.

Looking down, Maisie threw her cigarette into the grate and sauntered across the room.

As she approached, Ena saw for the first time since she'd been in the house that the pink blush on Maisie's left cheek was not rouge, but the start of a bruise. Her left eye was beginning to swell and her eyelid was turning blue. 'Ouch!' Ena said, 'that's going to be a shiner.' Reaching out, Ena lifted up Masie's chin. Maisie jerked her head and turned her face away. 'A gift from Arnold, was it?'

'None of your bloody business. Give me my money and get out!'

Ena had riled her, and would keep on doing so until she had Doreen's money. 'I'll make a deal with you, Maisie. I'll give you your wages if you give me the money you stole from Doreen this morning?'

Maisie shot a look at Ena that was somewhere between shocked and relieved. She took a step back, stumbled, fell onto the settee and buried her head in her hands. 'God forgive me. Oh my God, my God, my God,' she mumbled.

'Forgive you for what, Maisie? For killing Doreen?'

'Doreen's dead? No!' Maisie said. Her hand flew to her mouth and she lifted her head. Except for the purple bruising on her face and around her eye, she was deathly white. 'I didn't kill Doreen. We argued, yes. She came into the kitchen and saw me taking her money. She flew at me and I pushed her. She tripped. It was an accident. I didn't mean for her to fall; I swear I didn't. The last time I saw her she was sitting on the floor holding her head. On my kid's lives, Doreen was alive when I left her house.'

'So, you didn't drag Doreen, unconscious, to the oven and turn on the gas?'

'No!' she screamed. 'No, I did not. I swear on my kids' lives,' she said again.

'My associate and I found Doreen on her kitchen floor overcome by gas fumes. Another five minutes and she would have been dead.'

Maisie shook her head again. 'You're lying. You couldn't have. I don't believe you!'

'Why would I lie about something like that? Doreen is adamant that she doesn't want the Police involved because of the children. However, I don't have the same responsibility to her children, or to yours, so give me the money you stole and I might not go to the Police.'

'I can't.'

'What do you mean, *can't?*'

'I haven't got it.' Tears began to fall from the wretched woman's eyes. 'Arnold took it.'

'Then I'll have the money you earned doing double shifts at the Wellington!'

Maisie shook her head. 'He took that too. He took it all except—'

'Except?'

'A few bob the kids have in their money boxes.'

'That's something, I suppose.'

'He didn't know the kids had it.' Then Maisie took a sharp breath. Her eyes were wide as if she'd had a shock.

'What is it?'

'The kids were outside playing when Arnold arrived. He promised them he'd see them after school and came in the front door. I gave him Doreen's savings and he said we didn't need it because he had a plan that would make us rich when we got to Margate. He said we'd be living like royalty and Doreen's bit of money was chicken feed. When I left the house, he said he was going to give Doreen her money back to keep her quiet.'

'He tried to keep her quiet alright by knocking her out and putting her head in the gas oven.'

Tears streamed down Maisie's face as she rocked backwards and forwards staring into the fireplace, moaning and crying.

If Ena hadn't known her, she might have felt sorry for her. 'Maisie? Maisie!'

She jumped. 'What?'

'Was the money you took from Mr Walter's bureau yesterday the money Arnold took from you today?'

Pretending to be outraged, Maisie ranted that she hadn't stolen any money from Mr Walters and that it was Dolly the waitress who had stolen it, saying she had seen her take money before.

'Stop it!' Ena shouted so loudly that Maisie stopped immediately. 'Stop lying for once in your life!'

Maisie drew her feet up under her and hugging her knees cowered in the corner of the settee.

'Mr Walters knows it was you who took the money this morning.' Maisie opened her mouth to protest again. 'It doesn't matter now! All that matters is that money is now in Arnold Hardy's possession?'

Maisie resumed her rocking. Ena was exasperated, but exasperation was not going to get Maisie to talk. Ena took a calming breath and sat down in the chair opposite her. 'Mr Walters isn't going to the Police about the money you stole. He told me to tell you not to go back to The Wellington, which I'm sure you don't want to do anyway. Come on, Maisie, not only is he not going to the Police, but he's giving you your wages. And, I won't go to the Police if you tell me whether Arnold took the money you stole from Mr Walters when he took your savings?'

Maisie looked up at Ena. 'He won't go to the Police?'

'He said, he wouldn't as long as you stayed away from The Wellington. You're very lucky, Maisie. You made some bad decisions when you hooked up with Arnold Hardy, but you're being given a second chance. So, what's it to be? Come on, Maisie, it's important.'

'Yes!' she said. 'He took it all.'

Ena exhaled and got up to leave. As she passed Maisie, she threw the wage packet onto the settee next to her.

'Thank you,' she whispered.

'Don't thank me, Maisie. If you didn't have children to feed you wouldn't have seen that.' Ena pulled opened the door.

'Stop! Please!' Maisie ripped open the wage packet, took out the contents, and held half of it out to Ena. 'If I hadn't got the children, I'd give Doreen all of it. Tell her I'm sorry about what happened, about everything. I should never have got involved with Arnold. Tell her I didn't know what he'd done to her. I didn't, honestly,' she said, her eyes pleading with Ena to believe her. 'Tell Doreen I'll pay her back what he stole. They're taking people on at the canning factory, in Elephant. I'll get a job there and pay her back every penny.'

Ena wanted to shove the money down Maisie's throat, but Doreen needed to feed her children too.

'You will tell her what I said, won't you?'

'Yes.' Ena took the money, opened the door and stepped out into the warm sun.

***

'Would you stop at Barclays Bank?'

The taxi driver slowed down and reversed the cab into a space between two cars in front of the bank. Ena jumped out. 'I won't be long.' The short queue soon dispersed, She cashed a cheque for ten pounds and was back in the cab in a matter of minutes. Ten minutes after that the cab pulled up outside 27 Rutland Road.

Doreen must have seen the cab arrive as before Ena had time to knock on the door, it opened and she beckoned Ena into the house.

'How are you feeling?'

'My eyes keep running and my throat's still sore, but my head isn't as bad now.'

'I've got a taxi waiting. If you want to go to St. Thomas' to get checked over...'

'No, I'll be fine.'

'If you're sure?'

'I am.'

'Alright. I can't stop, but Mr Walters asked me to give you this.' Ena gave Doreen ten pounds. 'It's an advance on your wages. He said there's no rush, but your job is waiting for you when you're ready to go back.' Ena saw Doreen's eyes sparkle. 'No more tears,' Ena warned. Doreen shook her head. 'And this,' she said, giving her several notes, 'is half of Maisie's wages.'

Doreen stiffened. 'I don't want that woman's money.'

'It isn't her money, it's yours. Take it. Mr Walters wanted you to have all of it, but because of her children... Oh, and I have something else to tell you. Arnold didn't only hurt you and take your money, he walloped Maisie and stole the money she'd saved – and stolen – from the hotel. She's going to have one hell of a black eye.' Ena began to laugh and Doreen trying not to join in, pressed her lips together until she was unable to keep a straight face. She too laughed. 'And this,' Ena said, pushing another ten pounds into Doreen's hand, 'is towards what you're owed for the wonderful job you did getting the office knocked into shape for me, and for keeping it looking spick and span.'

'I'm not taking your money, Mrs Green.'

'It isn't *my* money. It's Dudley Green Associate's

money, and it's only a fraction of what I owe you.'

'But how will you manage at the office without me to do the cleaning?'

'Marigold do a very nice line in latex gloves. I shall buy a large pair for Artie.'

'And there's the investigation? I owe you for clearing my name.'

'Oh, yes, I'd forgotten about that.' Ena, pretending to be deep in thought, put up the fingers of her right hand one at a time as if she was counting. 'That's what you owe me. Hang on. Now,' she said, putting up the fingers of her left hand, 'that's the work you have done for Dudley Green Associates. I think that makes us even.'

Ena turned on her heels and ran down the path. 'Call in and see us any time,' she shouted over her shoulder before jumping into the waiting taxi.

CHAPTER TWENTY-FIVE

'Inspector Powell telephoned again.'

'Damn. I should have phoned him back.' Ena picked up the telephone and dialled the number for Bow Street Police Station. When she was through to the inspector, she apologised for not returning his call.

'It wasn't important,' he assured her, 'but I thought you'd like to know that O'Shaughnessy was found guilty on two counts of murder – Sid Parfitt and Hugh Middleton – and one count of attempted murder – Eve Robinson.'

'He's going to hang for killing Sid?'

'You sound surprised?'

'I am. Nick Miller told me it wasn't O'Shaughnessy who killed Sid, it was Helen Crowther.' For a fleeting moment Ena thought of Nick Miller and smiled. 'O'Shaughnessy wouldn't have been brought to justice without the help of the old rogue,' she said.

'He wouldn't,' the inspector agreed. 'Bending the rules sometimes pays off. Sir John Hillary said O'Shaughnessy didn't kick up about the sentence. I don't suppose he thought it was worth it. Brighton Police had enough evidence to hang him three times for Hugh Middleton's murder. Your testimony helped, but Hillary said it was Mrs Robinson's that was the clincher.'

'Thank you for letting me know, Inspector. I'll be in touch about the art theft case soon. I have two suspects, but at the moment I've as much gut feeling as I have proof. I need a lot more on them before I come to you. The Hardy investigation is over. Arnold Hardy has done a runner with Doreen's savings.'

'He has what?'

'Stolen every penny she had, but Doreen has refused to press charges.' Ena bit her lip. If she could trust anyone in this world it was Dan Powell. She had promised Doreen she wouldn't tell the Police, even so... 'You must give me your word that you won't take what I'm about to tell you any further.' The inspector didn't answer. 'Dan?'

'You have my word.'

'Thank you.' Ena still wasn't sure, but said, 'Arnold Hardy tried to kill her. He probably thinks he has.'

'What?'

'He didn't, and she's fine, so don't say anything!' Ena ordered. 'Some of the money he stole was what Maisie had given Doreen for looking after her children while she worked at the hotel. He promised Maisie he'd take her away and they'd set up home together.'

'Once he'd got rid of Doreen?'

'Precisely. However, after taking Maisie's savings – and smacking her about, leaving her with a bruised face and black eye, he left her too. The good news is that Maisie stole money on her last day working at the Duke of Wellington hotel and the notes were marked.'

'If we knew where he'd gone and could catch him splashing marked notes about, we could put him away again for stealing money from The Wellington, as well as from Maisie?'

'And he beat Maisie up?'

'I'm sure she could be persuaded to press charges if the Police didn't charge her for stealing the marked money in the first place.'

Inspector Powell laughed. 'Do we know where Arnold is now?'

'Maisie told me they were going to start a new life

in Margate.'

'I'll give the DI at Fort Hill a ring.'

'Another of your Hendon chums?'

'Unfortunately not, but no one likes scum like Arnold Hardy on their patch.'

'Don't mention Doreen's name, will you?'

'I gave you my word I wouldn't.'

'I know, sorry.'

'I'll let you know what the DI at Margate says.'

When Inspector Powell had finished the telephone conversation, Ena sat at her desk and laid her head on the ink blotter. When she sat up, she was smiling from ear to ear. 'I am pleased to be back in my office, in my chair, in charge of what I do and where I go instead of having some posh arse of a lawyer asking me loaded questions and twisting everything I say.'

'It was worth it,' Artie said, putting a cup of coffee in front of her.

'Yes it was. O'Shaughnessy was given a fair trial, which was something he didn't give his victims when he played judge, jury and executioner. You know,' Ena said, taking a sip of her coffee, 'at last I feel that Sid and your friend, Hugh, have got justice.'

'And when O'Shaughnessy is hanged it will be over.'

'It's over now.'

'I suppose it is. He'll never leave Wandsworth Prison. The building, yes, but not the grounds.'

'What have you been doing while I've been out?'

'I've just finished writing up Doreen Hardy's case. I'm glad we didn't have to show her the photographs I took of Maisie at the prison.' Artie stacked them. Levelling them on the desk like a pack of playing cards, he slipped them into a large brown A4 envelope.

'All dated – and the places and people in each photo are named.'

'Good. We need to keep everything in order.' Ena took a key from the drawer of the desk, picked up the envelope containing the Hardy investigation and crossed to the filing cabinet. Opening the top drawer, she pulled out the hanging files and placed the envelope in the section marked 'H' along with the rest of the Doreen Hardy paperwork. 'What next?'

'The poisoning of George's father.'

'I'll tell George what we've found and then, if she agrees, I'll turn what we've got over to the Surrey Police.' Ena took out the file and dropped it onto Artie's desk.

'Accidental Death of Mr Derby-Bloom?' Artie said, reading the title. 'The man was poisoned. How is that anything but murder?'

'The poison wasn't meant for him. His death was either an accident or a mistake, so his death is manslaughter.'

Artie opened the file and began to read. 'Looks to me like premeditated murder.'

'It was. Planned well in advance by someone quite clever and very evil. At first I thought it could be someone who knew about George and her father's activities in the war?'

'What, and they were *coincidently* in the same nursing home?'

'No. A thought crossed my mind that someone had been after him and found out that he was in the nursing home. He'd have been an easy target. But, you're right, it was definitely not a coincidence, nor was it someone taking revenge for the work he did during the war. So, it had to have been a mistake. There's nothing else it could it have been.'

'You don't need me for this one,' Artie said, handing back the Derby-Bloom file.

Ena took the file absentmindedly 'And then there are the art thefts,' she said sighing heavily.

'Do you have a suspect?'

'Two, and when I work out how it was done, I shall know which of them did it. Let's go and grab a sandwich and when we get back, I'll run through what I've got so far with you. You might see something I've missed.'

CHAPTER TWENTY-SIX

'Thank you for seeing us again, Nurse McKinlay. I was wondering if we might ask you a couple more questions?'

Nurse McKinlay smiled. 'Of course.'

'Did Mr Derby-Bloom say anything before he died?'

She looked at Ena thoughtfully and then her eyes widened and she took a long slow breath. 'Yes,' she said, 'he did.' She turned to George, 'I'm sorry. I was so upset when you were last here, I forgot.'

Ena looked at George. 'Do you remember what it was he said?'

The nurse looked up at the ceiling as if the words were written there. 'Yes, but I didn't hear everything he said. He was speaking German.'

'Are you sure it was German?'

'Yes, quite sure.'

'Try to remember what the words sounded like.'

Nurse McKinlay looked thoughtful. She took a shaky breath and said, 'I didn't understand him at first because what he said didn't make any sense.'

'Could he have been hallucinating?'

'No, I'm sure he wasn't. He reached out and took my hand. I couldn't hear what he was saying, so I leaned over him and put my ear near his mouth. It's been a long time since I've heard anyone speak German and I didn't catch the first couple of words, but it sounded like, sie hat mich getötet. Then, I'm sorry, he'd gone.'

George took a sharp breath, looked at Ena and then at the nurse. 'Sie hat mich getötet?'

'Yes. He spoke quietly, but that was definitely

what he said.'

'And in English?' Ena asked.

'She has killed me,' George said. 'Who did he think had killed him?'

Before the three women had time to discuss the meaning of Mr Derby-Bloom's last words, the nursing home's manager, Mrs Sharp, opened the door.

'Before you leave, Miss Derby-Bloom, would you pop into the office?' She left without waiting for George to reply.

'It'll be the fee for Dad's stay here,' George said, 'I won't be long.'

When George had left, Ena gave Nurse McKinlay a card. 'If you think of anything else, anything at all, however insignificant you think it might be, would you telephone me on this number?'

'Yes, of course.'

'I see from your badge you're a registered nurse.'

'I was with the First Aid Nursing Yeomanry during the war. I began nursing in 1937. I was one of the first recruits to train at the Nurses Preliminary Training School. Not all the hospital matrons approved of the training. Most preferred their nurses to learn on the wards, which I did eventually. It was a good foundation course, though. Two intensive months in the training school and we learned everything from medical and nursing theology to anatomy and physiology. But it isn't the same practising on life size dummies.'

'No. It must have been very different when you began working with real patients?'

'It was. I spent two years on the wards and when war was declared I joined up and became a FANY.'

'And, do you mind me asking where you learned to speak German?'

'Not at all. My first overseas assignment as a FANY was just after the Russian invasion of Finland in November 1939. I was one of forty FANY drivers in a convoy of ten ambulances that went to Norway. We arrived after the fighting in February 1940 but stayed on to help evacuate the hospitals and the refugees from Karelia.'

'Finland would be cold at that time of year,' Ena said.

'February is the coldest month of the year. It was between minus five and minus ten most nights, but we were too busy to think about it. It was in Finland that I learned to speak German. I worked with an Austrian doctor who had spent ten years as a surgeon in Germany. He was fluent in German and English – and the languages of the countries that border Finland – Russian, Norwegian and Swedish. When I got back to England, a friend who had returned from Scotland as a driver with the Polish fighting units told me about an organisation that trained people with languages as wireless operators. She went off to work in a grand old manor house in Banbury, and because I understood German I was sent to the east coast to listen to conversations between Luftwaffe pilots and the top brass giving the orders.'

Ena had been an engineer making small discs and dials for coding and deciphering machines at Bletchley Park, and Henry who was already at Bletchley Park, worked on top-secret codes, so Ena knew how important jobs like the one Nurse McKinlay did were. 'An interesting job,' she said.

'We coordinated what the wireless operators sent back with what we heard the pilots say, and the girls in the map room were able to plot their route within a mile, sometimes less.'

'I remember my husband telling me that the RAF was often given information that enabled them to stop the Luftwaffe over the Channel?'

'They were.'

'It must be gratifying to know that the work you did, stopping bombs from being dropped on factories and homes, saved lives.'

'I suppose it was. I didn't think about it at the time. None of the girls did. We just got on with it. I had learned Morse Code and hoped that with my knowledge of German, I'd be sent overseas to work as a wireless operator, but it didn't happen.'

'Your contribution to the war effort was of huge importance,' Ena said. 'I'm sure many operations were foiled because the RAF had information in advance of German air strikes.'

Nurse McKinlay smiled.

Ena liked her. She was easy to talk to. Now, Ena thought, would be a good time to ask her about the staff and the other residents in the nursing home.

'How long have you worked at The Willows?'

'Since 1945. Gosh, fifteen years at Christmas. My sister worked here until she became pregnant. She had terrible morning sickness that lasted most of every day. Anyway, they needed a qualified nurse to replace her and asked me to take over when she left. I've been here ever since.'

'Have most of the staff been here a long time?'

'Some yes, but not as long as me. We're short-staffed again now. The manageress says she's advertising for medically trained staff, but she hasn't found anyone in the last six months.'

'It's quite a big building. How many patients are there here?'

'Thirty-two. We have beds for forty, but we don't

have the staff for forty people at the moment.'

'What did you say the woman's name was who befriended Mr Derby-Bloom?'

'Mrs Thornton. She's very a nice lady. She's missing Mr Derby-Bloom. They had become quite attached to one another.'

'All paid. Paperwork done and signed,' George said, retuning and putting a large white envelope in her shoulder bag. 'I can now arrange for Dad to be taken to Surrey. In our religion the funeral should take place straight away. At the very latest within forty-eight hours, but because of the circumstances in which he died, I couldn't do that for him. Now it's urgent that he is laid to rest as quickly as possible.' She took a deep breath and let it out slowly.

'That's good. Hey,' Ena said, seeing tears in George's eyes, 'people will understand why there was a delay. Come on, let's get back to the theatre.' She turned to Nurse McKinlay. 'If you do think of anything?'

'I'll telephone.'

Ena shook the nurse's hand and said how nice it had been chatting with her. She left as George was thanking her for all she'd done for her father.

There was something edging its way into Ena's mind. A thought on the periphery of her consciousness that wouldn't show itself.

CHAPTER TWENTY-SEVEN

The restaurant where Ena was meeting Priscilla was a stone's throw from Mercer Street. Until today it might have been a thousand miles away. It was not a restaurant that Ena and Henry could afford to frequent. The menu was in a glass case on the wall at the side of the entrance. Ena's eyes widened. She didn't like anyone paying for her, but at these prices, she was glad to be Priscilla's guest.

Someone tapped her on the shoulder. 'You shouldn't look,' Priscilla, standing by her side, remarked. 'Come on, let's live a little.'

Ena followed her into the restaurant's foyer. 'Hello, James,' Pricilla called, as she swept past a middle-aged man in royal blue and gold livery. James bowed his head. His smile told Ena he knew and liked Priscilla.

'Mrs Galbraith?' The maître d' beamed Priscilla a welcoming smile.

'I'm lunching with my friend, Ena.' Priscilla gave Ena a child-like grin. 'Our husbands are working.' She half cupped her hand, put it up to her mouth, leaned close to the maître d' and whispered, 'Someone has to earn money for us girls to spend.' Then she burst into laughter.

On occasions like this, though there hadn't been many in Ena's life so far, she would have cringed at the kind of joke her friend had just made, but not today. There was something about Priscilla that Ena found endearing – childlike and fun – and charismatic. It was as if she was hungry to experience everything to the n'th degree.

'Your usual table is ready for you,' the maître d'

said, leading the way across the plush, maroon and gold restaurant to a table overlooking the gardens of the hotel. He pulled out Priscilla's chair and when she was seated, moved quickly and effortlessly to Ena. 'Madam,' he gestured, pulling out Ena's chair for her. He then gave both women a maroon leather-bound menu. 'Bon appetite, ladies,' he said, bowed and turned into the room. With the slightest flick of his hand, a waiter nodded and brought them the wine list.

'What would you like to drink, Ena?'

Priscilla was enjoying playing the role of hostess and, as Ena struggled to tell the difference between a Claret and a Bordeaux, she said, 'You choose.'

'Where do you come from, Ena? I can tell from your accent you're not a Londoner.'

'The Midlands, a small place called Foxden in Leicestershire. My father was the Head Groom on a country estate. We lived in a tied cottage on the estate surrounded by acres and acres of fields and woodland.' Ena laughed, 'And a lake the estate workers' kids were allowed to skate on in the winter. We didn't have any money and being the youngest of four sisters, my clothes were hand-me-downs. But looking back, with fields and woods as my playground, it wasn't so bad. Foxden Hall is now a hotel. My eldest sister and her husband own it with the Foxden family. The Foxdens don't have anything to do with the day-to-day running of the hotel.

'James Foxden and my sister, Bess, were very much in love during the war. Before his last mission, James gave Bess his signet ring with the Foxden family crest on it and asked her to marry him when he returned. Sadly, he didn't come back. I don't know the details, but as titled gentry, James, as Lord and Lady Foxden's only son would have one day inherited the title and the Foxden Estate. All Bess had left of him was his signet ring, which because it had been handed down through generations of Foxdens, she gave back to James' parents. Lord and Lady Foxden said if James gave Bess his ring and asked her to marry him, she should keep it. I think it was James parents' way of saying they accepted Bess as their son's choice. I also think that fighting a common enemy in the war narrowed the class divide and made people more equal.'

Priscilla laughed. 'Did it?'

'Not everyone changed, but the Foxdens did. Lord Foxden always treated his workers well. Lady Foxden was a snob to everyone except my father. She wouldn't hunt without Tom at her side.' Ena swallowed the emotion that always rose in her throat when she talked about her father. 'Losing her only son changed her completely,' Ena took a deep breath, 'and it broke Bess' heart. But our Bess is a strong woman and now has a lovely husband and a beautiful daughter.'

Ena took a drink of her wine. 'What about you? Where do you come from, Priscilla?'

'I was born in the slums of Salford. My playground was the back yards of derelict houses and filthy alleys, and puddles were my lakes. Dad worked for the Co-Operative Society and my mum, who came from Manchester, pestered him to ask for a transfer to Moss Side. He eventually plucked up the courage and a year later we moved to Caxton Street, Moss Side in Manchester. It was still a poor area, but Dad had a good job which meant my mother could give up her cleaning job and no longer took in sewing. I was sent to the local C of E school,' Priscilla laughed. 'We thought we were *it* then. After we moved to Manchester, Mum never left the house without a clean scarf round her head and she always kept a clean pinafore hanging on the back door in case anyone called. She used to put it on to hang out the washing.' Priscilla speared an asparagus head, but didn't eat it, 'She died six months after we moved to Moss Side. She died where she wanted to live.'

Ena could see in Priscilla's eyes that the death of her mother was as painful to her as the death of her father was to herself.

When they had finished eating and were drinking coffee, Ena asked Priscilla how she had met her husband.

Priscilla laughed, put down her cup with a loud clunk and laughed again. 'You wouldn't believe me if I told you.'

'Try me.' Priscilla tilted her head to one side and squinted at Ena as if she was deciding whether or not to share that piece of information with her. Ena laughed. 'Now you're teasing me.' Ena knew before she asked Priscilla about her and Charles, that their meeting would not have started as girl meets boy at a local dance.

'Oh, alright!'

Ena leaned forward, eagerly waiting to hear Priscilla and Charles' story.

'Charles saw me before I saw him and when I did see him, I didn't remember him.'

Ena shook her head, 'Why not?'

Priscilla giggled. 'When I was fifteen, my best friend and I used to walk into Manchester every Saturday morning. We had no money so...' Priscilla stopped speaking and bit her lip. 'You must promise not to judge me.'

'I wouldn't anyway, but I promise.'

'One of us would steal something from

Woolworths or C&A and the other one would take it back. We'd say that our mother had sent us because whatever it was that we'd stolen that day didn't work. We alternated between Woollies and C&A – and always went to a different assistant. If they didn't want to refund the money we'd start crying and say how we had six brothers and sisters and our mam was poorly. And, I'm ashamed to say, we got away with it every time. Well, as many times as there were shop assistants. Anyway, one Saturday we'd had pop and a sandwich for our lunch, spent what was left on sweets, and we were wandering around when we saw a poster advertising a funfair. It wasn't far away so we went to it.

'We wanted to go on the rides, but we'd spent our money so I picked the pocket of a posh looking lad.'

'And he caught you?'

'No, but I found out later that he saw me picking someone else's pocket. Anyway, I spent my few pennies on the shoot the duck stall. I was on my last round when I realised the posh lad who I'd pickpocketed was standing next to me on my right. He paid for a couple of rounds with a ten-shilling note and put the change in the left pocket of his coat.' Priscilla giggled. 'It was too tempting so I took it. I was useless with the rifle and missed every duck. He was a hotshot and won a teddy bear which he gave me.' Ena saw tears in the corner of Priscilla's eyes. 'That was the first and only teddy bear I ever had, and I've still got it.' She dabbed her eyes with her handkerchief and tutted. 'I'm getting sentimental in my old age.

'Anyway, in the war I worked in a munition's factory. The money was okay, but Dad had TB in 1917 and it came back that year. If he hadn't gone to a sanatorium he'd have died. So, we scraped together every penny we could find and off he went. I was twenty-one and took on the house so he had somewhere to come back to when he was cured. Travelling to the sanatorium and taking him fresh fruit, which cost a fortune – if you could get it – meant I often went without myself. I didn't care because I could see Dad was improving every time I visited, but I fell behind with the rent. The landlord had let me pay late several times, but the debt built up and he took me to court. I promised the magistrate I'd pay back the rent I owed. I can't remember how much in arrears I was, or how much I promised to pay back every week on top of the normal rent, but the magistrate agreed and I lived to fight another day.'

'How did you pay it?'

'I took in a lodger. Her rent paid the arrears and I was straight by the time Dad came home.'

'And how did you meet, Charles?'

'That's the part of my life you wouldn't believe. The chief magistrate was the father of the boy from the shooting stall at the fair all those years before. The boy was waiting outside for his father, saw me coming out of court and stopped me and said hello. I was then the age that he was when we first met. I didn't recognise him until he asked me if I still had the teddy bear he'd won for me at the fair shooting ducks. I almost cried there and then. Of course I still had it. How on earth he recognised me I don't know. He took me for a cup of tea and we talked for ages.'

'Was it love at first sight?'

'Charles said for him it was. He said he'd never forgotten the scruffy teenage girl at the fair. He said he put the change the man had given him at the duck stall in his left pocket so I could take it. He said he didn't want me to steal from anyone else in case I got caught.'

'That was lovely.'

'I suppose he felt sorry for me. He didn't say he did, but he's told me since that...' Priscilla laughed. 'I'm embarrassed to say it.'

'You can't stop now. Come on,' Ena said, 'it's a lovely story.'

'He said he was fascinated by me and that he had probably fallen in love with me when he saw me at the fair, but I was too young. He said, he often thought about the pretty girl who stole his money.' Priscilla laughed again and said, 'And the rest, as they say, is history.'

CHAPTER TWENTY-EIGHT

Ena was fascinated by Priscilla and overwhelmed by her honesty. 'What did Charles do for a job when you met him again outside the court?'

'He was at university. His dream was to be a defence lawyer. He'd have made a good one too. He understands people, always sees the good in them. He'd probably be a judge by now if it wasn't for me.' Priscilla's voice cracked with emotion. 'I have a Police record from my pick-pocketing days, so he joined his father's insurance firm. He says he doesn't care that he gave up the law, but I care.' Priscilla looked down at her wedding ring. 'I know I can be an embarrassment, but he refutes that. He says I keep him young. Poor Charles. He gives me anything I want. If I see something I like, he buys it for my birthday, or for Christmas.' An impish grin crossed Priscilla's face and her eyes began to sparkle. 'If I take something without paying for it, Charles either goes to the shop and buys it for me, or he returns the item. I'm well known in Regent Street and so is Charles. The shops I go to have his telephone number, and it's because he's such a respected man that shop owners don't embarrass me by accusing me of stealing. Instead, they telephone Charles.' Priscilla shrugged her shoulders. 'I wish I didn't steal things.'

'So why do you?'

'I don't know. Some people steal for the fun of it, the excitement, the thrill of getting away with it. I expect that was me once. Now it's a case of old habits die hard.'

Ena shook her head. Not from disgust, but because she didn't understand why someone with so much – and with so much to lose – would do something like that.

'I can see you're shocked. I'm sorry, Ena. I could say I steal because I didn't have anything when I was a child, which is true, I didn't, but that would be an excuse. Charles thinks I have a psychological problem.'

Kleptomania, Ena thought, but didn't say.

'I hope you'll forgive me, Ena. I don't want my unfortunate habit to spoil our friendship.'

'It won't, I promise. I don't judge anyone, especially if I like them.'

Priscilla beamed Ena a smile. 'I like you too, but now I want to ask you something. I've been totally honest with you, so you must be with me.'

Ena nodded. 'Ask away.'

'Why did you really accept my invitation to lunch today?'

Ena didn't answer immediately, but decided that since Priscilla had been honest with her, she would be honest in return. 'At first, but only fleetingly, I wondered if you might know something about the Hogarth that went missing from The Savoy and then mysteriously turned up at Bow Street Police Station. But I promise it was only for a second.'

Priscilla played with the brooch on her lapel. 'And that's because you saw me take the Gilou Donat from the display cabinet on preview night at La Galerie Unique?'

'Yes.'

'But I put it back.'

Ena laughed. 'Yes, you did. I was astonished – and I felt a fool when the brooch I'd seen you take out of the cabinet was suddenly back in its place when Giselle Aubrey went to look. It made me wonder how you'd opened the cabinet to take out the Donat and how, when you put it back, you had locked it.'

Priscilla laughed. 'That's easy. I told you on the night we had dinner at The Savoy that ordinary cabinets don't have individually cut keys. The display cabinet at La Galerie Unique didn't. Any old key would fit it. Charles' bureau key would have fitted it; my china cabinet key *did* fit it.'

'Maisie's china cabinet key!' Ena said, more to herself than to her companion. 'Priscilla, you've just solved a problem for me.'

'Anything you can share?'

'I would, but it's neither interesting nor important. You've tied up a loose end on a theft case I've been working on.' Ena lifted her glass. 'Thank you.'

'Don't you want to know why I put the Donat brooch back?'

'Yes, of course, why did you?'

'Because I knew you had seen me take it.'

'Touché!' Ena pulled a silly face. 'Mmm... better learn to be more discreet in my detection work in future.'

'You need a poker face, like this.' Priscilla made a thin line of her mouth and looked into the mid-distance, her eyes staring and emotionless. She couldn't hold the pose for long, laughed out loud again and said, 'Shall we go?'

'What about the bill?'

'Shush!' She looked around. 'I never pay bills. Follow me,' she said conspiratorially. 'We'll pretend we're going to the Ladies' lavatory and then sneak out of the back door. Come on.' Again, Priscilla couldn't keep up the pretence and laughing loudly, called the waiter, 'René will you put that splendid lunch on Charles' account.'

'Of course, Mrs Galbraith,' René said, pulling out

Priscilla's chair for her to stand, before doing the same for Ena.

Ena had been holding her breath. Relieved, she blew out her cheeks and laughing, followed Priscilla out of the restaurant.

While they waited for a taxi, Ena promised Priscilla that she and Henry would dine with her and Charles again. 'Next time we will invite you,' Ena said, to which Priscilla agreed. When a black cab came into sight, Ena flagged it down and Priscilla climbed into the back seat. After waving her friend goodbye, Ena set off at a brisk pace to the office.

Looking in the shop windows it seemed to Ena that every day there was another clothes shop in Leicester Square and Covent Garden. She stopped briefly to window shop as she passed by, noticing that the fashion was for skirts to be shorter. She spotted a beautiful dress and matching jacket in soft pink and wished she was brave enough to wear a skirt that short. In the next shop, window dressers were changing sleeveless summer dresses and sandals for autumn designs – dresses and skirts in orange, russet reds and greens. Jackets and coats in heavier fabrics and knee-high fashion boots.

It was still July, albeit the end of the month, but there was plenty of summer left and it was likely there would be a summer sale. Ena made a mental note to pop back to the shop the following week. Her wardrobe was dated, and besides, she needed to look smart in her job.

Ena was watching the window dressers taking summer clothes out of the window when loud music caught her attention. She glanced across the street to where a new coffee bar had recently opened and almost fell down the pavement in shock.

CHAPTER TWENTY-NINE

From a nearby doorway, she watched Louis Mantel, Giselle Aubrey's American sponsor at La Galerie Unique, arguing with an older man. Louis took a wad of notes from his pocket and offered it to the man, who pushed Louis' hand holding the money away and began to walk off. Louis quickly followed, grabbed the man by the arm and swung him round. The older man put up his hands as if to surrender. Louis pointed to the door of the café and the older man turned and went in. Louis followed.

Ena could no longer see them. She ran across the road to the telephone box, put in a handful of coins and dialled the number of the office. 'Come on, Artie,' she said, impatiently.

'Dudley Green Associates. Can I help you?'

'Artie, it's Ena.' She didn't wait for him to reply. 'Is your camera in the office?'

'Yes.'

'Good. Grab it and meet me at the top of Slingsby Street.' Ena put down the telephone and walked the short distance back to the top of the street. She'd only been on the telephone for a couple of minutes and was sure that Louis and his companion would still be in the café. She looked along Long Acre and then at her wristwatch. It should only have taken Artie five minutes to lock up and get to her, yet ten minutes had passed. Where the hell –? She scanned the road again, impatiently, and was pleased to see Artie running towards her.

'What's going on?' he asked, trying to regain his breath.

'Louis Mantel, Giselle Aubrey's sponsor from the

art gallery and another man were arguing outside the café. Mantel offered the man money. He refused to take it and started to leave, but Mantel caught up with him and said something that made the man change his mind. They're both in the café.'

'And you want me to do a bit of eavesdropping?'

'Yes. I'd do it myself, but Mantel knows me from the gallery's preview night. Have you got your camera?'

Artie tapped his document case.

'Good. Mantel's medium height, mid-thirties, long hair, with a loud American accent. I should think you'll hear him before you see him. The other man is around fifty and a bigger build. I'll see you back at the office.'

Ena watched Artie saunter along the street and pass the café. At Slingsby Place, he crossed the street and walked back on the opposite pavement. As he neared the café, he turned left and disappeared under an arch leading to a cobbled courtyard where vehicles parked when they delivered goods to the offices and cafés on Mercer Street.

Ena didn't have to wait long before he reappeared, strolled across the street and went into the café. Two girls, loaded down with bags from clothes and shoe shops on Oxford Street, followed Artie, as did a man and woman. Ena was itching to walk past the café window to see if she could spot Mantel and his companion, but she thought better of it.

There was no telling how long Artie would be. From the archway he'd probably taken photographs of the two men if they were sitting near the window. She hoped Artie was able to hear the conversation between Mantel and the older man now he was inside the café but that depended on how busy it was and whether there were any unoccupied seats near them. However, Artie was experienced in surveillance. He'd been successful working on more difficult and more dangerous cases for the Home Office. More recently he had unearthed the truth in the Doreen Hardy investigation through surveillance. 'So,' Ena said, aloud, 'leave it to him,' and she walked back to the office.

From the top of Mercer Street, Ena spotted Inspector Powell's black Wolseley parked next to her Sunbeam. She quickened her pace and arriving at the car tapped the driver's window. 'No WPC Jarvis to chauffeur you today?' she joked, as the inspector got out of the car. Ena knew Constable Jarvis wouldn't be driving the inspector if he'd come to impart information about La Galerie Unique, or one of the people involved with the gallery. She unlocked the outer door and crossed the foyer to the office. 'Come in, Inspector.' She ushered him in and went through to the kitchen. 'Tea or coffee?'

'Coffee, thanks,' the inspector replied.

When Ena returned with two steaming cups of strong coffee, Inspector Powell was seated at her desk. Using the blotter as a mat, she put both cups down, walked over to the filing cabinet, unlocked it and took out a buff-coloured file titled 'Gallery Profiles'. Returning to her chair she picked up her coffee and with both cups removed from the blotter she laid the file on it, before taking out several sheets of paper and handing them to the inspector.

'This is who I met on the night of the preview – and who I think could be involved in the art thefts. And this page is just my opinion of them, a kind of overview if you like. Read it with pleasure, but my opinion has changed since I wrote it.'

She drank her coffee while the inspector read her findings. 'Not a lot there that you don't already know,' she said when he had finished. 'However,' she said, her face lighting up. 'I have two interesting events to add. One, I've just had lunch with someone who was at the gallery on preview night. Her name's Priscilla Galbraith.'

The inspector looked up from the papers with surprise. 'The wife of Charles Galbraith whose company insures La Galerie Unique?' Ena nodded. 'And the other event?'

'My gut feel was that there was something untoward about Louis Mantel.' Ena took a box of cigarettes from her drawer, lit one and pushed the packet across the desk to the inspector. 'And I was right. Walking back to the office after lunch, I happened to glance down Slingsby Street and saw two men arguing. One of them was Louis Mantel, Giselle Aubrey's sponsor at La Galerie Unique. They were having quite a barney. Mantel gave the man money, which the man refused. He shoved the money back at Mantel and began to leave but Mantel grabbed him and after some discourse, they both went into the café. You know the one, it's opposite the cobbled courtyard.'

DI Powell nodded. 'Damn shame you couldn't have gone into the café and listened to their conversation, but Mantel would have recognised you.'

'There was no need for me to go in, I telephoned Artie and he's there now. Plus, he has a camera. He won't be able to take any snaps inside the café, it would look suspicious, but before he went in he ducked under the arch opposite the café. He'll have taken photographs from there so hopefully we'll be able to identify the man with Mantel when the film's developed. Do you have any news about the art thefts?'

'Nothing that helps this case.' The inspector looked again at Ena's notes and began to laugh.

'What is it?'

'You say here that people of interest in the art thefts are Priscilla question-mark and her husband.'

'I did, but not anymore. If you read on, you'll see that Henry and I had dinner with Priscilla and Charles, during which I changed my mind. And, after spending time with her today I'm a hundred per cent certain they have nothing to do with The Savoy theft or any other thefts.

'Whoever is at the top of this one is powerful, but it isn't Charles Galbraith.'

CHAPTER THIRTY

The sound of the street door opening and slamming shut halted the conversation. Ena and Inspector Powell turned at the same time to see Artie come crashing into the office out of breath and smiling like the proverbial cat that got the cream.

He flopped into his chair, put his briefcase on the top of his desk and rolled his shoulders.

'What happened? Did you take any photographs?'

'Oh yes, several from the street. The two men were sitting near the window. I got them both full-face. I went in, ordered a coffee and sat at the table next to them. I heard everything.'

Ena and the inspector turned their chairs to face Artie. 'Who was the older man?'

'The night security guard.'

'Are you sure? He wasn't on duty the night Henry and I were there. But then if he worked through the night he wouldn't necessarily be working when the gallery was open.'

'Are you sure?' Inspector Powell repeated Ena's question.

'Of course!' Artie rolled his eyes.

'Go on, Artie.'

Artie consulted his notes. 'The security guard's name is Selwyn Horton.'

'He's an ex-copper.'

'I heard him say he hadn't signed up for trouble.'

'So is Horton working for Mantel?'

'I don't think so.' Artie consulted his notes again. 'Mantel sounded worried, nervy. He said something like, "That's why you weren't there," and Horton replied, "I don't skive on the job. You know why I had to go." Mantel then said, "Yeah, sorry about that. My man was too enthusiastic. I've offered you compensation. Selwyn, old buddy, my advice to you is take the money and keep your mouth shut about last night." Then the café door opened and a tall bloke, black hair, built like the proverbial brick outhouse came in and sat at a table at the rear of the café. I didn't take much notice of him and don't think Mantel or Horton saw him. I glanced at him a couple of times and each time he was watching Mantel. Anyway, Mantel said, "You did the right thing not calling the Police. As far as you're concerned nothing was stolen." Horton's mouth dropped open. He looked shocked and said, "But nothing was stolen, was it?" Mantel laughed and said, "What you don't know can't hurt you, but what you do know could get you killed. The people I work for aren't the kind of people you mess with, okay? If they thought you couldn't be trusted, you wouldn't be around long enough to spend this." With that he placed a wad of notes on the table and covered them with a newspaper.'

'Did Horton take the money?'

'Not at first. Mantel told him to take it saying, "I'm sure there's stuff your daughter needs. Babies grow fast." At that remark the colour drained from Horton's face. When Mantel got up to leave he leant over Horton and said something like,' Artie looked into the mid-distance trying to recall Mantel's exact words, '"If you don't want anything to happen to your daughter and the kid, you'll take the money and keep your mouth shut."'

'So, Horton isn't involved. At least he wasn't until he took Mantel's money. Good work, Artie.' Inspector Powell stood up and shook Artie's hand. 'Will you let me know when you have the photographs? I should very much like to see them.'

'I'll bring them into Bow Street,' Artie replied.

Inspector Powell shook Ena's hand and thanked her for the work she was doing, saying he'd be in touch.

When he had left, Ena voiced her opinion to Artie. 'It sounds to me like the night security guy, Selwyn Horton, didn't want to be involved in Mantel's plan and only agreed to go along with it because Mantel threatened his daughter.'

'I agree. So,' Artie said, 'how are we going to play this?'

'If Horton works all night, he'll likely stop somewhere for breakfast on his way home.'

'I'll follow him tomorrow morning and if he does stop for breakfast, I'll have breakfast too.'

'And, if he's on his own...'

'Get chatting.'

Ena laughed. 'You and I make a good team, Artie.'

'So, did you have a nice lunch?'

'Lovely, thanks. Good food, good wine and Priscilla was fun. I haven't laughed as much in ages.'

'Do you think the magpie and her husband have anything to do with the thefts at the gallery?'

'Definitely not. Priscilla's husband is Charles Galbraith, the gallery's insurer. Galbraith's is a big insurance company. They insure millions of pounds worth of art.'

'They could be in on it though. What better way of knowing who has what and where?'

'Not on your life.'

'Mrs Galbraith did attempt to nick an expensive brooch.'

'Nicking a brooch is a far cry from being an art thief and a forger. Besides, not only would Charles have too much to lose, but he doesn't need the money.

He's a millionaire, or close to it.'

'That doesn't mean anything either,' Artie pondered.

'No, but having spent time with Priscilla, I don't think they're involved. However, I now know how Maisie Hardy opened the bureau at the Duke of Wellington Hotel.' Artie's expression went from uninterested to interested in a flash. 'I asked Priscilla how she unlocked the showcase at the art gallery and she said with the key from her china cabinet at home. Apparently, keys to china cabinets, drinks cupboards, bureaux and the like, are not individually cut like keys to houses and cars. She was positive that her china cabinet key would open an ordinary writing bureau – which in effect is what Mr Walter's bureau is.' Ena kicked off her shoes and leaned back in her chair.

'Damn! I forgot. I took a call just before you phoned asking me to go to Slingsby Street,' Artie suddenly recalled. It was from a Nurse McKinlay at The Willows Nursing Home. She said she had remembered something important and asked if you could telephone her as soon as possible.'

'Will you ring her for me? Tell her I'm on my way to see her.' Artie picked up Ena's telephone book. 'I don't know what's going on at that nursing home but I don't want the woman who runs the place listening in on our conversation.' Ena grabbed her handbag and shouted, 'See you later.'

CHAPTER THIRTY-ONE

Nurse McKinlay was waiting for Ena when she arrived. She opened the door before Ena had time to ring the bell and showed her into the dining room. 'We won't be disturbed in here.' She motioned to a table just inside the door, pulled out a chair and sat down. Ena did the same.

The nurse spoke in a whisper. 'I've remembered something Mr Derby-Bloom said. Like I told you and Miss Derby-Bloom, his voice was very faint. I didn't think I'd heard the first couple of words. Well, I didn't, not properly, but then I thought about it. The first word I definitely didn't hear. It would be wrong of me to guess what he said, but I'm sure I heard the second one. I recognised the word, it was on the tip of my tongue, but before I could grasp it, it had gone. I'm sorry not to have recalled the word before,' she said, closing her eyes. 'The second word was *En-kilin*. Mr Derby-Bloom said, 'Enkelin. Sie hat mich getötet.' Ena looked questioningly at the nurse. 'Granddaughter. Mr Derby-Bloom said something followed by Granddaughter. She has killed me.'

'Granddaughter?' Ena repeated the word several times and then said, 'George is an only child, she has no children, What could he have meant?'

'Someone else's granddaughter?' Nurse McKinlay offered.

'Mrs Thornton's granddaughter?'

The nurse nodded. 'Andrea was here that morning.'

'She'd have no reason to kill George's father. So, did she put poison in her grandmother's cordial and George's father drank it by mistake?' A thought crossed Ena's mind. 'Does Andrea stand to inherit her grandmother's money if she dies?'

'I don't know. She might. Last week I was dressing Mrs Thornton's arm. She cut it when she fell. Anyway, she told me that her granddaughter had been asking for money again. She has money from the old lady all the time. Mr Derby-Bloom used to say that Mrs Thornton spoiled her. The old lady agreed, but said it's because she hadn't been well, mentally, since she lost her parents. Her mother and father were killed in a car accident some years ago and I think it was after that that Andrea went to live with her grandmother. She now has a flat of her own, but she did live with Mrs Thornton immediately after her parents died. When I told my mum I was worried about Mrs Thornton, Mum said she remembered the accident. She said it was in all the newspapers.' Nurse McKinlay clasped her hands in front of her and cast her eyes down.

'What is it?'

'I don't want you to think I'm a gossip. I don't talk about the patients outside work, but I've been concerned about Mrs Thornton for some time.'

Ena waved away the idea that Nurse McKinlay was a gossip and shook her head reassuringly. 'Did your mother say anything else about the accident?'

'She said at the time there was a lot of talk that the crash wasn't an accident. That Andrea's father drove the car off the road and into a tree on purpose.'

'Good Lord. No wonder the girl's mentally disturbed. It's no excuse for murder though,' Ena said. 'Whereabouts did Mrs Thornton fall?'

'In her house. She fell down the stairs.'

'Did she?' Ena expected Nurse McKinlay to say the old lady had fallen in her bedroom at the nursing home. But falling in her own home? A dozen scenarios crowded into Ena's mind. None of them said accidental.

'She's due to leave here next week.'

'Will she go home?' Nurse McKinlay nodded. 'Is there anyone to look after her when she leaves here?'

'Only her granddaughter.'

'God help her.'

'She doesn't need professional nursing care. She's very fit for her age and she's really bright. It's only that she tripped over something at the top of her stairs and then fell down them. She was black and blue when they brought her here from the hospital.'

'It may be my suspicious mind, but I think Mr Derby-Bloom did mean Mrs Thornton's granddaughter. I don't think she'll try to harm her grandmother again. Not while she's here anyway. She'd be mad if she did. No, Mrs Thornton is safe for the time being.' Ena looked at Nurse McKinlay. 'It's when she gets home that worries me.'

***

Ena parked the car, ran back to Café Romano and bought a couple of rounds of sandwiches before going to the office.

'When was the last time you had something to eat?' she asked Artie, dropping the paper bags containing sandwiches on his desk.'

'About the time Noah was building the ark,' he said ripping open the first bag.

Ena went into the kitchen and made them each a cup of coffee, Giving Artie his, she sat down with her coffee at her desk. 'I'm going to see Inspector Powell. He should know what kind of poison killed George's father by now. While I'm gone, find out all you can about a fatal car accident in Surrey in 1950. Mr and Mrs Thornton were killed, but their teenage daughter, Andrea survived. The accident was reported in the local newspapers. Probably in the nationals as well, but check what the local papers said about it first. Ring the editors of a couple of the newspapers in Surrey and see if you can meet them or the reporters who wrote up the accident. I'd have thought someone would have been sent to cover the story pretty quickly. And have a word with the local Police if you can. I want to know everything there is to know about the accident and the people involved in it.'

'Journalists like to be wined and dined.'

'From memory they prefer pie and mash and a pint of beer at the local pub after work.' Ena waved the discussion away. 'Find a B&B and stay overnight if you have to. Do whatever it takes, but don't forget to ask for receipts. Right,' she said, picking up her handbag, crossing the room and swiping her jacket from the coat-stand, 'I'm off to see my favourite copper.'

'Before you go!' Artie called, stopping Ena in her tracks.

'What is it?'

'I'm supposed to be following the night security guy from the gallery when he finishes work tomorrow morning. I don't have the car, so I'm relying on the train. He'll finish early and there may not be a train to get into London in time.'

Ena groaned. 'I'll do it. Do we know which agency Horton's from?' Artie shook his head. 'Inspector Powell might know but if he doesn't, I'll ring round when I get back from Bow Street.'

***

'The dregs in the bottom of the glass you gave me contained hemlock.' Inspector Powell read from a note pad. 'Water hemlock to be precise. It's found in streams, ditches, any boggy or wet area, and there's no smell or taste apparently.'

'Killed by mistake,' Ena mused. Picking up her handbag from the floor she thanked the inspector. 'I'd better go.' She grimaced. 'I'm doing a surveillance job in the morning.'

'By the look on your face, you're not looking forward to it.'

'I'm not looking forward to getting up at dawn, no. I need to find out what time Selwyn Horton's shift finishes. I don't suppose you know which security agency La Galerie Unique got him from?'

'Sure Security Services.' The inspector picked up the telephone. 'Jarvis, give Sure Security Services in Leicester Square a ring. Don't tell them you're the Police. Say you're in London and you're enquiring about security. Ask about the hours night security guards work.'

'What do you know about the big chap on the gallery's door named Victor, Inspector?'

'Straight as a die and very protective of Giselle. He's known her from when she was a child. He was Flying Squad, took a bullet during an East End gang bust, which put him out of the force. I wouldn't want to upset him, he's a big man and fit.'

The telephone rang and Inspector Powell picked up the receiver. 'Thank you, Jarvis.' He put down the phone. 'You will be getting up early in the morning,' he said, laughing. 'Night security guards work from ten at night until six o'clock in the morning.'

Ena blew out her cheeks. 'Artie's on the Derby-Bloom case. He'll be in a lovely country pub this evening eating and drinking with local newspaper reporters. Damn! I told him to stay in a B&B overnight. He'll be back in the morning, but not in time to shadow Horton. Why didn't I go to Surrey instead?'

'I could get someone here to follow Horton.'

'No, it's okay. I'm hoping he stops off at a café for breakfast before he goes home. If he does, I'll be able to have breakfast too.'

'Won't he recognise you from preview night at the gallery?'

'No, Horton wasn't on duty that night.'

'Not many people are out and about at six o'clock in the morning. What's your cover story?'

'I haven't thought of one. How about I've been working in a strip joint in Soho and come into the café to have a fry up?'

Inspector Powell laughed.

'I don't know why you're laughing. I think it's a good cover.'

'Better you've just got off an overnight train from the north. You're going to a job interview, but the office where you're being interviewed doesn't open until nine o'clock?'

'Spoil sport.'

'You will be careful?' the inspector said.

'You know me.' Ena jumped up and crossed to the door.

'Which is why I'm reminding you,' the inspector replied.

'I promise to be careful. Thanks for finding out the name of the poison that killed George's father. I'm not sure yet how he came to drink poison. I think I know why, but not how. I'll let you know when I know,' Ena said, and left.

CHAPTER THIRTY-TWO

Without opening her eyes, Ena reached out, hit the bell on top of the alarm clock with the flat of her hand, groaned and turned over. She hated early mornings. With three sisters, a brother and a mother and father, every school day of her childhood meant getting up early to wash and dress to avoid being late for school. In the war too, it was up at the crack of dawn to get ready for work or risk clocking in late. When she was taken off the factory floor and given a desk in the boss' office, it was even worse. She didn't have to clock in, but she had responsibilities and felt she needed to set an example. A cold chill rippled through her when she thought of the danger she had been in every time she'd travelled on the train to Bletchley Park with Frieda Voight who, with her brother, Ena had exposed as spies.

Ena had taught herself to put Frieda in an imaginary box, close the lid and lock it. As she thought Frieda and her brother were dead, she had pushed the box and the memory of them to the back of her mind. It had worked for thirteen years. It would no doubt still be working except that last year she had seen Frieda again, and blaming Henry for her brother's death she had jumped from the roof of the church where he was buried, to her own death.

She rolled over and looked at the clock. Its round face showed it was ten minutes past five. If she was going to be at La Galerie Unique before the night security man left work at six, she needed to get moving. She pushed herself up into a sitting position, swung her legs over the side of the bed and stood up. Dragging on her dressing gown she left the bedroom.

Henry was crossing the hall from the bathroom to the sitting room. 'Good morning.'

'Is it?' Ena yawned.

He laughed. 'Welcome to my world.'

'Mmm... I'll be fine when I've had a cup of tea and a slice of toast,' she said, grinning at him before disappearing into the bathroom.

If she was going to hitch a lift into London with Henry there was no time for a bath, a quick top and tail would have to do. He was leaving for GCHQ at half-past five, she reminded herself and put a spurt on.

Dressed in a smart suit, the type she would wear for a job interview with just a little makeup on, she threw her lipstick into her handbag, dashed into the sitting room, took a swig of her tea and grabbed a slice of toast. 'Hang on, darling. Will you drop me somewhere near the Aldwych?' she asked, pushing her feet into high heeled shoes before putting on a red hat. With her handbag in one hand, her briefcase in the other, she followed Henry out of the flat.

Henry pulled up on the north side of Waterloo Bridge. 'Be careful, Ena?'

'Aren't I always?' Leaning across the gear stick she kissed him, leaving traces of lipstick on his cheek. 'See you later,' she giggled.

Henry drove off waving out of the car window. Ena waved back until he turned onto the Strand.

Life was so much better now she no longer worked for the Home Office. She had left behind government corruption and politics, spies and the undercover agents of the Cold Case department. Henry was happier at GCHQ too. MI5 had treated him appallingly and Special Branch would have made him a scapegoat if she hadn't intervened. Ena shook off the memories of those days and looked down at the Thames. It was deep and dark and held more secrets than the intelligence and security services which she'd grown to despise. At that moment the sun peeked out from behind a cloud, throwing a silver shimmer across the river. Ena had unhappy memories of the Thames, but she had some happy memories too.

***

Ena looked at her wristwatch, it was now five to six. She stepped into the doorway of a furniture repair shop and stood among posters advertising French polishing and furniture upholstering. She heard footsteps approaching from the left and leaned back into the shadows on the left side of the shop door. A man who Ena recognised from preview night passed by and walked down the narrow alley to the rear of the gallery. Two minutes later, Selwyn Horton appeared. So, the security man she had seen at the gallery on preview night was now working the day shift.

Horton came into view, turned right and walked down the street. He stopped suddenly and, leaning against a lamppost, lit a cigarette. Ena poked her head out of the doorway as a bus pulled up and Horton got on it. Holding onto her hat, Ena ran down the street. Beaming a smile at the driver she mouthed hello, and thank you for waiting, ran to the back of the bus and as Horton's legs disappeared up the stairs, she jumped on. She had no idea where he was going, nor where the bus was going for that matter.

The conductor rang the bell and approached her. 'Where to?'

'The end of the line,' she replied, attempting a joke.

'Angel and Islington. That'll be one and six.'

Ena paid, took her ticket and waited. Horton couldn't live too far away if he travelled by bus to Covent Garden each day, she thought, preparing herself to leave the bus at every stop.

'Smithfield Market,' the bus conductor shouted.

There was mumbling as people left their seats and the clatter of shoes as others clanked down the metal stairs of the bus. A woman left first and waited on the pavement for four young boys who, one after the other, piled down the stairs followed by Selwyn Horton. Ena hung back until everyone from the upper deck had alighted before she too got off.

She followed Horton past the derelict poultry market that had burned to the ground two years before and watched him go into The Tavern. It was only half-past-six and she was twenty yards away from the pub, but the aroma of fried breakfast made her mouth water. In case Horton had seen her on the bus, she took off her red felt hat, folding it and put it into her briefcase before going in.

In a costume, carrying briefcase and handbag, she stuck out like the proverbial sore thumb. Noticing an empty seat, she said, 'May I sit here?'

The rotund middle-aged man in a white coat that looked as if it was covered in blood laughed and said, 'Are you lost?'

'No, but I feel a bit out of place.' She bit her bottom lip. 'I came down from the north on the early train. I'm going to a job interview in Islington, but I think I got on the wrong bus. Not that it matters, I have plenty of time.' She smiled sheepishly at the man in the blood-stained coat. 'I saw this pub, or rather I smelt breakfast cooking.' She looked at the man's empty plate. It still had egg yolk on it. 'So, as I'm starving, I came in.' She leaned over the table. 'It is alright me being here, isn't it?'

The man laughed again. 'Course it is.'

'It's only, everyone's wearing white coats with…'

'Blood, love. We're all ere at this time a the mornin' 'cause we've all come in for breakfast after a twelve-hour shift at Smithfield's meat market. Most of the lads in here are Bummarees.'

Ena screwed up her face. She didn't have a clue what a Bummaree was.

'Bummarees are porters. We haul the meat from the lorries when they deliver at night and in the early hours, take it to the butcher's stalls and then when it's sold to butchers for shops, hotels, market stalls and the like, we take it to the individual butcher's vans. We push it on carts or haul it on our shoulders. I'm a Bummaree. Harry,' he said, offering Ena his hand.

'Ena,' she replied, shaking Harry's hand. 'I've never heard the word Bummaree until now. Where does the name come from?'

Harry burst into laughter. He laughed so much his fleshy cheeks wobbled. 'Well,' he said, when he had recovered, 'The lads at Billingsgate fish market reckon it comes from the French word, "bonne maree." But that means, fresh seafood,' Harry said knowledgeably. 'Here at Smithfield, the word goes back hundreds of years to the days when if a cow was stubborn; wouldn't leave the lorry or follow the other cows into the market, porters would prod them on their posteriors. Get it? Bum and rear?' Harry laughed again and two men on the table next to him who had been listening to the conversation laughed with him.

Ena pretended to see the funny side of Harry's explanation of Bummarees. In all honesty, she felt sorry for the cows.

Harry picked up his glass and drained his beer.

'Yes, when we've done, we come in here and have a full English and a couple of pints before we go home to bed.'

Harry looked around the room and Ena did the same. She glimpsed Selwyn Horton at a table with two men in blood-stained white coats. He was leaning forward, his left hand at the side of his mouth. He was speaking quickly, his face animated, yet serious.

'Can I get you anything, Harry?' Ena asked, getting up and putting her briefcase on her chair. She didn't want to lose her seat. Being near the door she would be able to leave quickly if she needed to.

'I'm alright, darlin, I've a pint o stout in.'

Ena went to the counter and ordered eggs, bacon, tomatoes, toast and a cup of tea. She paid and said, 'Harry has a pint of stout in. I'm sitting with him if you'd like me to take it over?' The barman pulled on the beer pump and filled a pint glass with black velvety beer. 'I've left a head on it. If he complains, tell him it was to make it easier for you to carry.'

Ena thanked him and, assuring the barman she'd relay his message, she made her way back to where she was sitting with her new friend. She placed the dark beer in front of him. 'Sorry it's not quite a full pint, but the barman was worried I'd spill it.'

Harry took a drink. 'Perfect,' he said, leaving froth as a white moustache on his top lip. Before taking her seat, Ena glanced again at Horton. He looked no happier as he ate his breakfast.

She didn't have to wait long before her own breakfast arrived. There was a lot of it. Two eggs, three thick rashers of bacon — with plenty of crispy fat on them — and goodness knows how many tomatoes on fried bread, two thick rounds of buttered toast and a half-pint mug of tea. Ena stared at the feast before her.

'If yer get that lot down ya you'll be set up for the day,' her Bummaree friend, Harry remarked.

'If I get half of it down me, I'll be doing well.' While she ate, Harry drank his beer. When she'd finished, Ena put her knife and fork down on her plate and Harry rose from his seat. Not only did he have a large girth, but he was well over six feet tall.

'I had better be off,' he said, consulting his wristwatch. 'My wife's only a little un, but she'll give me what-for if I'm late getting 'ome. She'll accuse me of stopping off for breakfast and a couple of pints. As if I would,' he said and winked at Ena. 'Good luck with your job interview. If you get the job we might see you in ere regular.'

Ena got to her feet, shook Harry's hand and said, 'I'd love that. Job or not, I'll see you again sometime.'

CHAPTER THIRTY-THREE

Several men left the pub at the same time as Harry, including the two Bummarees who had been sitting with Selwyn Horton. Ena wondered whether, because he was on his own, it would be a good time to approach him. Her thoughts were dashed by the barman ringing a bell and calling last orders. A sudden surge of burly men in white stained coats left their seats and pushed their way to the bar. Horton wasn't one of them. He got up when the others did, but instead of going to the bar he walked towards the door. Ena picked up her handbag and made for the door at the same time. Then, suddenly remembering her briefcase was hanging on the back of her chair, she turned round and bumped into him.

'I'm so sorry, Mr Horton,' she said, 'I left my briefcase on the chair.' She stepped away from him, picked up the briefcase and hooked it over her arm. 'Oh,' she said, turning back and seeing Horton standing in the doorway. 'I almost bumped into you again.'

Horton was staring at her. Ena looked past him to his left and then his right. 'Excuse me, Mr Horton, you're blocking my way.'

'Do I know you?'

'I don't think so. Unless you were on duty the night of the art viewing at La Galerie Unique.'

Ena watched the colour drain from Horton's face.

'Mr Horton, my name is Ena Green, of Dudley Green Associates. I'm a private investigator. I'm not here to accuse you of anything. In fact, I can help you. I want to know why Louis Mantel threatened you and forced you to take his money.' Ena motioned to the chair that Harry had vacated. 'May we talk?'

'If it's about stolen paintings, I know nothing about them. I swear on my granddaughter's life.' Horton shuddered. 'I mean, I swear on my life.' He began to perspire and was breathing heavily. He took a handkerchief from his trouser pocket and mopped his face.

When he pushed the hanky back into his pocket, Ena said, 'I know. I saw you yesterday in Slingsby Street talking to Louis Mantel. I saw him offer you money and I saw you refuse it. When you walked away, he came after you. He said something to you that made you change your mind and you then accepted his money.'

Horton took a bunch of notes from the inside pocket of his jacket. 'He gave me this.'

Ena looked around cautiously. 'Put the money back in your pocket, Mr Horton, before anyone sees it.'

'He threatened me,' Horton said, returning the money. 'And he threatened my daughter and her baby. He said he'd get me the sack if I told anyone what happened that night.'

'I don't understand. You said you didn't do anything, so how could Mantel get you the sack?'

Horton got up. 'They'll be chucking us out soon. The pub's been open since four o'clock this morning. The staff have to clean up and have a rest before they open at eleven for the lunch time customers.' Ena picked up her bags and followed Horton outside. He took a packet of cigarettes from his pocket and offered one to Ena. She declined, though she'd have liked one, but out of habit she didn't smoke in the street. Horton cupped his hands around the match and lit his cigarette. It wasn't windy. Ena guessed that was his habit.

He took a drag of his cigarette, inhaled deeply and blew out a stream of smoke that disappeared into the morning air. 'My daughter telephoned the gallery at midnight. She said Lily – that's her little girl, my granddaughter – was poorly. I told her there was five pounds in the drawer of my bedside table and to get a taxi to the hospital, but she began to cry. She begged me to go home. I told her I couldn't leave the gallery and then a man's voice said, "If you want to see your daughter and granddaughter again, you'd better do as she asks." Well, that was it, I knew I shouldn't have left, but my daughter's life was at stake. So, I took the keys from the office, let myself out and locked the door behind me. I thought, five minutes by taxi to get home, five minutes to sort out whatever it was that was going on at home and five minutes back. I would never have left unless I thought it was an emergency – and this was.' Horton dropped the spent cigarette on the ground, stamped it out and took another from the packet. After he'd lit it, he said, 'When I got home, the thug who had barged into my house and threatened Linda was gone.'

'And your granddaughter?'

'In her cot fast asleep. He hadn't even been in her bedroom. She knew nothing about what had happened. Linda, on the other hand, was hysterical. She threw herself into my arms as soon as I walked through the door. She was terrified.'

'Was your daughter able to describe him, the man who threatened to hurt her and the baby?'

'Better than that, she drew a picture of him. Before you ask, no I didn't recognise him. I'd never seen him before and I haven't seen him since.'

Ena nodded. She believed him. 'Then what?'

'I got my neighbour to take Linda and the baby in for the night and I returned to the gallery. No sooner had I let myself in than I felt a sharp pain on the back of my head and everything went black. I didn't know what had happened until I woke up with a hell of a headache and blood all over my shirt and jacket. I got up and managed to stumble to the washroom. I then grabbed a towel, put it under the cold water tap and held it on my head until it stopped bleeding. Eventually, when I was able, I went to the front of the gallery and checked the main entrance doors. They were locked. I went to the back door. That was locked too and all the windows were secure.'

'Did you call the Police?'

'No!' Horton looked terrified by the idea. 'The bloke at my house made it clear to Linda that I wasn't to say anything to the Police. Besides, I went into every room, checked each painting against my lists and they were all there. So, because whoever hit me over the head knows where I live, and more to the point because Linda and Lily live with me, I decided not to say anything to anyone. Not only that, I can't afford to lose my job, which I'd be sure to do if Miss Aubrey knew I'd left the gallery.'

'Did you check the jewellery display cabinets?'

'Yes. There was nothing missing.'

Selwyn Horton looked pleadingly at Ena. 'Does Miss Aubrey have to know? Because whoever hit me – and I'd put money on it being the bloke that held Linda hostage – probably thought he'd killed me and scarpered.'

'Maybe.' Ena wasn't convinced.

'I don't know what would have happened to my daughter and the baby if the paintings had been stolen and I went down for it.' Horton gave a cynical laugh.

'Jailbirds love bent ex-coppers.'

'Don't worry, even if something is missing, I'll do my best to make sure you don't go to prison. As I see it, you had no choice but to leave the gallery because your daughter and her child were being held against their will by someone.' By one of Mantel's men, Ena thought, but remained silent because as yet she had no proof.

'God knows what would have happened if I hadn't agreed to go home.'

'Don't think about it, you did go home and your family are safe. I suspect what happened was, as soon as you said you were on your way home, the man holding your daughter left your house and while you were in a taxi heading away from the gallery, he was in a car going towards it. Whatever the so-called burglar wanted he had got by the time you returned. It was bad timing on his part and bad luck on yours that you arrived back as he was leaving. If you'd been two minutes later, he'd have been gone and you'd have been spared a crack on the head.'

'Who would believe it?'

'I would, it's too ridiculous to be anything but true.'

'I should never have taken Mantel's money.'

'He was blackmailing you. I saw Mantel force the money on you.'

'I told him I didn't want it. I was going to give it back to him last night, but he didn't come to the gallery.'

'Give it to me,' Ena said. 'It's evidence.'

Horton took the money from his pocket and handed it to her. 'I didn't want to take it.'

'I know. I told you I saw you and Mantel. I saw you refuse his money and walk away.' Ena looked into the security guard's eyes. 'What did Mantel say to you that made you change your mind about taking his money before you went into the café with him?'

The colour drained from Horton's face. The look of relief that he'd displayed minutes earlier was replaced by a look of fear. 'He said if he can't tell his bosses that I was onside; that I was willing to close my eyes to paintings being stolen from the gallery and…'

'Replaced by forgeries?'

'Yes. How did you know?'

'It doesn't matter. Carry on.'

'Mantel said if I didn't work with him, he couldn't guarantee the safety of Linda and the baby. I begged him not to hurt them, that it was me they should take it out on, but he said he had no influence over what his bosses on the continent did.'

'Mr Horton, I know you weren't working on the night the gallery previewed paintings that were going to auction. How well do you know the security guard who was working that night?'

'Quite well. His name's Bob Smith.'

'Do you know which agency he's with?'

'The same as me. Sure Security, in Leicester Square.'

'Was it Bob Smith I saw arriving today just before you left the gallery?'

'Yes. He was working the night you were there, but he's on days now. He messed up the day before the preview. He was in charge of transporting paintings from The Savoy to the gallery and he lost one of them. It was found by someone staying at the hotel and they took it to Bow Street Police Station. After that Miss Aubrey had someone come in and authenticate it.'

'Who knew the painting was being authenticated that evening, do you know?'

'I didn't. I was on days then. Bob might have known and Miss Aubrey would have told Mantel.'

That's why the painting that went missing wasn't replaced by a forgery, Ena thought, and Henry authenticated it because it was a real Hogarth, as were the others on show that night. 'It's beginning to make sense to me now.'

'I wish it made sense to me,' Horton said.

'The less you know, the better, don't you think?' Horton nodded. 'I need to go back to the office. You go into work tonight as normal and for the time being, do as Mantel says.' Ena took a card from her pocket and gave it to him. 'Don't take this into the gallery, leave it at home. It's my office telephone number. If you ring and I'm not there my associate, Mr Mallory, will be. You can leave a message with him.' She took a pen from her handbag and scribbled down her home phone number on the back of the card. 'My job doesn't allow me to keep office hours, but if you can telephone during the day it would be better. If you can't, ring this number. If I don't pick up keep trying. Alright, Mr Horton?'

CHAPTER THIRTY-FOUR

Ena was at her desk drinking coffee when Artie arrived. 'Good morning.' She put on a comical frown. 'You look as if you've had a rough night.'

'Reporters can't half put the beer away.' Artie went to the kitchen and came back with a mug of coffee. 'I met the editor and the only reporter on the Brickham News. It's a local news and views paper. The reporter was the first on the scene after the accident. He's a local man and said rumours about the accident were rife. Mrs Thornton's son and his wife were taking their daughter, Andrea, back to boarding school in the Surrey Hills area. He didn't say which boarding school. Anyway, he said the daughter didn't want to go. She was fourteen and a bit of a tearaway by all accounts. She looked older than she was, liked the boys and was often seen hanging around the pubs with a couple of local lads.

'She, Andrea that is, told the Police that her father was shouting at her because she didn't want to go back to school, lost control of the car and it careered off the road into a tree.'

Artie consulted a newspaper cutting. 'The report is pretty much what we already know, but a couple of weeks after the accident the guy I spoke to wrote another report. There's a quote here from the grandmother. "My granddaughter has survived the accident, thank the Lord, Mrs Thornton said. She has no physical injuries, but she isn't the same child. Seeing her mother and father killed and her little brother so badly injured, has broken her heart and her spirit."'

'Brother? There's been no mention of Mrs

Thornton having a grandson. So, he survived the accident too?'

Artie scanned the rest of the page and turned to the next. 'Got it. It says here that Mr and Mrs Thornton's daughter, Andrea, dazed and in shock, left her small brother in the back of the car while she went to get help.' Artie put down the newspaper and rolled his eyes.

'You don't look convinced.'

'I'm not. I did as you suggested and took the reporter to the pub. He told me that some months later he spoke to the lads Andrea ran around with and they told him that the accident happened not because her father lost control of the car, but because Andrea, in a fit of anger, grabbed the steering wheel. It was her fault the car went off the road and hit a tree. She was thrown clear, her father died at the scene, her mother who was in the back of the car with the six-year-old boy died on the way to the hospital. The boy's legs were broken so badly he was in a wheelchair. The reporter said the boy hasn't been seen since his grandmother fell down the stairs and went into the nursing home. He didn't say it, but I knew by his tone the reporter thought the old lady's fall was suspicious.'

'I do too. So,' Ena said, 'at the time of the accident Andrea would have been fourteen, too young to inherit her parents money. She'd also be too young to live in the family home on her own, especially with a disabled brother.'

'What are you thinking?'

'If Mrs Thornton sold her son and daughter-in-law's house and invested the money for the children when they were older and Andrea wanted her share now...'

'... she might have tried to kill her grandmother,

but instead killed George's father?'

'Nurse McKinlay said Mr Derby-Bloom's last words were, *Granddaughter. She has killed me.* What if he meant *me* opposed to Mrs Thornton. Andrea had been to see her grandmother the day George's father died. What if she put poison in her grandmother's glass and the glasses were accidently switched?'

'In which case, Mr Derby-Bloom wasn't the intended victim, but Mrs Thornton was. We'd better get over there. I'll telephone DI Powell, ask him to let the Surrey Police know what we've found out – and that we're going to the nursing home – and you telephone George, ask her if we can meet next week.'

When they had each finished speaking on the telephone, Ena grabbed the car keys, Artie the office keys. While he locked up, Ena ran across the road to the Sunbeam. Got in and gunned the engine. 'DI Powell is going to let Surrey Police know what's going on,' Ena confirmed. Artie jumped in the car as Ena backed out of the parking space and drove up Mercer Street.

'I told George we'd had a breakthrough. She said her father's funeral is on Tuesday.'

'I'll go to it. I'd rather you stayed in the office in case Selwyn Horton phones. You didn't want to come with me, did you?'

'No. Someone needs to be in the office.' Artie leaned back in the passenger seat and sighed. 'Everything seems to happen at once. I've a pile of paperwork to catch up on. So have you.'

'Don't remind me.'

***

Ena parked at the side of the nursing home to keep the

drive at the front free. 'No Police cars yet,' she said, locking the Sunbeam.

As they entered the lobby, the door to the manager's office opened and Mrs Sharp came out.

'Mrs Green?' she said, exhibiting her usual pinched look. 'What can I do for you?' She looked Artie up and down.

'Mr Mallory and I,' Ena said, by way of introducing Artie, 'would like to speak to Nurse McKinlay and Mrs Thornton.'

'As you didn't make an appointment, I wasn't expecting you. If you'd be kind enough to come into my office and explain to me why you wish to speak to one of my staff and a resident.'

'Mrs Sharp, we're wasting time. It's important that I speak to Nurse McKinlay.'

The nursing home's manageress threw her hands in the air. 'Nurse McKinlay is working. I can't have her abandon patients every time you come here. You should have telephoned first!' she said, holding Ena with a defiant look.

Ena took a deep and calming breath. She was losing patience with Mrs Sharp and her rules and was getting very close to telling her so.

The manageress was first to back down from the stand-off. 'Very well, I'll send for her. But Mrs Thornton is in her room, resting. She is not to be disturbed.'

The door to the resident's lounge opened and Nurse McKinlay appeared pushing an elderly man in a wheelchair.

Nurse McKinlay smiled at Ena.

'Mrs Green would like to speak to you, Nurse.'

'Thank you, Mrs Sharp, I'd like to speak to Mrs Green.' The manageress gave her a curt nod. 'I'll take

Mr Carlisle to his room and get him settled. I'll be five minutes.'

'You can wait for Nurse McKinlay in my office.' Mrs Sharp didn't wait for a reply, she turned her back on Ena and Artie and opened the door.

'As Nurse McKinlay said she'll be five minutes, I'll pop to the toilet,' Ena said, turning on her heels and heading along the corridor leading to Mrs Thornton's room.

'No need to go all the way to the resident's wing when there's a perfectly good toilet here.' Mrs Sharp jabbed a forefinger at the door next to her office marked private.

'Even better. I should have gone before I left London.' Ena pushed open the toilet door and disappeared inside, closing it with a considerable thud. When she heard the door to the Mrs Sharp's office close, Ena tiptoed out of the toilet and closed the door quietly. Waiting until she was certain she wouldn't be heard, she then ran down the corridor towards Mrs Thornton's room. Hearing voices inside, she tapped the door gently. There was no reply so she opened it. Mrs Thornton was in her armchair, her granddaughter was sitting on her bed. They both turned and looked at her.

'I'm terribly sorry to have disturbed you,' Ena said, 'I was looking for the toilet.'

'The next door along,' Mrs Thornton's granddaughter said.

Ena tutted. 'Of course it is.' She smiled at Mrs Thornton, apologised once more, and left, closing the door behind her.

Before going into Mrs Sharp's office, Ena popped into the small private lavatory next door, flushed the toilet and washed her hands. 'That's better,' she said, nodding at Artie as she entered. No sooner had she sat down than Nurse McKinlay knocked on the door. Without waiting to be told by her superior to come in, she entered and crossed the room to Ena, showing her a glass with what looked like lemon and barley water in it. 'I swapped the glasses. This is the first glass, the one I gave to Mrs Thornton earlier. I was called away...'

'Thank you, Nurse McKinlay, good work.'

'Would someone tell me what is going on!' Mrs Sharp spat, puffing out her chest. She looked at Nurse McKinlay as if she had something unpleasant stuck to her top lip.

'Before Mr Derby-Bloom died, he said, "Granddaughter. She has killed me." He didn't have a granddaughter. Mr Derby-Bloom was not referring to a grandchild of his, he—' Before Ena explained further, there was loud knocking at the front door.

Mrs Sharp left her seat and looked out of the window. 'It's the Police!'

CHAPTER THIRTY-FIVE

Ena was nearest the door. 'Shall I let the Police in?'

'No!' Mrs Sharp snapped. 'This is still my nursing home.' The manageress barged past Ena, marched across the entrance foyer to the street door and yanked it open.

'Inspector Reed, Surrey Constabulary,' a plain clothes policeman announced. 'This is DS Myers and WPC Elliot. We'd like to speak to Mrs Thornton.'

'This is most irregular. May I ask why?'

Ena heard the inspector hesitate before saying, 'We have reason to believe that her life is in danger.'

Mrs Sharp's hand flew to her mouth and she gasped. Ena thought she might faint and took a few steps towards her in case she needed to show the Police to Mrs Thornton's room. She needn't have bothered. Seeing Ena approaching, Mrs Sharp quickly recovered. Summoning Nurse McKinlay she said to the inspector, 'If you would like to follow me.'

Ena watched as Mrs Sharp led the Police Officers down the corridor. Five minutes later, the detective sergeant and the female Police constable were walking so quickly they were almost running, As they left the building the inspector appeared holding a glass of lemon and barley, which Ena suspected was the glass Nurse McKinlay had swapped for a fresh drink of cordial.

No longer than a minute later, a nurse was pushing Mrs Thornton in a wheelchair and Nurse McKinlay was at the old lady's side holding her hand and speaking to her in calming hushed tones. Ena couldn't hear what she was saying but assumed the compassionate nurse would be saying something to comfort her. No sooner had they arrived at the main exit than they were met by two ambulance men who took over, leaving both the nurses and Mrs Sharp watching, speechless. In shock, Ena thought. She exhaled. At least the old lady was alive, but where was her granddaughter?

'Back to work, ladies,' Mrs Sharp ordered, leaving them to secure the front door. As the nurses turned to resume their duties, Ena opened Mrs Sharp's office door a little wider, attracting the attention of Nurse McKinlay. Upon seeing Ena, she jerked her head in the direction of Mrs Thornton's room. Ena nodded and as Nurse McKinlay headed back down the corridor, Ena quietly pulled the office door to, and prepared herself for an onslaught of questions from Mrs Sharp.

The inspector entered the office first, with Mrs Sharp hard on his heels. She looked understandably worried. 'It was Mrs Green,' Mrs Sharp said, pointing to Ena, 'who first suspected Mrs Thornton's life was in danger and it was one of my nurses who alerted me.'

The inspector acknowledged Ena with a professional smile. 'Perhaps I could use your office to interview the staff?' Mrs Sharp didn't look at all happy by the inspector's request. 'It will be quicker for them and cause less concern to your patients if I speak to them in here.' Mrs Sharp pursed her lips but didn't answer. 'Of course, it would be easier for me to interview them at the station…'

'No, no, no. I can't have them out of the building. We're short staffed as it is.' She looked at her wristwatch. 'No, my office is at your disposal,' she said sitting down.

'I'm sure you have a great deal of work to be getting on with, so, I'll start by speaking to Mrs Green. Would you give me an hour? It shouldn't take longer.'

'Of course.' Mrs Sharp got up and pulled on the lapels of her jacket. 'I shall be in the staff room if you need me. Along the corridor, first door on the right.' She cleared her desk of paperwork with such speed the documents might have been top secret. With files and folders under her arm, Mrs Sharp left her office. 'Call me if you need me,' she said, as the door swung shut behind her.

Inspector Reed introduced himself to Ena and Artie and took a notepad and pen from his briefcase. 'I understand from Detective Inspector Powell at Bow Street that one of the residents here has already been poisoned and you suspect Mrs Thornton's granddaughter?'

'I think it was the granddaughter and I think it was accidental,' Ena explained. 'I believe Mr Derby-Bloom died because he drank Mrs Thornton's lemon and barley water by mistake. I also believe he realised what he'd done and that he knew his friend's life was in danger. He told one of the nurses as much before he died. He said, "Granddaughter, she has killed me." Except he said it in German.'

'Is the nurse German?'

'No, she worked with a German doctor after the Russian invasion of Finland in 1940. She was also a translator in the war. Mr Derby-Bloom worked with German students, Jewish students. Nurse McKinlay is a caring, and understanding woman. I think they had spoken about the work they had both done in the war and they had the German language in common. I'm guessing Mr Derby-Bloom trusted Nurse McKinlay, which is why he told her. I believe he told her in German in case anyone was listening to their conversation.'

'Where can I find Nurse McKinlay?'

'The last time I saw her she was heading back to Mrs Thornton's room.'

The inspector stopped writing and looked up at Ena. 'It's a coincidence that the nurse who was with Mr Derby-Bloom when he was murdered was also with Mrs Thornton and her granddaughter today?'

'I was worried that having failed to poison her grandmother once, Andrea Thornton would try again, so I asked Nurse McKinlay to watch her and if Andrea went anywhere near her grandmother's cordial to replace it immediately and keep the glass so the contents could be analysed.'

'Since you recruited the nurse who was with Mr Derby-Bloom and Mrs Thornton to work for you, perhaps you'd like to find her and tell her I need to speak to her,'

Ena felt the heat of embarrassment creep up her neck. As she thought, Nurse McKinlay was in Mrs Thornton's room looking out of the window. 'The inspector would like to ask you a few questions,' Ena said, poking her head around the door.

Nurse McKinlay turned and followed Ena along the corridor. 'Mrs Green,' she said, before she and Ena entered the manager's office. 'I need to give you this.' She took a piece of paper with two addresses on it from her pocket. 'The first is Mrs Thornton's address, the other is the address and telephone number of her granddaughter, which she gave the office when she signed as her grandmother's next of kin.'

Ena's eyes widened. 'Did you give the Police these addresses?'

'No, I assumed Mrs Sharp would.'

'When did Andrea Thornton leave?'

'Not long after you came into her grandmother's room. I couldn't go after her or come and tell you because I didn't want to leave Mrs Thornton. By the time the Police arrived Andrea had disappeared. I looked everywhere for her, but...' Nurse McKinlay shrugged her shoulders.

Ena noted the addresses. 'Thank you. I'll go to one address and Artie the other.' Ena stopped. 'Damn, we only have one car. Is there a taxi company nearby?'

'No, but I have a car. It's old and doesn't go very fast, but you're welcome to borrow it.'

'I couldn't...'

'I insist. That young woman killed a lovely gentleman. Wait here.'

Ena took several deep breaths. She looked at the door to the staff room and prayed the manageress wouldn't come out of it.

'Here,' Nurse McKinlay pushed the keys to her car into Ena's hands. 'It's the green Morris Minor in the car park at the back of the building. Drop it back here when you've finished with it. I'm working until 8 o'clock tonight.'

'Thank you,' Ena looked at Nurse McKinlay's name badge, 'Jeanie.' Ena pressed he lips together. 'I don't know how to ask you this, but could you do me another favour?'

'Of course.'

'When Artie and I leave, the inspector will interview you. Would you wait a couple of minutes to give Artie and me a head start before you give him these addresses. If you don't want Mrs Sharp to know you took them from her office, say they were in Mrs Thornton's room.'

Jeanie nodded.

'Mrs Thornton has a grandson. If he's at her house I want to speak to him, find out if he's in cahoots with his sister in trying to kill his grandmother. Because he's younger than Andrea, she may have coerced him.

'I'm Ena, by the way.' She reached out and took hold of Jeanie's hands. 'I'll see you later when I return your car,' Ena said and entered the office behind Jeanie. The inspector was writing. Ena looked at Artie, who rolled his eyes.

'If you've finished with my associate and me, we've got work to do,' Ena said, giving the inspector her card. 'If you need to see either of us again, give the office a call.' As she passed Jeanie, she gave her a conspiratorial wink.

CHAPTER THIRTY-SIX

Ena took the keys to the Sunbeam from her shoulder bag and gave them to Artie. She then took out a notebook and pen and wrote down the addresses of Andrea Thornton and her grandmother. 'Take my car and go to Andrea's flat. She hasn't seen you before, so if she's there, ask for a different name and then leave when she says the person isn't at that address. She's dangerous. I'm going to the old lady's house.'

'How, if I take your car?'

'Nurse McKinlay has loaned me hers. Now get going. She's going to give the addresses to the inspector so both houses will be swarming with Police in an hour.'

The green Morris Minor looked old, but drove perfectly. It had obviously been well maintained. Having got to know Jeanie McKinlay, Ena wasn't surprised.

***

Ena didn't know the area but she found Mrs Thornton's house quite quickly. She drove past the half-moon shaped drive. There were no cars in front of the house. She turned the Morris around, parked twenty yards down the road, got out and walked the short distance to the three-storey red brick Victorian house. At the front were two bay windows and between them steps with a metal rail on either side leading to the front door. Mounting the steps, Ena knocked on the door. There was no reply. She knocked again, but still no one answered.

Ena glanced over her shoulder. On either side of

the drive, tall shrubs made it difficult to see the neighbouring houses, which in turn would make it difficult for the neighbours to see Mrs Thornton's house. As the house appeared to be deserted, Ena lifted the flap of the letter box and peered in. A light shone from one of the downstairs rooms, its stark beam reflected a harsh glare across the polished wooden floor of the hall.

Checking again that she wasn't being watched, Ena walked down the steps, continued along the side of the house and looked through the first window she came to. She was right, a standard lamp without a shade shone brightly. The rest of the furniture in the room was covered with white sheets.

Was Mrs Thornton going to sell the house, Ena mused, or was it her granddaughter that was going to sell it? Ena wondered if Mrs Thornton knew what was happening in her absence. Her heart began to thump. Jeanie had said her granddaughter was Mrs Thornton's next of kin. Was she also the beneficiary of the old lady's will? Ena hoped not.

Ena looked through the next window and the next along the path leading to the back garden. Every piece of furniture in each darkened room was shrouded in sheets. Only the kitchen looked as if it was being used. Ena put her hand up to shade her eyes from the sun's reflection on the glass and pressed her face against the window. There was a cooker and a sink on the right. She looked across the room to a table and then recoiled in horror. A boy tied to a wheelchair was looking back at her. Ena's heart began to race and she stumbled backwards.

Seeing the boy alone in his wheelchair in the sparsely furnished kitchen had given her a shock. He must be Mrs Thornton's grandson, Andrea's brother.

What kind of person does that to her brother? Ena took several calming breaths, braced herself and looked through the window again. She gasped with horror. The boy had a makeshift gag of white cloth in his mouth. He stared at Ena wide-eyed and began shaking his head and rocking the wheelchair from side to side. From the little she could see of the boy's face he looked terrified. Clearly he was in distress. She needed to help him, but to do that would mean breaking in.

Ena put her elbow against the bottom pane of glass in the kitchen door, brought it forward and thrust it back sharply. She heard a crack but the glass hadn't broken. She elbowed the pane again, this time there was a crash and not only the glass but the wood moulding holding it in place splintered. Ena knocked wood and several shards of glass out of the door frame, put her hand inside and unlocked the door.

As she entered the kitchen, she felt a severe drop in temperature. It was a sunny day, hot outside, but the kitchen was cold. The boy was shivering. His feet were bare and his thin cotton shirt and slacks were stained with food. As she approached him the acrid smell of stale urine filled her nostrils.

Ena reached out to him. He flinched, his eyes flashed with fear, as a wild animal's might when trapped. Shaking his head from side to side, he tried to speak but his words were inaudible beneath the cloth in his mouth. 'My name's Ena. I know your grandmother,' she said reassuringly, but the boy kept rocking from side to side. 'Don't be frightened, I'm not going to hurt you, I'm going to get you out of here.'

Moving quickly to the back of the wheelchair Ena untied the knot in the makeshift gag, pulled it from the boy's mouth and he screamed, 'No!'

That was the last word Ena heard before waking

up with a splitting headache, tied to a kitchen chair next to the boy. She looked at him. Staring into the mid-distance, his eyes dull and full of tears, he looked defeated.

'I'm sorry,' Ena whispered, 'I should have looked to see if your sister was here before—'

'Shut up!' Andrea shouted from behind her. She walked around the table, made a fist and slammed it down hard, making Ena jump. In her other hand she clutched a knife, and pointed the blade at Ena.

Ena swallowed hard. She needed to get Andrea talking and keep her talking to stop her from using the knife. 'I don't think you wanted to hurt me,' she said, as calmly as she was able. 'Hurting me would make things worse for you.'

'I said, 'Shut up!' Andrea walked around the table again. Ena could feel her eyes burning into the back of her head. 'My associate knows I'm here, Andrea,' she said, observing her out of the corner of her eye. 'The nurse who takes care of your grandmother knows I'm here too. She was going to give the Police this address as soon as I left the nursing home.' Ena's heart was beating ten-to-the-dozen and the pulse at her temples began to throb. 'If you make a run for it now, you've got a good chance of getting away. Stay here and you're bound to be caught. By my reckoning, the Police will be here any minute.'

Andrea stopped walking when she got to the front of the table. She leaned on it, sliding her elbows forward until the top half of her body was on the table and her face was level with Ena's. 'You're lying,' she said, pressing the knife against Ena's throat. 'No one knows I'm at dear old Granny's house. I told the old bitch at the nursing home the house had been sold and Granny was going to live with me when she got out of the old folks' home.'

Andrea pressed the tip of the blade into the muscle on the side of Ena's neck beneath her ear. She felt a sharp pain and then warm blood trickled down her neck. 'No one will come looking for you here.'

'Yes, they will!' Artie shouted, throwing a sheet over Andrea's head. She fell to the floor and Artie fell on top of her. Holding her arms tightly beneath the sheet, Artie made every effort to tie a silk curtain tieback around her. The tieback was thick and shiny, the fabric slipped and Andrea began to struggle free. 'Keep still,' Artie shouted, but like a wild cat Andrea twisted and turned, lashed out at Artie and began to sit up. 'I didn't want to do this,' Artie said, punching Andrea beneath the sheet. As she fell back groaning, Artie tied her arms against her body. What was left of the tieback he knotted round her ankles.

With Andrea trussed up like a turkey, Artie untied Ena and then the boy.

'Water, please,' the boy wheezed. Artie went to the sink, took a glass from the cupboard above, filled it and gave it to the boy. He gulped the water down and choked. Artie took the glass from him, patted his back, and held the glass for the boy to take several more sips. He exhaled loudly when he'd had enough and whispered, 'Thank you.'

'Listen!' Artie laughed. 'I never thought I'd be happy to hear the wailing sirens of Police cars.'

'You're safe now,' Ena said to the boy.

The Police sirens grew louder, the cars arrived, and a dozen policemen, truncheons raised, burst into the house via the front door. Inspector Reed followed the uniformed men in and behind him were two women constables. The WPCs pulled Andrea to her feet, untied her and took off the sheet. Ena looked at Artie and raised her eyes. Andrea had a bright red mark on her chin and her face was beginning to swell.

As the WPCs took Andrea away, Artie turned to Ena and whispered, 'Whoops!'

'She must have bumped her face when she fell,' Ena said.

The inspector looked from Artie to Ena. 'So, Mrs Green, this is the work you were so eager to get back to London to do?'

'I didn't actually say London, Inspector.'

The conversation between Ena and the inspector was interrupted when two ambulance men arrived. One asked her if she was alright. She said she was. The other asked the boy his name, something Ena hadn't thought to do, but now wished she had. He answered in a tired voice, 'Rory.'

The ambulance man asked him about his health, the reason he was in a wheelchair and other questions which Ena didn't hear because the second medic was asking her questions, which she answered quickly and succinctly. He looked at her head and said she should go to the hospital. Ena had no intention of going to hospital. She was more interested in what was going to happen to Rory and ignored the medic.

'Thank you,' Rory said, as he drew level with Ena. She forced back her tears and the emotion she felt for the boy and smiled. 'Is my Gran alright?' he asked.

'Yes. She's fine.' Ena turned to the man pushing Rory. 'Which hospital are you taking him to?'

'St. Marks.'

'I'll let your grandmother know where you'll be.'

'Thank you,' he said, again. The first medic pushed him to the back door where a St. John's Ambulance nurse was waiting. She lifted the undercarriage of the wheelchair and the chair cleared the step. As the first medic pushed Rory towards the ambulance, the second one turned to Ena.

'I'll get a chair. Miss.'

'There's no need. I'm fine. I don't need a chair and I'm not going to the hospital.'

'You've had a whack on the head, you ought to get it checked out,' Artie said.

'My head hardly hurts and I'm not seeing double. If I feel at all unwell later, I'll go to my local outpatients.'

The medic looked at Artie. 'Sir?'

'I'm not hurt at all. And,' said Artie glaring at Ena, 'I'll drive her home and stay with her until her husband gets back from work.'

'If she shows any signs of nausea, dizziness, memory loss…'

'I'll take her straight to the hospital.'

The medic nodded and turned to leave, but Ena called him back. 'The boy, Rory, he will be alright, won't he?'

'We won't know until the doctors have seen him. He's dehydrated, looks as if he needs a few good meals, but he's young. Kids of that age bounce back. There's obviously a reason why he's in a wheelchair, but if he has no other underlying health problems, he should be fine.'

'Thanks, I'd like to give his grandmother some positive news. Oh, and what will happen to him when he's released from hospital, where will he go?'

'I don't know, Miss. It'll be up to the hospital and the welfare people.'

'Thank you. Sorry to hold you up. Come on,' Ena said to Artie when the medic left, 'let's get out of here.'

CHAPTER THIRTY-SEVEN

'You're not driving!' Artie said, taking the keys to the Morris from Ena. 'I'm taking you home. I'll come back for the nurse's car later.'

'When Henry gets home? I don't think so. He'll be hours yet. He may not come home at all tonight. No,' Ena said, 'take me to The Willows in Jeanie's car. She was good enough to lend it to me, it isn't fair to keep her waiting. You can come back for the Sunbeam when you've dropped me off.'

Artie opened his mouth to argue but gave in. 'Okay, at least if you're at the nursing home and you feel ill, there'll be people there to look after you.' Artie took Ena by the arm. At the beginning of the short drive, Ena and Artie saw Inspector Reed running up the steps at the front of the house. When he saw them, he stopped, put up his hand and jogged back to meet them. 'Someone will telephone,' he said to Ena, 'to arrange for you and Mr Mallory to come down to the station and give a statement.'

'Nothing would give me greater pleasure!' Artie looked at Ena. 'She'd have killed Ena if I hadn't stopped her,' he said, nodding at Ena, his eyes widening.

Ena suddenly fell into what Artie wanted her to say. 'That's right,' she said, 'the girl caught me off guard, hit me on the back of the head and knocked me out. Thank God Artie arrived when he did. She had tied me to a chair and was about to cut my throat when he intervened.' Ena pushed her hair away from her neck and turned sideways to let the inspector see the wound on her neck.

The inspector leaned forward and scrutinised the

wound. 'Did it bleed?' he said with a twinkle in his eye.

'Yes!' Ena and Artie said in unison.

'I pressed my hanky on it.' Ena dug into her pocket and produced the bloody handkerchief.' With as much emotion in her voice as she could muster, she said, 'God knows what she'd have done if Artie hadn't got her off me.'

'With considerable force, by the look of the bruise on Miss Thornton's chin.'

Ena, with a bemused look, said, 'Bruise? Oh, that must have happened when she wriggled out of Artie's arms. She slipped and the fell on the floor, didn't she, Artie?'

'Yes,' Artie nodded, 'that's when she must have bruised herself, Inspector.'

Inspector Reed looked from Artie to Ena. 'If you say so.'

'I forgot you decked her,' Ena said when the inspector was out of earshot.

***

Artie dropped Ena off at the front of The Willows, parked the Morris and walked back to the front door.

Ena and Jeanie were on the way to the staff room. 'Jeanie is going to make a pot of tea. I bet you could do with a cup?'

Artie declined the offer. 'I want to collect your car and get you home,' he said, giving Jeanie her car keys. He took the keys to the Sunbeam from his trouser pocket, threw them in the air and caught them. 'Look after her, Nurse McKinlay,' he said and left.

'That's a nasty cut on your neck, Ena.'

'It might have been a whole lot worse. Mrs

Thornton's granddaughter had her brother gagged and tied to his wheelchair. I went into the house, and as I was taking off the gag she hit me from behind. When I came round, I found myself tied up too. She was about to make this cut a gash when Artie threw a sheet over her and wrestled her to the ground.'

'She has serious problems, that's for sure.' Jeanie looked more closely at Ena's neck and exhaled loudly. 'She could have done a lot of damage if she hadn't been stopped. The cut is close to an artery. I'll clean it up and put something on it to stop it from becoming infected.'

'It's not that bad, is it?' Ena asked, unable to hide the panic in her voice.

Jeanie rolled her eyes. 'I bet you don't go to the doctor unless you really have to, do you?'

'No, I don't. The place is full of sick people. I'd likely catch something in the waiting room.'

Jeanie laughed. 'Well, you won't catch anything here. If any of the staff has as much as a cough, they're sent home. Most of our patients are vulnerable, some are susceptible to catching the slightest thing. The home has to be kept sterile.'

'Like Mrs Sharp.'

Jeanie laughed again. She pushed open the staff room door for Ena to enter first and then followed her in.

'Take a seat.' Jeanie went to the cupboard and took down the First Aid kit. 'This might sting a little.'

'That's what they all say. Ouch!'

'Almost done,' Jeanie said, dabbing Ena's neck with what smelled like a strong astringent. There, the cut is clean now. I'm just going to put a dab of Germoline on it.'

'I hate the smell of antiseptic creams.'

'It will soon wear off.' When she had applied a plaster to Ena's neck, Jeanie washed her hands, dried them and flicked on the kettle. While it boiled, she spooned tea into the pot and when the tea was made, joined Ena at the table. 'Mrs Thornton is in St. Jude's. She hadn't ingested anything harmful, so they're sending her back here tomorrow. We'll only be able to keep her here for few days, a week at most, then she'll have to go home. As I told you, she is quite capable of looking after herself.'

'More so now her granddaughter is in custody. But she may not be able to look after her grandson,' Ena said, 'not a young man in a wheelchair. What's going to happen to him?'

'I have some holiday due, I'll take it and call on Mrs Thornton for the first few days she's home. If nothing else, I can take her to the hospital to visit her grandson. When he comes out, I'll help her sort something out.'

Artie poked his head around the door. 'Excuse me, Nurse, but I think it's time I took this one home,' he said to Jeanie. Then, turning to Ena, 'What time does Henry get back from work?'

'How long is a piece of string?' she said getting to her feet. 'Thank you for lending me your car, Jeanie, and for patching me up. Stay in touch, will you?'

Jeanie promised she would and said, 'I'll let you know how Mrs Thornton and her grandson get on, if you promise you'll go to the nearest hospital if you begin to feel unwell.'

Ena promised and Jeanie saw her and Artie out of the nursing home. Before she got in the car, Ena looked across the tarmacked drive to the front door to wave goodbye. Jeanie wasn't there. She had no doubt already returned to her duties.

CHAPTER THIRTY-EIGHT

'Here you are, strong and sweet,' Artie said, placing Ena's tea in front of her. She turned her nose up at it. 'It's good for shock, so get it down you.'

'I had two cups with Jeanie at The Willows. Can't I have a scotch?' Artie looked to the heavens. 'I'll be swimming in bloody tea soon,' she mumbled and took a sip. 'I hate sugar in tea, but thanks. And thank you for going back for the Sunbeam. God knows what I'd do without you.' Ena was grateful to Artie and very pleased to be home.

'Telephone your pal at Durden Cameras and ask him if he's developed the photographs of Mantel and Horton?'

'I only took the film in yesterday.'

'I know, but the quicker I can get them to Inspector Powell, the sooner he'll send someone to watch Horton's house.' Artie went to the telephone. 'If he hasn't developed them yet, tell him you'll give him a fiver to do them today. I need those photographs.'

While Artie spoke to his friend at Durden Cameras, Ena took a bottle of Teacher's Whisky from the sideboard cupboard and poured a measure into her tea. 'Want some?' she asked, pushing the bottle towards Artie when he had finished the call.

'Thanks. He's developing them now,' Artie said, adding a capful of whisky to his tea. 'I'll pick them up on the way to work tomorrow morning. You know they're likely to incriminate Horton, not exonerate him.'

'I saw Horton give the money back to Mantel and walk away.'

'Yes, but he had Mantel's money in the café when

I was taking photographs.'

Ena reached for her handbag at the side of the settee, opened it and produced the money Mantel had given to Horton. 'He doesn't want Mantel's money.'

'Okay! Let's thrash this out and see what we come up with.'

'Horton told me when I followed him to the Tavern at Smithfields that he wasn't involved in transporting the Hogarth paintings from The Savoy to the gallery so he couldn't have had anything to do with the painting that went missing. And, secondly, he doesn't want anything to do with Mantel.'

'But he works for Mantel?'

'No, Horton works for Giselle Aubrey. Mantel is her sponsor, and he's blackmailing him.' Ena took a drink of her tea. 'I'd bet my last penny that the four Hogarths going to auction are forgeries and the real paintings are winging their way to France or Germany. And I don't think they'd have been the first to be replaced either.'

'Since Mantel's been the gallery's sponsor? Okay, could Henry get into the gallery and check the other paintings?'

'I could ask him. I'm sure Horton would let us in, but,' Ena slowly shook her head, 'Henry wouldn't do anything illegal.'

'Would it be illegal? You'd be helping the owner out in the long run, or is she involved in the scam?'

'I don't think she's involved. I think she's a little smitten with Mantel. He's a smooth operator, a charmer. He's what my mother would call a lady's man.' Ena grimaced. 'Not my cup of tea. No,' she said thoughtfully, 'Giselle isn't involved in the thefts or the forgeries, I'm sure of it.'

'Horton said no paintings were missing that night.'

'They could have been stolen and replaced with forgeries while he was at home.'

Ena took a drink of her tea. 'Horton's worried about losing his job so he's obviously hoping nothing was taken. He thinks the burglar panicked after hitting him and did a runner before he had time to steal anything. The more I think about it the more I'm sure that the bloke who rang Horton from his house threatening to hurt his daughter, is the same bloke who knocked Horton out.'

'He must have left Horton's house soon after talking to him.'

'I think he left immediately he put the telephone down, went to the gallery and he had already swapped the paintings by the time Horton got there. I think he was probably leaving as Horton came in.'

Artie sipped his tea thoughtfully. 'Strange that the painting that went missing on the day of the preview that you and Henry attended was found and authenticated by Henry as original.'

'The original was put on show for Henry's benefit. Mantel would have known Henry was going to look at the painting. Giselle Aubrey had no reason to suspect Mantel of dodgy doings. She'd have told him in all innocence.'

'So, Mantel swapped the forgery with the real thing, and when the gallery closed, swapped it back?'

'That's one scenario. However it happened, the Hogarth that Henry saw that night was genuine. The other three in the set were also genuine.'

'So, after thrashing out the possibilities, are you any the wiser?'

Ena blew out her cheeks. 'No, but I hope to be when I've dragged Henry back to the gallery to look at the display for the next pre-auction viewing.' Ena and

Artie's heads turned at the sound of the front door opening. 'We're in here, darling,' Ena shouted.

'Artie?' Henry said, entering the room. 'Good to see you.' The two men shook hands. 'Hello, darling.' Henry kissed Ena and frowned. 'You look pale. What's the matter?'

'It's a long story,' Artie cut in. 'I don't suppose she'll tell you,' he said, pouting disapprovingly at Ena, 'so I will. She has had a bump on the head, so, if she feels unwell or shows the slightest sign of concussion, take her to the emergency department of your local hospital.'

His frown deepening, Henry looked at Ena and then Artie. 'I'll see you out,' he said, following Artie to the hall and then the front door. 'Thanks for bringing her home.'

'Artie's taking my car,' Ena shouted from the sitting room.

Henry picked up the keys to the Sunbeam from the hall table and gave them to Artie.

'I can walk to Stockwell station and get the Underground.'

'I'll bring Ena into work in the morning, she won't need the car.'

When Henry returned to the sitting room, Ena was pouring a glass of whisky. Henry took it from her. 'Concussion and you're drinking scotch? I don't think so. You need food?'

'We've got a dozen eggs, cheese... there's plenty of food in the refrigerator.'

'Cheese omelette, coming up. I'll fry last night's leftovers and make bubble and squeak,' Henry leaned over Ena, kissed her and took the glass with whisky in it with him.

***

'I wondered whether you'd be in today,' Artie said passing Ena coming out of the cloakroom. He ran into the office and picked up the ringing telephone on Ena's desk. As she entered, he was holding the telephone out to her. 'Surrey CID,' he whispered.

Ena mouthed, 'damn', took the telephone from Artie and said, 'Ena Green here, can I help you?'

'Mrs Green, DI Reed. I was wondering if it would be convenient for you and Mr Mallory to come down to Police headquarters today?'

'Headquarters?'

'Surrey headquarters. We're in Guildford, Mount Browne. Sandy Lane.'

Ena scribbled the address down on a notepad.

'Would you hold for a moment, Inspector?' Ena put her hand over the telephone's mouthpiece. 'Did you pick up the photographs?' Artie nodded. 'Good. We'll go through them now and then you go down to Guildford. I'll hang on here, I need to make a few calls. If there's time I'll take the photographs to Bow Street. If not, I'll go tomorrow.' She took her hand away from the telephone and lifted it to her mouth. 'Mr Mallory will come to Guildford this morning. It will take him time to get to you. Shall we say between eleven and twelve?'

'Fine.'

'Good. I'll come down this afternoon. We're only a small agency, I'd rather not close the office for too long.'

'Perfectly understandable, Mrs Green. Until this afternoon then. Goodbye.'

Artie brought in two cups of coffee and put them on the table before taking the envelope containing the surveillance photographs and spreading them out in the order they were taken.

Ena put the receiver on its cradle and joined him. 'I've no idea where bloody Mount Browne is in Guildford.'

'I was a stone's throw from there yesterday.'

'In that case, you go down by train and then get a cab from Guildford railway station. I'll take the road map and drive down.' She looked at Mantel's photograph. 'Smarmy tyke.'

'Look, Martel has his hand on Horton's shoulder and he's smiling at him. That's what I meant when I said the photos wouldn't clear Horton.'

Ena went to her desk and took a magnifying glass from it. She scrutinised each photograph in turn and picked out three. 'Use this,' she said, handing the magnifier to Artie. 'Look closely at these three and tell me what you see.'

Artie leaned over the photographs and lifted the magnifying glass to his left eye. 'Mantel isn't smiling at Horton at all, he's grinning menacingly. And his hand isn't on his shoulder in a friendly gesture. Mantel's applying pressure to the muscle running down the side of Horton's neck with his thumb. Horton's grimacing with pain, the poor bugger.'

While Artie was focusing on the photographs of Mantel and Horton, Ena scanned the rest. 'There's a man in the background of most of the photographs you took from the street. Did you see him?' Ena pointed to a broad-shouldered man in a dark jacket with dark, probably black hair, holding a cup. She flicked through the rest of the photographs. He was in half a dozen of them – and he wore the same expression and was holding the same cup. Did you see this man when you were inside?'

'Yes, but I didn't take much notice of him. I remember him being there. Now, come to think of it, he left at the same time as Mantel and Horton and walked off in the same direction as Mantel. Why, do you know him?'

'Yes, his name's Victor. He's the doorman at the gallery. He greets people when they arrive. If La Galerie Unique was a nightclub he'd be a good bouncer. I wonder why he was there,' Ena mused. 'He's very protective of Giselle Aubrey. Perhaps he's also suspicious of Mantel. Good work, Artie.'

Artie smiled. 'Thanks, boss. Oh,' He looked at his wristwatch, 'I'd better get moving if I'm going to be at the nick in Guildford before twelve o'clock.' He went to the desk and ripped the address of Surrey Police Headquarters from the notepad. 'So,' he said, 'what's the story?'

'The truth. Tell the DI exactly what happened. Don't lose your temper and don't get emotional, stick to the point.' Ena laughed. 'Claire taught me a good lesson when she and I were caught coming out of O'Shaughnessy's house in Brighton last year. A detective sergeant and constable took a dim view of two women breaking into someone's house on their patch, even though they knew O'Shaughnessy had a rap sheet a mile long. Misdemeanours mostly. Anyway, we drove behind them to Brighton nick where an old pal of Inspector Powell's gave us the third degree.' Ena laughed again. 'He was alright really. On the way, Claire said, don't volunteer anything, just answer the questions you're asked and don't elaborate.'

'I'll remember,' Artie said. He picked up his attaché case and made for the door. 'By the way,' he said turning back to Ena. 'You are coming down this afternoon, aren't you?'

'Yes. I need to make some calls. If I have time, I

want to pop into Bow Street and see Inspector Powell. I need to update him on the case and show him these photographs. I think Horton will help us if he knows a plain clothes policeman is keeping an eye on his daughter and granddaughter. I'll telephone Horton and arrange to meet him at Bow Street tomorrow morning.'

'I'll get a cab to Waterloo station.'

Ena gave Artie ten pounds from the petty cash tin. 'I'll drive down. By the time you've given your statement it'll be getting on for one o'clock. I might be a little longer giving my statement because I'll run through George's father being poisoned. If I'm done in time, I'll bring you back. If you're done early and there's no sign of me get the train back. Either way we'll meet later, if not in Guildford, back here.'

Artie saluted and pushed open the office door.

'Good luck!'

CHAPTER THIRTY-NINE

The desk sergeant at Mount Brown telephoned through and told DI Reed that Ena had arrived. A young WPC took her upstairs to the DI's office and asked her to wait in the corridor. She knocked and entered without waiting to be asked. A minute later Artie came out, followed by the WPC.

'If you'd like to go in, Mrs Green?' The WPC held open the door. Ena got up and as she drew level with Artie said, 'There's a café a couple of doors down on the right. Get something to eat. I'll see you as soon as I'm done here.'

Ena entered the DI's office followed by the WPC who pulled out the chair opposite the inspector. When Ena sat down, the Police woman picked up a notebook and pen and sat down next to her, her pen poised to take down Ena's statement.

'Thank you for coming in, Mrs Green. Have you recovered from your ordeal at the hands of Andrea Thornton?'

'Yes. My head has stopped aching and my neck is healing.' She had a scarf around her neck which hid the plaster that Jeanie McKinlay had put on to keep the cut clean. Had the cut been bigger, deeper, she'd have shown him. Aware that the woman Police constable was writing down every word she said, Ena began with the death of George's father. 'I was commissioned to investigate the death of Mr Derby-Bloom by his daughter and, during my enquires I learned that he had picked up Mrs Thornton's lemon and barley drink by mistake and taken it to his room where he drank most of it.'

Aware that the WPC was writing, Ena paused to

let her catch up. She turned the page and waited for Ena to resume speaking.

'Because I found Mr Derby-Bloom's death suspicious I had what remained of the drink he'd ingested on the day he died analysed. It contained water hemlock. Mr Derby-Bloom's death was tragic and unnecessary. A mistake. I believe the poison was meant for Mrs Thornton, the grandmother of Andrea.

'My associate, Artie Mallory, interviewed the reporter who was at the scene of the accident when Andrea Thornton's parents were killed. The reporter told Artie she had a disabled brother. When I got to house, I looked through the kitchen window and saw the boy, Mrs Thornton's grandson, Rory, gagged and tied to his wheelchair.'

'Which is why you broke into the house?'

'Yes. I couldn't leave the poor boy. He was in a terrible state. He had clearly needed the toilet while his sister was at the nursing home, his clothes were filthy and he looked half-starved. So, yes, I broke in. I was trying to take the boy's gag off when Andrea knocked me unconscious. When I came round, she had tied me to a chair.' Ena shuddered. 'I dread to think what she'd have done to me – and her brother for that matter – if Artie hadn't shown up.'

'Quite.' Inspector Reed glanced at the WPC. When she had stopped writing she nodded. 'Did you witness Mr Mallory using more force than was necessary when he restrained Miss Thornton?'

'No. She had a knife aimed at my jugular. She'd have stuck me with it in a second if he hadn't thrown a sheet over her. He pulled it down and held her arms at the side of the body. She'd have used the knife on him if she'd got the chance. She went wild. She thrashed about and eventually fell, taking Artie with her. But you know all that.'

The inspector looked at the policewoman again. When she stopped writing he thanked her and asked Ena to read what the WPC had written and if it was correct to sign her name on the bottom of the last page. Ena glanced through the statement and signed.

'Thank you for coming in, Mrs Green.' The inspector stood up and shook Ena's hand across the table. 'The WPC will see you out.'

'For the record, Inspector, Artie Mallory saved my life,' Ena said from the door. She followed the policewoman down the stairs, thanked her and left.

Ena spotted Artie sitting in the window of the café tucking into a plate of fish and chips.

'You were quick.'

'You'd probably already told him everything he needed to know after you arrived at the house. Could I have the same,' she asked the waitress who came to take her order. 'And a cup of tea?'

'I did tell him everything, damn right I did. Did the DI tell you that cheeky mare has made a complaint against me? She only wants me done for GBH. She told the inspector that I put a sheet over her, tied her up and then punched her.'

'You did. I mean, you hadn't tied her up by then, but you did give her a thump to stop her wriggling.' Ena began to laugh.

'Not funny! I only punched her because I thought she'd escape. She was like a bag of bloody eels. She'd have done more than punch me if she had got free.'

'So, what's going to happen about her complaint? Did the inspector believe you?'

'Yes, after I reminded him that you'd told him she'd fallen when I got her off you.'

The waitress brought Ena's lunch on a tray,

placing a knife and fork on the table before the plate of fish and chips. When she had put down the cup of tea, Ena thanked her.

'The desk sergeant told me she attacked the DC who brought her in.'

'That was a bit of luck. At least now Inspector Reed knows what she's like.'

'I'm guessing you didn't have time to take the photographs to DI Powell?'

'No, he was about to go to a meeting with the Chief Constable. He said he'd see me tomorrow morning.'

'On your own or with Horton?'

'I want half an hour with him first, so I'm meeting Horton there at ten. I telephoned him. He was reluctant at first and took a bit of persuading. He's worried that Mantel will find out and there'll be repercussions.'

'His daughter and her child?'

'Yes. I said I'd get someone to keep an eye on his house, make sure the thug who threatened the daughter before, doesn't do it again.'

'I'd be happy to watch the place, but I wouldn't be much good in a fight.'

'I wasn't suggesting you do it. I think Horton and his daughter would be happier with a woman.'

'You?'

Ena laughed. 'I was thinking more along the lines of WPC Jarvis, from Bow Street. She isn't much older than Horton's daughter, and she might like to get out of her uniform. I shall suggest it to Inspector Powell. I think he'll go for the idea.'

Ena put down her knife and fork and finished her tea. 'Come on, let's get back to London. We'll have a quick look at the flat, see how it's coming along, and then go to the Lamb and Flag for a drink.' Ena got up and stretched. 'It's already been a long day.'

***

'Do we need anything from the office before tomorrow, Artie?'

'I don't but you need the photographs to show Inspector Powell. I'll get them. You go up to the flat. I'll be with you in two minutes.'

Ena ran up the stairs and switched on the landing light. Her and Henry's new home at 8a Mercer Street was twice the size of the flat in Stockwell. She heard the street door open and close, and then Artie's footsteps on the uncarpeted stairs.

'In here,' she shouted, making her way along the corridor to the main bedroom. It was almost finished. The woodwork had been painted white and the walls a soft cream. All the room needed now was carpet and furniture. She left the main bedroom and poked her head round the door of the guest bedroom. Nothing had been done in there except the walls had been stripped of the old wallpaper and it had been plastered. The bathroom was the same. The kitchen when she went in took her by surprise. It had been fitted with a sink and draining board, washing machine, refrigerator and two high stools under a counter along the far wall.

'Ooo,' Artie came in and ran his hand along the smooth Formica top above the high stools. 'Very swish. This is fabulous; like one of those counters in a trendy coffee bar.'

'It is a bit, isn't it?'

'The sitting room is modern too. Or it will be when it's finished.' Ena pushed up a hatch, designed to look like a small window in the kitchen wall. 'That's the dining room end of the sitting room,' she said, poking her head through. 'It's for when we entertain, don't you know?' Ena said, putting on her best posh voice.

They both laughed. 'Well,' she said, pulling down the hatch, 'we won't be able to afford to move again for a very long time, so we thought we'd have what we wanted. To be honest we've been making do in the small flat in Stockwell for a couple of years now. The rent is high and it will never be ours. So,' Ena opened her arms and twirled, 'this is it!'

'And it's going to be FAB when it's finished.'

Ena laughed again. 'You're getting very modern in your old age, Artie, but yes, I think it is going to be *FAB*.'

'Where does this door lead?' Artie pulled on it, it was locked.

'The back yard.'

'Can I see it?'

'I don't have a key. Follow me and I'll show you.' Ena led the way to the sitting room, opened the window and looked out. 'We don't have a garden, but there's an ornate staircase behind the kitchen door that leads to a sizable yard at the back of the building. The stairs are steep and narrow, but Henry and I can doseydoe down them in the summer with a glass of wine. We can have lunch alfresco as the continentals do. We can't sit out now. The couple who lived here used it as a dumping ground for everything they didn't want to take with them when they left, but the builders said they'll clear it and clean the paving slabs, so next summer...'

'Maybe even sooner. They're getting on really well with the renovations.'

'They are.'

'You know the latest trend in city dwelling is flowers in big pots.'

Ena laughed. 'Can you see Henry sitting in a deckchair surrounded by pots with flowers in them?'

'Yes, actually, I can. Though it might be a bit noisy.'

'Not on Sundays. There's nowhere open. Apart from the odd coffee bar, everywhere else is shut. There'll be a few buses, but no cars,'

'When the yard's been cleared, I'll come shopping with you for pots and plants.'

'That's a date. But now, we're going to have a drink at The Lamb.'

CHAPTER FORTY

'Selwyn Horton's only crime,' Ena said to an attentive Inspector Powell, 'if you can call it a crime at all, was leaving the gallery and going home because someone was in his house threatening to hurt his daughter and her baby.'

'Ena, he didn't call the Police about the break-in.'

'Because when he came round after he'd been hit on the head, he checked the art against the list he'd been given and nothing had been stolen.'

'Paintings could have been stolen and replaced by forgeries.'

'I know that and you know that, but he didn't know that. Security guards don't know enough about paintings to tell which are genuine and which are forgeries. You said yourself the forgeries were good. They were so good that some owners who'd had their paintings stolen didn't notice they'd been replaced by forgeries.'

The inspector didn't reply immediately. When he did, he said, 'You obviously think Selwyn Horton is straight.'

'I do.'

'He should still have informed us that there had been a break-in.'

'I know, and he knows he should have too. And, if the same thing were to happen again, he would inform the Police, but he panicked. All he could think about was the safety of his family. He was also worried that he'd lose his job, which he would have done if Giselle Aubrey knew he'd left the gallery.' Ena looked at the inspector. 'You can trust him. I'm sure he'll help us if we ask.'

Ena thought she had explained Selwyn Horton's predicament well enough to get the DI onside. 'There's just one thing. Artie has offered to keep watch on Horton's house to make sure the bloke who threatened Horton's daughter doesn't come back. But I think Horton would be happier working with us if he knew someone from the force was in the house with his daughter while he was at work. I thought maybe a WPC would be better than a male officer.'

The inspector nodded thoughtfully but said nothing.

'Anyway, have a look at these.' She pushed the paper wallet containing the photographs that Artie took of Mantel and Horton across the inspector's desk. 'Before you look at them, you'll see Mantel give Horton this.' She took the money from her bag and put it on top of the photographs. 'Horton didn't want it then and he doesn't want it now.'

The inspector opened the envelope that Ena had put the money in. 'How much is in here?'

'I didn't count it. But there's enough to make Mantel thinks he's bought Horton.' The inspector looked up at her. 'And before you ask, no, he hasn't. I saw Mantel foist the money on him.'

'Horton could have refused it.'

'He did, twice. He walked away from Mantel, and Mantel followed him. He took the money because Mantel told him that he had no control over what his bosses would do to Horton's family if he couldn't tell them that Horton would help him.'

'There's no end to what Mantel will do and say to get what he wants.'

'I expect he's as scared of his paymasters as Horton is.' The inspector picked up the photographs and slowly looked through them. He held one up, picked up the next and did the same. 'That's Victor in the background. He's in this photograph too. Mantel needs to watch his step. If Victor knows what he's up to, Mantel's bosses will be the least of his worries.' He put down the photographs. 'What time will Horton be here?'

Ena looked at her watch. 'Anytime now. I said I'd meet him outside. I'd better go down in case he's early. I don't want him to think we don't believe him.' At the door, Ena looked back, the inspector had picked up the telephone. 'You do believe him, don't you?'

'Assure him that a WPC will be with his daughter and granddaughter while he's at the gallery.'

As she closed Inspector Powell's office door, Ena heard him ask WPC Jarvis to come to his office. She exhaled with relief, ran down the stairs and out through the street door.

'Selwyn?' she called. He was on the other side of the road walking briskly. Ena called him again and this time he turned round and looked at her. She waved and ran across the road to join him. She had no intention of asking him if he was leaving, but said, 'Sorry to keep you waiting.' Then, before he had time to reply, 'DI Powell is going to arrange for a woman Police constable to stay with your family while you're working at the gallery.'

Horton took a deep breath and sounding relieved, whispered, 'Thank you.'

'I'll take you up to his office.' Ena could sense there was something wrong. 'You haven't changed your mind, have you?'

'No, not at all...'

'Then what is it?'

'Does the DI know I went home the night of the break-in at the gallery?'

'Yes, and he knows why you went home. Any decent father would.' Ena could see Selwyn needed more persuading. 'I've given him my account of how Mantel coerced you and is now blackmailing you and he has seen the photographs that Artie took. You've nothing to worry about. Inspector Powell knows the predicament you're in and he's grateful that you're going to help us with the investigation. Come on, I'll take you to his office.'

From the corridor outside the DI's office, Ena could hear voices. She gave Selwyn an encouraging smile. WPC Jarvis opened the door and asked them to go in. Inspector Powell welcomed Selwyn by shaking his hand – and Ena could tell by the way Selwyn's shoulders relaxed, that he felt better about being there. Ena, an onlooker now, stood at the back of the room by the door while the inspector assured Selwyn that WPC Jarvis would ensure that his family would be safe.

'Ena has brought me up to date with what has been happening at the gallery, as well as Mantel's threats to you. Can you add anything that you think might help our enquiry?'

Selwyn cleared his throat. 'Last night Mantel let himself into the gallery after Miss Aubrey had left. I was in the office putting the new itinerary in order. As paintings come in, Miss Aubrey adds them to a list, the jewellery too. I find it easier to start at the front of the gallery with room one, list one, and work my way to the back of the building,' he explained. 'I was about to leave the office to start checking when I saw Mantel putting a suitcase and a leather suit-carrier in the storeroom. I didn't want him to know I'd seen him so I went back to the desk and pretended I was still putting the lists in order. When he didn't appear, I went out into the corridor. He was nowhere to be seen. I gave the storeroom door a tug but it was locked. Mantel didn't come past the office or I'd have seen him, so I guessed he'd gone out the back. I switched the light off and poked my head out of the back door. I was looking along the alley behind the gallery when I heard the front door bell ring. I shut the back door sharpish, put the light back on and ran to the front door. When I opened it, Mantel was standing there. He pushed past me saying he'd left his key at home. He asked me if Giselle was in the office. I told him no, Miss Aubrey had left for the day, which he knew anyway. He said, "Good, I need to make some calls." Then he winked at me and said, "You haven't seen me tonight, old buddy, okay?" I nodded that I understood, turned into room one, and he set off along the corridor to the office.

'I started checking the paintings against my list and when I'd done, I went to room two. But instead of going in, I slipped along the corridor to Miss Aubrey's office and listened at the door. I could hear Mantel talking on the telephone. Whoever he was talking to didn't appear to understand him. He kept repeating "Saturday, Saturday night." Then he shouted, "This weekend!" When he put the phone down, I heard him say, "God damn frogs!" I expected him to come charging out of the office in a rage, so I moved away from the door and went back to room two. When I'd finished in there, I had to pass the office to room three. I glanced in and saw Mantel putting something in Miss Aubrey's desk. She uses the top drawer for important documents and Mantel uses the second drawer.'

'Did you see what he put in the drawer?'

Horton's brow furrowed in thought. 'It was a fairly big oblong envelope, thick like the ones the photography shop gives you when you've had a film developed, but bigger. There was writing on it.' He brought his hands from behind his back and let his arms hang down by his side. 'Red!' he said suddenly. 'The writing on the envelope was red and the envelope was white. I can't tell you what is said, I only glimpsed the envelope when Mantel dropped it in the drawer. When he left, I went to the office and gave the drawer a tug, but as I thought, it was locked.'

'Tomorrow's Saturday. We don't have much time. The word 'frogs' sounds as if he's going to France, tomorrow.' The inspector rubbed his chin. 'Which airport is he flying from? Is he flying at all? If he took the ferry, would he be in France by Saturday night?'

'He'll fly, surely?' Ena said.

'Yes, you're right, Ena. But from where and to where is anyone's guess. That envelope will probably contain an airline ticket, his passport, and money. He'll need some Francs.' Inspector Powell looked at Horton. 'If we knew the name of the airline, we could check the times of the flights to France. At least then we'd have some idea which airport he's flying out from and at what time.' The DI got to his feet, walked around his desk and sat on the corner of it, keeping one foot on the floor. 'How easy would it be for you to get into Mantel's desk drawer tonight and look at what's in that envelope?'

'I don't know. There's a keyring hanging up in the office that has a key to every room, but I don't know if there are keys to open the drawers in Miss Aubrey's desk.'

The inspector stood up, took a key from his desk drawer and went to the safe in the corner of the room. Unlocking it, he took out a leather holder no bigger than a coin purse and gave it to Horton.

Ena felt her cheeks blushing red with embarrassment. She knew exactly what the inspector had given Selwyn – lockpicks. Her sister Claire had used them to break into Shaun O'Shaughnessy's house in Brighton the year before. She looked away.

'You won't know the size of the lockpick needed to get into Mantel's drawer, so take them all. One of them will fit.' Selwyn nodded and put the case of lockpicks in his inside jacket pocket. 'Good. The quicker you get the job done, the safer it will be for everyone.'

'As long as I don't get caught with the lockpicks on me. I don't want to be done for breaking and entering,' Selwyn said, laughing nervously.

'Nor me,' Inspector Powell added. 'Asking someone to pick a lock is not in the Police Procedure Handbook.' Both men laughed.

Ena had been worried about Selwyn when she saw him walking away from the Police station. She wasn't now and exhaled with relief. The inspector and the ex-policeman seemed to be at ease in each other's company. If not at ease, they understood one another. Ena caught WPC Jarvis's eye. The woman Police constable gave her a reassuring smile.

'The minute you know what's in that envelope, telephone me here.' The inspector gave Selwyn his telephone number. 'WPC Jarvis will be at your house at seven o'clock tonight and she'll stay there until you get home, which should be shortly after we get to the gallery.'

Selwyn got up. 'Thank you, Sir. Until tonight, then.' As he passed Ena he nodded and put out his hand. Ena shook it and he said, 'Thank you, Mrs Green.' He didn't give Ena time to reply. He turned to WPC Jarvis, thanked her and said, 'I'll see you tonight, Miss.'

Ena watched the man who only yesterday carried

the weight of the world on his shoulders walk confidently out of Inspector Powell's office.

WPC Jarvis said goodbye and left closing the door behind her.

'Right!' Ena said, 'what do you want me to do, Inspector?'

'Nothing, Ena. As far as the Louis Mantel case is concerned you've done all you can. I'll take it from here.'

Ena felt deflated. She should have responded with an 'okay' or 'that's good' as any professional investigator would have done, but somehow she felt cheated. She got up and sauntered over to the door. Instead of leaving she turned back to the inspector who was writing. She waited. Then the telephone rang and he picked up the receiver. 'Yes, Sir. Yes, Sir.' He looked across the room at Ena. His face relaxed into a smile. Then he shook his head and looked up at the ceiling and said, 'Thank you, Sir.' Ena left.

CHAPTER FORTY-ONE

'Artie, while Henry and I are at Mr Derby-Bloom's funeral, would you check which security agencies Bob Smith has been with? They might have had him on their books as Robert Smith. He's the security guard who left the Hogarth painting in the alley behind The Savoy. There are a couple of security agencies in Leicester Square. Ask if Smith has been on any of their books. If he has, why did he leave them; was there trouble with clients, or did he leave of his own accord? Get as much background information on him as you can.' Ena flicked through her diary. 'Selwyn Horton said he's now with Sure Security, but check out West End Security as well. Both have ex-coppers and firemen on their books.'

'Credible agencies then.'

'You'd like to think so, but I'm not sure. Horton is the real McCoy, but I don't think Smith is. I think he's working with Mantel but I can't prove it, yet.'

Artie pushed back his chair and rose to his feet. 'I'm not leaving a trip over to Leicester Square until tomorrow. I'm going now, it's quieter.'

'Leicester Square, quieter?' Ena said, laughing.

'No, it's quieter here, now. The telephone hasn't rung for an hour.' Artie sighed loudly. 'As I was saying, I'll do my Sherlock Holmes act now and then I won't have to leave the office tomorrow while you're away at the funeral. I have plenty to do.' Artie put the file he'd been writing up into the filing cabinet and as he passed Ena's desk, he stopped. 'Why don't you go early? There really isn't much that needs doing here. Have a rest, you look all in.'

***

Ena put the sealed manilla envelope containing the details of the investigation into the death of George's father in her briefcase and Henry put it in the boot of his car with their overnight cases. Ena dropped onto the passenger seat.

'Thanks for coming to the funeral with me,' she said, and yawning, slid down in the comfortable leather seat of Henry's Humber.

'I had every intention of taking you, darling. I put in for the day off as soon as you told me the date.'

'I didn't give you much notice.'

'I didn't give the office much notice, but I explained the situation to Colonel Smith and he was fine about it. Anyone else he might not have been, but he's always had a soft spot where you're concerned.'

'Mmmm...Well, thanks anyway,' Ena replied. Henry's Humber was much newer than her Sunbeam and with less wear and tear, it purred along smoothly at any speed.

Ena marvelled at Surrey's rich green grasslands and heaths, the woodlands, rivers and later the rolling chalk downs. 'This part of Surrey's beautiful,' Ena said, looking out of the passenger window. 'How much further to Thurston Water?'

'A mile, maybe two. Do you want to call at the house first, or go straight to the hotel?'

Ena wondered whether they might be in the way if they went to George's house. 'There'll be people in and out all the time delivering food. And Natalie's there. She drove down last night with food. She's staying at the house so she's on hand if George needs her. No,' Ena said, 'Betsy's there too. We'll be in the way. Let's go straight to the hotel.'

Henry glanced at the clock on the dashboard. 'It's only eleven, why don't we find a hotel, put our bags in our room, and have something to eat.'

'Good idea. That's another reason for not going to the house. George would insist on making us food.'

As they drove along the High Street, Ena spotted the Manor Hotel, an imposing four-storey building painted white with black window frames and ledges. Half barrels painted black and filled with summer flowers decorated the pavement at the front of the hotel. 'The Manor Hotel looks nice. Let's go in and see if they have any vacancies.' Henry slowed the car and when there was no oncoming traffic turned right under the archway in the centre of the building to a car park at the back. More tubs and pots with colourful flowers, as well as tables and chairs shaded by large striped umbrellas – the kind you see on the coast – were placed in a line, roped off by thick black cord linked every now and again to brass poles. Ena got out of the car and began walking towards the road. Henry took the bags from the boot and followed her under the arch to the main front door of the hotel.

The receptionist told them they were lucky as there were only two rooms left, saying that today was the funeral of a well-respected local man. Describing the two rooms; one overlooking the main road and one, slightly bigger, overlooking the car park – both had bathrooms, Henry plumped for the bigger of the two rooms that overlooked the car park.

'The right choice,' Ena said, flopping onto the large double bed. Henry put the bags down by the wardrobe and joined her. Turning over and laying on his side, Henry brought his knees up behind Ena's knees, put his arm around her and kissed the nape of her neck. She half turned and sighed and his warm lips moved from her neck to her ear.

'There isn't time if we're going to have lunch,' she

whispered, hoarsely.

'I know,' Henry said, unzipping her dress and caressing her.

Ena turned and faced him. 'Aren't you hungry?'

'Yes,' Henry said, pulling her to him.

***

'Ena? Ena?' Henry called, 'wake up, darling.'

Ena moaned softly and smiling, opened her eyes. 'Oh, my God!' She sat bolt upright. 'I fell asleep. Henry, we can't be late for the funeral.'

'Relax, there's plenty of time,' he said, wheeling in a two-tier tea trolley and kicking the door shut behind him. Taking off his shoes, Henry climbed onto the bed, settled into a comfortable sitting position and pulled the trolley as close to the bed as was possible. Ena leaned towards him and craned her neck for him to kiss her.

'I was thinking that after the funeral we could have a drink in the hotel bar and then find a local restaurant. Go out for dinner instead of eating in the hotel. What do you think?'

Ena, her mouth full of a ham and tomato sandwich, nodded her agreement. When they had finished eating, they drank coffee – and when the pot was empty, Henry leapt from the bed, collected the used crockery and piled it onto the trolley. 'I'll put this outside the door.'

Ena used the bathroom, washed and put on her makeup, giving Henry just enough time to change into his suit before leaving for the synagogue.

Walking along in the sunshine, Ena put her arm through Henry's. Still feeling the glow of their lovemaking, she bit her bottom lip and said, 'Making love on the day of a funeral doesn't seem right somehow.'

'But it is, Ena. When someone dies, it's a reminder to the rest of us that we must live life to the full. Life is precious. And you,' Henry said, stopping and looking into Ena's eyes, 'are the most precious thing to me.'

Ena exhaled slowly and lovingly. 'I love you, Henry Green.'

CHAPTER FORTY-TWO

The synagogue at Thurston Water was a short walk from the hotel. The Church of St. Saviour was on one side of the small town, the synagogue was on the other. At its heart was the market place where shops and cafés had been built around a cobbled square. An impressive, almost circular, 18th Century town hall stood between a bank and a museum. On the right, as they approached the square, was a florist, bakery and haberdasher. On the left a café, ironmonger and Ye Olde Oak Inn. The spire of St. Saviour could be seen from anywhere in the town. The synagogue couldn't be seen, nor was it easy to find. Today the church bells rang out in celebration of the life of a Jewish man who had been loved and respected in the town by Christians and Jews alike.

They were met at the door of the synagogue by a young man who gave Henry a kippah. Henry placed the skullcap on the crown of his head and the young man nodded slowly, once. Inside the synagogue a beautiful gold Menorah displayed seven candles. There were decorative wall coverings; a tapestry of The Star of David, God's hand representing all the faiths called The Hamsa had been embroidered on another, the third was The Lion of Judah and the last, a tapestry of two square tablets with rounded tops, called, The Tablets of Stone, which Ena knew represented the two tablets on which Moses wrote the Ten Commandments at Mount Sinai. And, on the east wall, the holy ark where behind its beautifully engraved façade the Torah Scrolls were kept.

Ena wondered if this was a synagogue that didn't allow men and women to sit together. Some didn't.

Her question was soon answered. She looked around and saw couples with their heads bent in prayer. Suddenly aware that someone was waving, Ena saw Natalie sitting on her own. She nodded to Ena for them to joined her.

George entered the synagogue with Betsy ahead of a simple pine coffin born by six men who carried her father to his place of worship for the last time. The service started with a eulogy read by the rabbi. Prayers followed and then hymns and psalms. Natalie, being Jewish, was able to participate in the service, while Ena and Henry sat and listened.

The service took less than an hour. When it had finished, Natalie drove Ena and Henry to the cemetery. Ena felt for George as she watched her father's plain pine coffin lowered into the ground. The rabbi sang a psalm in Hebrew and then chanted softly with some of the women. When he had finished, George, clinging to Betsy, followed by a dozen or more men and women in their mid to late thirties, left the graveside. Ena and Henry took their cue from Natalie and, without speaking, followed her back to her car.

Ena had cried in the car, she always cried at funerals. They reminded of her own father's funeral. Unlike today, it had been bitterly cold. There had been a severe frost, a hoar frost, and the fog and mist hadn't cleared by the time her father was interred. The ground was hard, and leaving him on his own in the frozen earth was one of the worst things she had ever experienced. She dried her eyes and dabbed her nose with face powder before leaving the car. Feeling emotional but knowing she must neither show it nor express emotion, Ena entered the house without offering her condolences.

'Thank you for coming,' George said, taking in

both Ena and Henry. She introduced Betsy to them saying she didn't know what she'd have done without her. Betsy shook Ena's hand and then Henry's, before giving George a caring smile. 'Nor you, Ena,' George added. 'Thank you for all you have done for my father and me.'

Ena took George's hands in hers. 'She wanted so much to tell her how sorry she was, instead she smiled, let go of her hands, and turned to Betsy. 'I'm sorry it's under such sad circumstances.' Ena bit her tongue. 'I'm pleased to meet you,' she said, 'I've heard a lot about you from my sister, Margot.'

Moving out of the way to allow other people to enter the Derby-Bloom house, George, Ena and Henry walked slowly through a long spacious room with floor to ceiling bookcases and out through French windows onto a patio where they were offered wine and a selection of canapés. Taking a glass of wine, but having recently eaten sandwiches at the hotel, Ena politely refused the delicious-looking food. Henry took a square of bread topped with smoked fish and they crossed a tailored lawn to a large marque with an open front.

A string quartet played sombre music. Ena looked around the small gathering of people who, with the rabbi, had been with George on the front of two rows of people at her father's grave. Some were seated, some stood by the marque's entrance, others were outside.

Ena and Henry turned to see Natalie walking across the lawn to them. She said quietly, 'The coffin bearers and the people you saw with George at her father's graveside are some of the students that escaped Germany in the war. Not all of them could be here, so there is going to be a memorial in a year's time.'

'Mr Derby-Bloom will be remembered for a very long time,' Ena said, 'not only by the people he helped escape the Nazis, but by their children and their children's children.'

There was a buffet on two tables – one table on the left side of the marque and one on the right. The table on the left had only bowls of boiled eggs and plates of bagels on it.

'It is traditional after a Jewish funeral to offer guests round food like boiled eggs and bagels, which must be prepared and cooked by the family of the deceased,' Natalie said.

'Did George and Betsy do all the food themselves?'

'Not quite. It's why I came down yesterday. Because I am Jewish, I was able to help them.' Natalie pointed to the table on the left. 'Round food, like hard-boiled eggs symbolise the continuity of life. Once the mourners have eaten the symbolic food, they can eat other food. There is some very tasty food on the table over there,' she said, pointing to the right. 'A variety of breads and biscuits topped with smoked fish, cheeses and spreads – and hummus. Do you like hummus Henry?'

'I don't think I've ever tried it.'

'Then you must. I'm sure you will like it.'

'What's it made of?' Ena asked.

'Chickpeas. There isn't much preparation needed. You soak the chickpeas overnight and cook them slowly until they are soft. Then you mix them with tahini.' Natalie looked at Henry and laughed. 'I can see by the look on your face Henry that you've never had tahini either.'

'I'm a meat and two veg man. Not very

adventurous, I'm afraid. So, what is…?'

'Tahini is ground hulled sesame. It's a large part of the hummus. It's mashed with chickpeas and garlic and it's mixed together until it's a paste. You add lemon juice and salt and pepper to taste. I'm sure you'll love it. After your boiled egg of course,' Natalie said, winking at Ena.

After the first glass of wine on entering the Derby-Bloom residence, which Natalie said wasn't a Jewish tradition, nor was it against the tradition, they ate food and drank tea.

CHAPTER FORTY-THREE

Unable to eat anything after the delicious food served at the wake, Henry and Ena decided not to go for a meal. They changed into the clothes they had driven down in, and after a drink at the bar, went for a quiet stroll.

Along the High Street, a quarter of a mile from the hotel was a gated park. 'It closes at ten,' Henry said, reading a notice attached to one side of the gate. 'That gives us plenty of time for a wander around.'

At the end of an avenue of horse chestnut trees, Ena and Henry stopped to watch a raft of ducks heading for the long reeds on the far side of a pond. They passed an empty bird aviary and then sat beneath a rose bower in the park's walled garden.

Ena laid her head on Henry's shoulder. 'Balmy,' she said.

'Who, you or me?'

Ena giggled. 'I was referring to the warm night air, but yes, you definitely are and I?' she said, 'must be to have married you.' Henry pulled her to her feet and hand in hand they ran from the walled garden to the path leading back to the north side of the park where they had entered earlier. A beam from a torch shone in the distance.

'Looks like we've just made it.'

'No, it doesn't,' Ena said, 'we're going to be locked in.'

'No, he's seen us. Hello?' Henry called, 'Excuse me?' As they drew near the north gate a short man dressed in what looked to Ena like a station master's uniform was looping a thick chain through the two halves of the ornate wrought iron gate. 'Would you keep the gate open?'

The man ignored Henry and waited until he and Ena were standing next to the gate before turning the key in a padlock attached to a chain.

'Would you let us out?' Ena said.

'Gates close at ten!'

'It's a good job it is only two minutes to, then, isn't it?' Ena said looking at her watch.

'Come on, old chap,' Henry said, in a friendly manner, 'You saw us running to the gate before you locked it.'

Ena leaned forward and smiled into the man's podgy face. '*Please.*'

Muttering under his breath the officious little man crouched down and with sigh, unlocked the padlock and pulled off the chain. He held the gate open just enough for Ena and Henry to squeeze through in single file.

'I'm glad we didn't have to go back to the other gate and walk all the way round the park,' Ena said, yawning. Henry put his arm around her shoulder and she snuggled into him. 'I'm tired.'

After undressing, washing and cleaning her teeth, Ena put on her nightdress. By the time Henry had finished in the bathroom she was asleep. Trying not to disturb her, Henry switched off the light and crept into bed. He pulled up the bedclothes, tucked them around Ena's shoulders and whispered goodnight.

'Night,' she said sleepily, 'love you.'

***

As she opened the curtains sunlight filled the room.

'Darling, let's make an early start.' Henry turned over and squinted into the bright sunshine. 'I don't think I should give George my invoice yet. It's too soon after the funeral.'

'I thought you'd arranged to see her today?' Henry said, sleepily.

'No, I told Natalie we wouldn't be going round. She agreed it would best to leave it for a while. I'll ring George in a couple of days, ask her how she is and I'll post the invoice. What do you think?'

'Sounds good to me, darling,' Henry said, agreeing as he usually did when Ena asked him a question that she didn't require him to answer – at least not an answer that differed from hers. Henry turned his back on Ena and the morning sun.

'Come on,' she said, pulling the eiderdown and blankets off him. He clung onto the sheet and buried his face in the pillow groaning. 'Time for breakfast,' she sang, 'aren't you hungry?' Ena didn't give him time to answer that question either. Her mind was elsewhere. 'If we leave the hotel at nine, we'll be in London before eleven. I want to know what Artie found out about the security chap at the gallery,' Ena said, her mouth forming an 'O' shape as she applied lipstick. She leaned into the dressing table mirror, pressed her lips together and began combing her hair.

Henry stumbled out of bed and crossed the room to her. He put his arms around her waist and rested his chin on her shoulder. 'Ugh!' she said, peering at his reflection. 'You need a shave.' Henry rubbed the stubble on his chin on her shoulder and she squealed.

Laughing, he went to the bathroom and Ena, when she had finished her hair, sat on the bed and waited for him. She took the details of the work she'd done investigating Mr Derby-Bloom's death from her handbag and read through them. Convinced that so soon after the funeral was not the time to present

George with an invoice, she put the envelope back in her handbag.

'You go down,' Henry shouted from the bathroom. 'Order me coffee – and eggs, bacon and toast. I'll be with you in five minutes.'

'Don't be any longer then, I'd really like to get back,' Ena said, leaving the bedroom. As she walked along the corridor to the stairs leading down to the lobby, she thought about Selwyn Horton and his family. She was itching to know that Artie hadn't found anything suspicious about Horton while he'd been snooping around the job agencies. It was Bob Smith – if that were his real name – the gallery's daytime security guard, that Ena suspected of being on Louis Martel's payroll.

CHAPTER FORTY-FOUR

'Ena? Aren't you coming up to see the flat?'

'Yes, but I need to check in with Artie first.' Ena could see the disappointment on Henry's face. 'I won't be long, I promise. You go up and I'll join you in a minute.'

Henry took out his keys and let himself into number 8a Mercer Street as Ena let herself into the office at No 8.

'You're back early?' Artie gave Ena a welcoming smile and looked past her. 'Who were you talking to?'

'Henry. He's gone upstairs to see how the work on the flat is coming along, make sure it's going to be ready for us to move into at the end of the month. I said I'd join him, but first I want to hear how you got on at the security agencies, yesterday.'

'Want a cup of tea? Coffee?' Artie said, getting to his feet.

'I'd love one, but I promised Henry I wouldn't be long.' Ena crossed to his desk. 'Stop teasing and tell me.' She put her hands on his shoulders and pushed him back into a sitting position. 'What did you find out?'

Artie sighed loudly. 'You were right, of course. Selwyn Horton is as clean as the proverbial whistle. Bob Smith, on the other hand, is a very dubious character. One agency,' Artie consulted his note book, 'The West End Agency said they took him off their books because he had a Police record.'

Ena dragged the chair from the front of Artie's desk and sat next to him.

'The woman I spoke to said she thought it was a bit unfair. Apparently, Smith got involved with the wrong crowd when he was a kid. Some older boys broke into an old fella's house and stole some stuff. She didn't know the details, but said that if he had told the agency when he applied to go on their books, they might have overlooked it because it was a long time ago. Unfortunately for him he didn't, and when they found out about it they had no choice but to let him go.'

'What about the other agency?' Ena looked over Artie's shoulder, 'Sure Security?'

'Sure Security, who your boy Selwyn Horton is with, was really helpful. I got talking to one of the guys waiting to find out where his next placement was going to be and he said that Smith was a braggart. He said he'd been spouting off about being in the big league now; bragging that he wouldn't be needing security work after the weekend. He told them he was getting the hell out of London.' Artie glanced down the page and then looked up at Ena. 'I won't go into detail but the gist of it was that he wouldn't be sitting about waiting to earn peanuts like them anymore because he would soon be earning hundreds of francs every week.'

'Well, well, well, he's also going to France!' Ena said.

'Yep! He told them that the first thing he was going to do was visit The Follies Bergere and said he'd send them a post card.'

'Selwyn told DI Powell that Mantel had a long envelope, which, by its description, the inspector thought was probably an airline ticket. He said Mantel locked it in the drawer of Giselle Aubrey's desk in the office. Did the bloke you spoke to have any proof that what Bob Smith told him was true?'

A grin spread across Artie's face. 'Oh, yes! The idiot showed him his ticket. He said it had BEA written on it and he was flying tonight from Heathrow to Orly. When Smith left, he told them he'd be waking up in Paris on Saturday morning.'

'Which means, he'll be flying tonight with Louis Mantel to Orly Airport, Paris. We need to let Inspector Powell know it's tonight they're leaving, not tomorrow.' Ena picked up the telephone, dialled Bow Street Police Station and asked to speak to Detective Inspector Powell.

'Inspector, it's Ena Green,' she said without preamble.

'Ena, when Horton opened the drawer in the office at La Galerie Unique, the envelope had gone.'

'And the suitcases too?'

'Yes, but he won't get away. I've got men at all the airports and to be on the safe side, at the railway stations and shipping ports.'

Ena was pleased her friend wasn't able to see the smile that had spread from ear to ear across her face. 'Mantel isn't flying out tomorrow, he's flying from London Airport tonight.' She heard the inspector take a sharp breath. 'I don't know whether Mantel will be on the same flight as the daytime security guard, Bob Smith, as I'm not sure how many flights there are to Paris tonight, but Smith will be on a BEA flight to Orly.'

'Good God! How do you know?'

'Trade secret.' Ena laughed.

'Thank you, Ena.'

'Don't thank me, it was Artie who found out.'

'Tell him I owe him a large drink.'

Ena laughed again. 'He'll hold you to that.'

'What about Horton?'

'Clean.'

'I'm glad. He was a good copper.'

Henry opened the office door and cleared his throat, loudly.

'I have to go, Inspector.'

'I'll let you know what happens.'

'Thank you.' Ena put down the telephone receiver. 'You're in the inspector's good books,' she called to Artie. 'He said he owes you a large drink.'

Artie appeared in the doorway to the kitchen. He blew on the nails of his right hand and polished them on an imaginary lapel.

Henry was leaning on the door frame of the office looking displeased. 'I was on my way but I thought I ought to let Inspector Powell know… Never mind, how's the flat coming along.'

'What's been done looks good. The plaster's dry in all the rooms. Some of the woodwork has been painted and some of the walls too. There's still wallpaper to hang, so it might take a little longer than we'd hoped. The decorator's a man short.'

'He wasn't the day before yesterday. What's changed?'

'One of the men has gone down with the flu.' He said he's been in touch with everyone he knows and they're all too busy to help him out.'

'Alfred Hardy needs a job.'

'Yes, but you can't just get anyone to—'

'Alfred Hardy is not just anyone. He has been working with his neighbour who is a painter and decorator. And,' Ena said, with her hands on her hips, 'have you forgotten that he is the young man who saved you from being convicted of murder last year. You might have been hanged but for the Hardy boys. The poor lad wanted to do an apprenticeship with his uncle, but he died.' Ena hoped she wasn't laying it on too thickly. 'Then, he thought he'd be working with his father, and we know how that turned out. Oh, Henry, it's time that family had a bit of luck. Darling?' Ena said, walking across the room to Henry and kissing him lightly on the lips. 'Would you go back upstairs and have a word with Mr Jones. Tell him that Alfred Hardy is a good lad, works hard and ask him to give the boy a chance.'

'How can I refuse,' Henry said, opening his arms and shrugging his shoulders.

Ena made a cup of coffee and when she had finished it, said, 'Henry's been up there a long time, don't you think?' Artie didn't reply, he had his head down writing. Impatient to know what the decorator had said, Ena scribbled something on her notepad and ripped out the page. Leaving the office, she called, 'I'll be back in a jiffy, Artie, stick the kettle on, there's a love.' She crept up the stairs to the flat and listened to the conversation between Henry and Mr Jones from the landing outside the sitting room. She heard Henry say, Alfred Hardy is a good lad and a hard worker, I don't suppose you'd consider giving him a trial? Just for a week or two, until the flat's finished.'

'We could do with another pair of hands.' Mr Jones looked across the room to the decorator working with him. He nodded.

Ena was willing Henry to be more assertive. Just as she was about to enter the room, she heard him say, 'I'll pay the lad's wages for the next two weeks, three weeks if necessary.'

Ena put her hand over her mouth to stop herself from shouting with joy and crept down the stairs. Once she was back in the hall by the front door, she ran up the stairs. 'Hello,' she said, out of breath. 'Did Henry mention Alfred Hardy, tell you what a hard working lad he is?'

'Mr Jones is going to give Alfred a job so he can get the flat finished on time.'

'That's wonderful. Thank you, Mr Jones. Alfred won't let you down. Oh,' she said, pretending she had just found a piece of paper in her pocket. 'This is Alfred's address. Henry could go and see him now, if you want.' Ena gave Henry a cheeky grin. 'You could pop in and see him on your way back to Stockwell, couldn't you, darling?'

'There's no need, Mr Green.' Mr Jones looked up after reading Alfred Hardy's address. 'I know this street. It isn't out of my way. I'll call tonight.'

'That's perfect. Alfred's mother is a friend of mine.' Ena started to leave and then thought, in for a penny… 'I don't suppose you'd consider taking him on as an apprentice? I mean, if he is good enough. If he—'

'Mrs Green, shall we start by asking him if he's free to help finish the work on your flat? If he is, and he's as good as you and Mr Green say he is, I'll think about an apprenticeship.'

Ena squealed and flew across the room. Putting her arms around Henry, she said. 'We'll be able to move in to our lovely new home at the beginning of September as planned.' She then turned to Mr Jones and the other decorator and shook both their hands. To the boss she said, 'Thank you, Mr Jones, I promise you won't be disappointed with Alfred.'

The decorator laughed. 'I'll let you know. Now!' he said, firmly, 'would you let us get on with our job? The lady we're working for is expecting us to finish at the end of next week.'

'And you don't want to get on the wrong side of her!' Henry said fielding blows to his arm from Ena.

Pretending to be annoyed with her husband, Ena

made an 'O' of her mouth, 'I'll see *you* later,' she said, 'and I'll see you tomorrow,' she said to Mr Jones, taking in the other decorator at the same time.

Laughing with excitement, Ena left the flat and returned to the office.

'Did you make me another coffee?' she asked Artie, falling into her chair.

'One of these days you'll meet yourself coming back,' Artie called from the kitchen.

'I think I just have,' Ena mumbled, taking a couple of calming breaths. 'What's this?' She picked it up a folder, took an invoice from it and said, 'Artie, what's the Duke of Wellington Hotel's folder doing on my desk?'

'You need to send Mr Walters the invoice for the work you did for him,' Artie said, returning from the kitchen with two mugs of steaming coffee. He put Ena's mug on her desk, went to his own desk and picked up three small brown envelopes. 'Quarterly electric bill, quarterly gas, and this month's mortgage. And it will soon be time for the rates.'

Ena wrinkled her nose. 'You're right. I have George's invoice in my handbag too.'

Artie looked up at the ceiling. 'The whole point of you taking it with you was to give it to George.'

'Don't start!' She put up her hand. 'Giving George an invoice for discovering who killed her father on the day of his funeral didn't feel right. I'll post it tomorrow when I post Mr Walters his invoice,' she said, taking a drink of her coffee.

'I'll let you off for not giving George her invoice, but seriously, Ena, you do need to send clients their invoices as soon as the work is completed.'

'And I will in future. I just didn't want to give George hers yesterday.'

'I know. How was the funeral?'

'Different. There are a lot of rules to observe. Not for Jewish people, they're brought up with them, but for me and Henry there were. I could tell George was upset. Unfortunately, she wasn't able to show her emotions during the day. I expect she would have done later when there was only Betsy and Natalie there.'

'Is Betsy George's, *friend?*'

'If you're asking if the two women live together, yes, they do. They've been together since they were young dancers at the Prince Albert Theatre in the war. I think George is a little older that Betsy. If Betsy is in her late thirties, George must be about my sister Margot's age – forty-two.'

She took the invoice that she'd typed up for Mr Walters from the folder leaving the carbon copy for her own records. She laid the invoice on her desk, took the folder back to the filing cabinet and slipped it in the section marked 'D' for Duke of Wellington Hotel. She then went to the stationary cupboard and took out two smaller envelopes. Writing the address of the hotel on the first envelope she added a first-class stamp. She did the same to the envelope containing George's invoice. Conscious that, although Dudley Green Associates needed the money, the invoice would still arrive too soon after George's father's funeral, she put a second-class stamp on it.

Artie reached over and snatched up both envelopes. 'I'll post them on my way home.'

CHAPTER FORTY-FIVE

Artie dropped several envelopes onto Ena's desk. 'More bills?'

Ena flicked through the mail picking a Wedgwood blue envelope from between three buff coloured ones. 'No. At least this one isn't a bill,' she said, slicing it open with the letter-opener.

'You hope.'

'Don't be such a cynic. You're like a bear with a sore head this morning. Had a bad weekend?'

Artie flicked his hair back and mumbled something Ena didn't hear. She looked at the name of the sender on top of the page before reading the letter. 'It's from Jeanie McKinlay, the nurse at The Willows. Oh,' she said surprised, 'she's left the nursing home.'

'Good for her,' Artie said, 'she was wasted there.'

'She certainly was.' Ena went back to reading Jeanie's letter. '*I have been visiting Mrs Thornton and her grandson, Rory. They are both doing very well. Mrs Thornton is in good health. She rarely speaks of her granddaughter and if her name comes up, which it has done recently in letters from the girl's psychiatrist, she gets upset. I don't know whether Andrea will ever be tried for the murder of Mr Derby-Bloom or the attempted murder of her grandmother. If she is tried, it won't be for a long time, as she is currently in a secure ward at The Hibbert Hospital for the mentally ill.*

Rory is having physiotherapy. The house is very big and there are several rooms on the ground floor that weren't being used. One room, in particular, has an adjoining door to Rory's bedroom. The physiotherapist and I have turned that room into a keep fit room.' Ena laughed. 'Good girl, Jeanie. *The physiotherapist has had parallel bars installed for Rory to hold onto. I've been assisting by helping Rory stand up. In the beginning, he was frightened to try, which was to be expected, but after a couple of weeks, he could stand for a few seconds. Now he holds onto the parallel bars without Gerry or me supporting him. He's amazing.'* Ena looked at Artie and giggled. 'I wonder who's amazing, Rory or Gerry the physiotherapist.' She read on. *'The physiotherapist has every confidence that Rory, in time, will walk again.'* Ena put down the first page, began reading the second and gasped.

'What is it?'

'She says, *I have decided to retrain. Working with Rory, I now know my vocation lies in orthopaedics. I couldn't be a physiotherapist, like Gerry. The training would take too long, and, although I'm fairly strong, I don't think I have the physical strength to do the job properly. But this last couple of weeks, helping Rory and seeing how the work Gerry has done with him has helped him – and it really has, Ena. It has made a huge difference to Rory's confidence and to his life. To mine too. I now know I want to work in the physical injuries and pain management field.'*

Ena laid the second page on top of the first and began reading the last page. *'Mrs Thornton is very grateful to you where her grandson is concerned, Ena, and extends an open invitation to you and Mr Mallory to visit the house anytime.*

I'd like to keep in touch with updates about Rory. He is a remarkable young man. I shudder to think how his life would have turned out if it hadn't been for you. Yours faithfully, Jeanie.'

'Well, that's a turn up for the books. Jeanie will have to lift patients on an orthopaedics ward.'

'But not on her own. Like at The Willows, if residents weren't able to get out of their chairs, there were always two nurses to lift them – one on each side of the person.' Ena put the letter back in its envelope. 'Jeanie's address was at the top of the first page. I'll keep in touch with Jeanie too. I'll write back to her when I get a minute.'

Ena leaned back in her chair. I wonder how DI Powell got on Friday night. I hope Smith was with Mantel, and the inspector arrested them both. I'd have given anything to see Mantel's face when DI Powell arrested him. Little squirt that he is.'

'Telephone the inspector and find out.'

'No. He'll telephone us when he has time.' Ena's fingers were itching to pick up the telephone and ask DI Powell about Mantel's arrest.

'Go on, you know you want to,' Artie teased.

'Shut up, Artie. I don't want to push it. He'll think we want thanking or something.'

'After handing him an international art thief on a plate, who wouldn't want thanks?'

'It was you who found out they were leaving the country; the flight details and the destination, not me. I only telephoned the inspector with the information.'

'And by doing so you saved him from deploying dozens of coppers to every railway station, shipping port and airport in Christendom. Which, I might add, saved the Metropolitan Police a small fortune in overtime.'

'True.'

'And,' Artie said, as much to himself as to Ena, 'with a saving like that, the inspector could afford to pay us.' Ena chose to ignore him. 'I'd send the lovely DI Powell an invoice if I were you.'

'Well, you're not me.' Ena got up and crossed the

room to the door. 'I'm not sitting here waiting for the damn telephone to ring.' She took the office keys from her handbag, but left her purse. 'You can buy me a cup of coffee at Café Romano.'

As Artie got up from his seat the shrill ring of the telephone on Ena's desk began to echo around the room. He stepped back and looked at it as if was about to burst into flames. 'Come on, Ena, quickly. It could be the inspector.'

Ena ran to the phone, took a deep breath and picked up the receiver. 'Dudley Green Associates, Ena Green speaking.'

'Mrs Green, it's Doreen Hardy here.'

Artie had left his seat and was standing next to Ena to listen to the conversation.

She moved the telephone from her right ear to her left and looking at Artie said, 'Hello Doreen.'

Artie took a deep breath, exhaling loudly and letting the air that escaped his mouth reverberate against his lips.

Ena glared at him. 'What can I do for you, Doreen?'

'Nothing, Mrs Green. I wanted to tell you that I have returned to the Duke of Wellington Hotel. I am working around taking and fetching Gerald and Billy to and from school, but the reason I'm telephoning is to thank you for asking your painter and decorator to give my boy a job.' Ena could hear the pride in Doreen's voice. 'Alfred did so well that Mr Jones said when the apprentice he's got now qualifies, he's going to take Alfred on as his apprentice.'

'Doreen, I'm so pleased for Alfred and pleased for you too. Give my regards to Mr Walters, will you?' Ena looked at Artie and put up her thumb. 'And what about Maisie?'

'She's working at the canning factory. She's paying me back a bit each week. She's doing her best to make amends.'

'I'm glad to hear it, Doreen.'

'Thank you, Mrs Green. That's really all I wanted to say. I know you're busy so I won't keep you – and I'm ringing from the hotel, so I'd better get on. Good bye.'

'Good bye, Doreen.' Ena put down the telephone. 'So, Doreen is back at the hotel and her eldest, Alfred, has been offered an apprenticeship by Mr Jones, our decorator.'

'I'm glad things have turned out well for her.'

'So am I.' Ena looked at Artie, thoughtfully. 'We're a good team, you and I, don't you think?' Seeing Artie's eyes moisten, which usually meant he was about to get emotional, Ena took her handkerchief out of her handbag and pushed it into his hands. 'Don't go all soppy on me, not before you've made me my morning coffee.'

'What about going to Café Romano?'

'Mmm... Let's have coffee here, the inspector might ring.'

Laughing and at the same time dabbing his eyes, Artie got up and went into the kitchen. 'You're a hard woman, Ena Green.'

'That's a splash of milk and one sugar, please,' she called after him. 'I need a boost of energy. Last night Henry and I polished off a half bottle of Teacher's.'

Hearing the flap of the letter box snap shut, Ena went out to the front door. Two letters. She opened the first walking back to the office. A bill for the rates. She slipped it into her handbag before Artie saw it.

'Was that the post?' Artie asked, coming from the kitchen with two mugs of coffee.

'Yes. Only one letter.' Ena sliced it open. 'It's from the London Electricity Board.'

'It's not a bill, is it?'

'No, it's telling us when they're coming to read the meter.' Ena tutted at him. 'Stop worrying.'

'Alright, I won't say another word!' Artie took a swig of his coffee. 'So, what were you and Henry celebrating last night that was worth a half-bottle of scotch?'

'We weren't celebrating really. We just had a laugh. While we were sorting out our wardrobe we found some weird and wonderful articles of clothing, an old hat of Henry's that's like a deerstalker. He looked silly in it when he bought it, he looked even sillier last night. You know how you get when you start laughing about something and you can't stop. Until you wear yourself out, everything you do and say seems funny. It was like that last night.

'We eventually stopped laughing and went out for a walk. We popped into the pub for a quick drink, went home and had an early dinner, which made a nice change. Apart from the night of the Derby-Bloom funeral, we've been like ships that pass in the night for months. And,' Ena said, 'Henry has warmed to the idea of moving to Covent Garden.'

'That's good, as he'll be living smack in the middle of it in a couple of weeks.'

'It is, isn't it?' Ena crunched up her shoulders and chuckled. 'In fact, I'd go as far as to say he's looking forward to moving into the area, and to living in the flat upstairs. I didn't think he'd come round to living in town. When we first moved to Stockwell, he said it was too busy. And, since we went to La Galerie Unique, he's been talking about taking up painting again.'

Artie's eyes sparkled with surprise.

'Henry was a very good artist before the war, after the war too, for a while.'

'You should hang one of his paintings upstairs when you move in.' Artie looked at each of the walls in the office. 'A couple of pieces of artwork wouldn't go amiss in here.'

'His paintings are at his parent's place up in Lowarth. I might suggest we bring one or two back the next—'

The sudden ring of the doorbell stopped Ena mid-sentence.

Artie got to his feet. 'I'll get it.'

CHAPTER FORTY-SIX

'Inspector?' Ena jumped up as Inspector Powell entered the office. 'It's good to see you.' She motioned to him to sit in the chair on the other side of her desk. 'Drag your chair over here, Artie.'

When both men were seated, Ena asked Inspector Powell how the arrest of Louis Mantel went on Friday night.

'Did you arrest Bob Smith at the same time?' Artie asked.

'Sorry to bombard you with questions, but Artie and I are dying to hear about Mantel's arrest at London Airport.'

'Well, Inspector. Did you arrest him?'

'No.'

'No?' Artie and Ena said at the same time.

'Why not?' Ena asked. 'Our intelligence pointed to Mantel and Smith leaving from London and flying to Orly airport in Paris.' Ena looked at Artie. He nodded in agreement. She brought her attention back to the inspector. 'Did we get it wrong?'

The inspector shook his head. 'Your intelligence was spot on.'

'Then what went wrong?' Ena asked.

'Why didn't you arrest him?' Artie said at the same time.

Inspector Powell leaned back in his chair. He gave Artie a business-like smile. 'Thanks to you we got to the airport before Bob Smith met up with Mantel and arrested him.'

Ena saw Artie's shoulders relax. She was delighted that Artie had given Inspector Powell good intel. Good for Artie and good for the reputation of Dudley Green

Associates.

'And he's singing like a bird,' the inspector said, 'which is thanks to you and Mr Mallory.'

'What about Mantel?' Ena asked.

'He caught the BEA flight to Orly. And, if he was worried that Bob Smith hadn't turned up, he didn't show it.'

'So, Mantel got away,' Ena said, feeling hugely disappointed.

The inspector looked at Ena for some time without speaking. Then he cleared his throat. 'I shouldn't be telling you this but as you have played a large part in the investigation – in exposing Mantel and Smith – and I know what I tell you will go no further.' He looked at Ena and then Artie.

'Of course not.'

'You have my word, Inspector,' Artie added.

'Mantel, while a bigger fish than Smith, is a small cog in a very large international wheel. The Met has been working closely with Interpol for two years in order to discover who is behind the thefts of masters and antiquities in England, France, Italy, Germany and other countries on the continent. The headquarters, Interpol thinks, is in Paris, but no one knows where. So, we let Louis Mantel board the BEA flight to Orly and the French Police – and Interpol, who have been working on countering cultural property since 1947 – will let him leave Orly Airport.'

'But they will follow him?'

'Of course. Mantel will be followed wherever he goes until he leads Interpol to bigger fish, and hopefully, those fish will lead to even bigger ones. And every time it will take Interpol a step nearer to finding and breaking up one of the biggest gangs of art thieves and forgers in Europe.

***

Ena closed the door and leant against it. What would she have done without Doreen Hardy's help? She had said it before when Doreen was in the office on the day the furniture arrived and, in Ena's absence, had galvanised Artie into action. Between them, they had cleaned the office, the kitchen, the furniture, even the windows. And, Doreen had done it again. Without her help, today Ena would not have had time to make food.

She mounted the stairs of her new home at No 8a Mercer Street and went into the sitting room. She counted the bottles of wine on the sideboard. Surely eight would be enough. Henry had also bought twenty-four bottles of IPA, which he had stored in the spare bedroom, taking six bottles from the top crate and putting them on the sideboard. There was enough beer Henry had said, but he wasn't sure if there was enough wine and had gone to buy a couple of bottles from the Seven Dials Inn on Shelton Street.

Ena levelled the stack of drink mats. She hoped people would use them if they put their drinks down, but she wasn't going to make a fuss. She felt sure a good polish tomorrow would restore any surfaces in the event of a splash or two of alcohol. She ran her fingers along the dust-free top of the sideboard and secretly hoped her guests would hold onto their drinks and not put them down.

It was a big room that looked even bigger with the settee and armchairs under the window. Pushing the furniture back against the wall had been Doreen's idea. She'd said there would be more space, and she was right. She also said it was better for those who wanted to sit down because they wouldn't have people moving about behind them. Ena had agreed. However, they both thought people would prefer to stand. Ena hoped so, then they would mingle.

With friends and work colleagues, there would be a dozen guests. Still unsure whether there was enough food, Ena crossed to the dining table and took off the tablecloth that she had covered the buffet with. Between them, she and Doreen had made twenty rounds of sandwiches – ham and tomato, cheese and pickle and tinned salmon and cucumber. In the middle of the sandwiches, Doreen had placed a tomato in the shape of a lily. There were also two dozen finger rolls – ham and mustard, grated cheese and onion, and egg and cress. At each end of the table was a plate of sausage rolls and half a grapefruit. Doreen had cut cheddar cheese into small chunks – added a cocktail onion – and speared them both through with a cocktail stick which she then stuck into the skin of the grapefruits. Ena told her she should go into catering. She laughed and said that was what they did at the hotel when they catered for parties.

Doreen had insisted Ena get changed for the party while she put the finishing touches to the buffet. She'd placed the silver salt seller, pepper pot, mustard dish and small spoon on a tray with dishes of sliced beetroot, gherkins and green olives. The olives were a gift from her friend and neighbour, Mr Bellucci at Café Romano. He wasn't able to come to the party but said, "The oliva like-a the Italian coffee is-a the fashion. Everybody eats-a the olivas."

Ena heard the door to the street open and close. 'Henry, I'm in here,' she called, replacing the tablecloth over the food. There weren't any flies in the flat that she could see, but it had been a warm day and while she had cleaned, she'd opened the windows.

Henry kissed Ena on the cheek and the wine

bottles clinked against each other in the shopping bag she had given him to transport them. He stepped back. 'Did I tell you how lovely you look in that slinky trouser suit?'

'Yes, before you went for the wine, but there's no reason why you can't tell me again.'

'You look lovely, darling,' With a bottle of wine in each hand, Henry kissed Ena full on the lips. She kissed him back.

'Mmm...' he sighed, 'I'd better put these in the refrigerator.'

'You better had,' Ena agreed.

Kneeling on the settee, she pushed up the sash window. It was a warm night, an Indian summer sort of night. It had been a long summer with lots of sunny days. During most of them Ena had been rushing from one place to another, juggling one investigation with the other but her hard work, Artie's too, had paid off. She slid down onto the settee and leaned back. The slightest of breezes came through the open window. The window faced east and the sun flooded the room from sunrise to lunchtime, but in the evenings the room was cooler.

Ena thought about the last five or six months and smiled. A lot had changed since she and Henry had bought Nos 8 and 8a Mercer Street. A new home and a new job – and both were everything she had hoped they'd be.

Dudley Green Associates, Private Investigators was at last in the black. No profit yet, but Artie had been paid and so had the bills – this quarter anyway. She hadn't dared take any wages for herself, but she was sure the agency would soon be in credit. Until then Henry paid for everything they wanted in their new home.

CHAPTER FORTY-SEVEN

The doorbell rang. 'I'll get it,' Ena shouted, as Henry came out of the bedroom. She pulled herself off the settee, quickly straightened the cushions and ran onto the landing at the top of the stairs. 'You've scrubbed up well, darling,' she said. 'You too look lovely. No time for kissing,' she remonstrated as Henry turned to her. 'Go into the sitting room and get the drinks sorted, I'll go down and open the door,' she said, running downstairs.

'Artie?' she said, opening the door. Rupert Highsmith was behind him. She threw her arms around Artie and gave him a hug. 'Thank you for suggesting I ask Doreen to help me with the food for the party. I'd never have done it without her.' She took Artie's jacket. 'Hello, Rupert, how are you?' she asked, shaking Rupert Highsmith's hand. 'I'm so glad you could come. Let me take your coat.' She helped Rupert out of his lightweight coat. 'It's good to see you.'

'And you, Ena,' Highsmith said, beaming her a smile.

The street door to the flat opened into a hall that was about twelve-foot square. Ena left the door ajar and led the way upstairs. 'Henry's in the sitting room. He'll get you both a drink.' At the top of the stairs, she craned her neck to see Henry standing next to the long sideboard and taking the corks out of bottles of wine. 'There's enough food to feed an army on the dining table at the far end of the room. Help yourselves.'

Rupert Highsmith, head held high, stood to the side of the door to let Artie enter first. Highsmith stood six inches taller than Artie, and Artie wasn't short by any means. No wonder he thought he was a cut above the rest of humanity. What did her old colleague Sid call him? Mr High-n-Mighty. Ena felt a pang of sadness. She still missed her friend, Sid Parfitt.

'You alright, Ena?'

'Inspector?' Ena moved towards him to hug him – she was in a hugging mood – but she was still holding Artie's and Rupert's coats. She laughed. 'Take your coat off, stick it on top of these and I'll take them to the spare room and lay them on the bed. Go through to the sitting room, Henry will get you a drink. Oh,' she said, stopping the inspector in his tracks, 'WPC Rhoda Jarvis is coming with her young man. I hope it was alright to invite her?'

'Of course, it was.' The inspector's eyes twinkled. 'I didn't know she had a young man. She's a sly one, that WPC of mine.' He leaned forward and whispered, 'I'll let you into a secret, Ena. Jarvis won't be a WPC for much longer. I've recommended her for promotion. She may soon be Detective Sergeant Jarvis.'

Ena pulled a surprised but happy face. 'I'm so pleased.'

'But don't say anything. It hasn't been authorised yet.'

'I won't say anything if you promise not to pull her leg about her young man at work on Monday.'

'Oh, I can't promise I won't do that,' the inspector said, laughing good-heartedly.

'In that case, I might have to tell her about her promotion.'

'Alright. You win,' the inspector conceded. 'I'm going to find Henry, I'm in need of a drink.'

After laying the coats on the spare bed in the unfurnished guest room, Ena joined Henry in the sitting room. He poured her a glass of wine, which after one sip she put down when the door-bell rang.

'Do you want me to get it?'

'Would you?'

Henry planted a kiss on Ena's cheek and poured a glass of red wine. 'Take this to Dan Powell. Won't be long.'

When Henry returned it was with half a dozen guests. Among them were her friends Natalie, George and Betsy.

After excusing herself, Ena left the inspector and ran to greet them. 'I don't believe my eyes,' she said, kissing each of them in turn.

'I hope you don't mind Betsy and me gate-crashing your house warming party,' George said.

'Mind? I'm delighted. I wanted to invite you both, but…'

'I know. Natalie telephoned and said you felt that in the circumstances it wouldn't be appropriate. But it is appropriate.' George looked at Betsy who, smiling, nodded in agreement. 'We're so happy for you and Henry; happy to be here to share and to celebrate your new home.' George gave Ena a gift. It was the size of a shoebox and very heavy, wrapped in silver paper. 'For you and Henry, from Betsy and me.'

'George, you shouldn't have.'

'And this is from me,' Natalie added, giving Ena a similar box wrapped in the same paper, but square in shape and lighter.

'I told you no house warming presents. I told Natalie not to bring a housewarming present,' Ena repeated to George and Betsy. 'We have everything we need.'

Natalie put her hand to her mouth and snatched a breath. 'I forgot.' She looked at George and Betsy who burst into laughter. 'I promise you won't already have these gifts.'

Ena looked at her friend quizzically.

'But if you don't want it, I'll give it to Henry...'

'No! There's no need to go that far.' Ena eyed the gifts. 'I'm intrigued,' she said, feeling the box, hoping for a clue to its contents. She pressed her lips together and gave Henry a sideways glance. 'I suppose you can open one of them.' She looked from one to the other of her friends. 'Thank you.'

'I'll open this one.' Ena chose the biggest. 'Henry, you open this,' she said, handing him the smaller box.'

'You open them both, darling, and I'll get the drinks.' As Henry asked the three women what they wanted to drink, Ena moved several bottles and glasses to the end of the sideboard and put down the two parcels. Taking the ribbon from the first, she pulled on the overlapping wrapping paper to reveal a white marble mortar and pestle. 'Henry?' she called, 'look at this!'

'It's beautiful, George, thank you, and thank you, Betsy.'

'That isn't all,' Betsy said, 'there's something else in the wrapping.'

Ena looked closer and saw the corner of white paper. She tugged it to reveal a sheet of thick writing paper with *Hummus Recipe* written on it in beautiful handwriting. 'Hummus, Henry, it's a recipe for hummus.'

'Now open this,' Natalie said.

'Natalie, you shouldn't,' Ena said, tearing the paper off Natalie's gift. She caught her breath. 'A silver dish and spoon. It's beautiful, Natalie.' Ena felt tears in the corners of her eyes and wiped them away with the back of her hand.

'Can I put them somewhere for you?'

'I'll take them to our bedroom while Henry

finishes getting your drinks.'

Returning to the sitting room she found WPC Jarvis and her boyfriend in conversation with Inspector Powell, George and Betsy talking to Henry who was nodding in agreement and Natalie had joined Artie and Rupert at the buffet – a plate of food in one hand and a glass of wine in the other. Ena surveyed the room, delighted that her friends were able to share in her and Henry's happiness. It seemed everyone that she and Henry knew in London was there. She crossed to the sideboard and picked up the wine she'd abandoned earlier, and wished her sisters could have been with her. She swallowed the emotion she felt and raised her glass to them. As she took a drink, she noticed Artie watching her and she said, 'Cheers!' He looked unhappy. 'Are you alright?' she mouthed.

Artie said something to Rupert and Natalie, which Ena wasn't able to lip read, left them and crossed the room to her.

'What's up?'

'Rupert's been getting threatening letters.'

'Anonymously?'

'Yes. I know it isn't professional, what with Rupert and me being … you know, but can I look into it?'

'Of course. And if you need my help you only have to ask.'

'Thank you, Ena.' Artie grinned at her.

'What is it? Go on, spill the beans.'

'Well, Rupert isn't a, you know, demonstrative sort of person.'

Ena almost choked on her drink. Was she going to hear about Rupert Highsmith's softer side? Did he even have a softer side? 'Oh?'

'And he doesn't show his feelings in public.'

'I can feel a *but* coming.'

'But,' her friend said pointedly, 'he wants me to move in with him. Live with him.' Artie wrinkled his nose and blushed scarlet.

'What are you screwing up your face for? Isn't that what you want?'

'Well, yes, it is…'

'So, I don't see a problem.'

'There isn't one,' Artie said, laughing.

'Can I give you a piece of advice?'

'I'm all ears.'

'Don't let him turn you into a cook, cleaner and bottle washer.'

Artie laughed again. 'I don't think he'll expect me to do any of that. I told him in no uncertain terms when I left GCHQ that it was because he treated me like a servant. Don't worry, he got the message.' Artie giggled.

'Have you told him you'll move in with him?'

'No, I said it was a big decision. I said I needed to be sure it was what I wanted, and that he must be sure it's what he wants too.'

'And are you, sure?'

'I am now. Thank you, Ena. I'll get us another drink and, as soon as we're on our own, I'll tell him.'

Ena hadn't seen Artie as happy for a long time. He was due some happiness, someone to care for him, love him. He almost skipped over to Henry for more wine. As arrogant as Rupert Highsmith could sometimes be, he and Artie were a good match. Her smile faded. The fact that Rupert was being sent threatening letters would affect Artie, and Ena couldn't help but feel worried for Artie. She decided to talk to him about the anonymous letters on Monday when they were in the office. Her thoughts were interrupted by Inspector Powell.

'I don't want to talk shop tonight, but I thought you'd like to know, Arnold Hardy was picked up in Margate yesterday trying to rob a Post Office. The Police searched his lodgings and found several hundred pounds under his mattress, which I hope will go back to Doreen.'

'I'll drink to that,' Ena said, raising her glass.

'And, the Chief Constable is happy with the work you did on the art theft case.'

'So, Giselle Aubrey is his goddaughter, is she?'

'She is. And,' Inspector Powell continued, 'if there is anything in the future, would you be prepared to work with the Met?'

'With you and Detective Sergeant Jarvis,' Ena teased.

'Shush! But yes.'

'Do you know our rates, Inspector?' Artie asked.

'I do, Mr Mallory.'

'Artie!' Ena said, shocked by his forthrightness.

'And, so do I, Ena,' Rupert Highsmith said, joining them.

'To Ena and Artie and the Dudley Green Investigation Agency.' Henry shouted, popping the cork on a bottle of champagne and pouring it into a row of champagne flutes.

'And to Ena and Henry,' Artie shouted in reply, raising his glass.

"To Ena and Henry!"

THE END

ABOUT THE AUTHOR

Madalyn Morgan has been an actress for more than thirty years working in repertory theatre, the West End, film, radio and television. She is a radio presenter, writes poetry, and has written many articles for newspapers and magazines.

Madalyn was brought up in Lutterworth, at the Fox Inn. "The pub was a great place for an aspiring actress and writer to live, as there were so many different characters to study and accents to learn." At twenty-four Madalyn gave up a successful hairdressing salon and wig-hire business for a place at E15 Drama College and a career as an actress.

In 2000, with fewer parts available for older actresses, Madalyn taught herself to touch type, completed a two-year correspondence course with The Writer's Bureau, and started writing. After living in London for thirty-six years, she has returned to her home town of Lutterworth, swapping two window boxes and a mortgage for a garden and the freedom to write.

As an Indie Author, Madalyn has successfully published seven novels: Foxden Acres, Applause, China Blue, and The 9:45 To Bletchley are set during WW2 and tell the wartime stories of Bess, Margot, Claire, and Ena Dudley. Foxden Hotel and Chasing Ghosts are post war. There Is No Going Home is set in 1958.

Madalyn is a member of The Society of Authors, the Romantic Novelists Association and Equity. Her books are available on Amazon - in eBook and in paperback at www.amazon.co.uk/Madalyn-Morgan/e/B00J7VO9I2/

FUTURE BOOKS

The only Dudley sister who doesn't have a sequel is Margot (Applause), but that is about to change. My work in progress is called Christmas Applause. Set in The Prince Albert theatre, Christmas 1960, it will be a celebration of Margot's life as London's leading lady and ENSA's Sweetheart in World War Two. The story brings together the Dudley sisters, their daughters - now young women - and Margot's dancer friends from the war.

Christmas Applause begins in 1960 and goes back in time to the 1940s, to the London Blitz, to the late-night clubs and the problems Margot had with alcohol and prescription drugs. It also goes back to Margot's survival, how she conquered her demons to become the The Prince Albert Theatre's leading lady and Talk of London.

I have never before written a duel-time novel. Nor have I written a feel-good Christmas story. Christmas Applause will be both. Two firsts for me - and two challenges.

I am also writing a Memoir. It will be a record of my work as an actress and as a writer. I have worked with some interesting people, I a collection of poetry, articles and biographies - with photographs of the characters I played when I was an actress. I think a collection of work would make a good memoir. It will be different, but I hope interesting to read.

OUTLINE OF EARLIER BOOKS IN THE DUDLEY SISTERS SAGA

FOXDEN ACRES:

Foxden Acres, the first book in the saga, begins on the eve of 1939 when twenty-year-old Bess Dudley, the daughter of a Foxden groom, bumps into James Foxden the heir to Foxden Estate. Bess, a scholarship girl, lodges at Mrs McAllister's boarding house in London while studying to be a teacher.

With offers of a teaching job in London and Foxden, Bess opts for Foxden, to be near James. However, when she is told that James is betrothed to the socially acceptable Annabel Hadleigh, Bess accepts the teaching post in London.

When war breaks out and London's schoolchildren are evacuated, Bess returns to Foxden to organise a team of Land Girls and turn the Foxden Estate into arable land. James, having joined the RAF, is training to be a bomber pilot at nearby Bitteswell Aerodrome.

German bombs fall on London and Mrs McAllister's house is blitzed to rubble. South Leicestershire is scarred too when an RAF plane carrying Polish airmen crash lands in a Foxden field. Traditional social barriers come crashing down when Flying Officer James Foxden falls in love with Bess. But is it too late? During the time Bess has been back at Foxden she has grown to like and respect Annabel Hadleigh. How can Bess be with James knowing it would break her friend's heart? Besides, Bess has a shameful secret that she has vowed to keep from James at any cost.

APPLAUSE:
Applause is the second book in the saga. In the early years of World War Two, Margot (Margaret) Dudley works her way up from usherette to leading lady in a West End show. Driven by blind ambition Margot becomes immersed in the heady world of nightclubs, drink, drugs and fascist thugs – all set against a background of the London Blitz.

To achieve her dream, Margot risks losing everything she holds dear.

CHINA BLUE:
China Blue, the third book, is Claire Dudley's story. At the beginning of World War II Claire joins the WAAF. She excels in languages and is recruited by the Special Operations Executive to work in Occupied France. Against SOE rules, Claire falls in love. The affair has to be kept secret. Even after her lover falls into the hands of the Gestapo, Claire cannot tell anyone they are more than comrades.

As the war reaches its climax, Claire fears she will never again see the man she loves.

THE 9:45 TO BLETCHLEY:
The 9:45 To Bletchley is the fourth book in the Dudley Sisters Saga. In the midst of the Second World War, and charged with taking vital surveillance equipment via the 9:45 train, Ena Dudley makes regular trips to Bletchley Park, until on one occasion she is robbed. When those she cares about are accused of being involved, she investigates, not knowing whom she can trust.
While trying to clear her name, Ena falls in love.

FOXDEN HOTEL:
The war is over. It is time for new beginnings.

Celebrating the opening of Foxden Hotel, New Year's Eve 1948, and an enemy from the war years turns up. He threatens to expose a secret that will ruin Bess's happiness and the new life she has worked so hard to create. Bess's husband throws the man out. So is that the last they see of him? Or will he show up again when they least expect?

Bess had hoped fascism was a thing of the past, buried with the victims of WW2. Little does she know the trouble that lies ahead, not only for herself but also for her family.

CHASING GHOSTS:
1949. After receiving treatment for shell shock in Canada, Claire's husband disappears. Has Mitch left her for the woman he talks about in his sleep? Or is he on the run from accusations of wartime treachery? Claire goes to France in search of the truth, aided by old friends from the Resistance.

THERE IS NO GOING HOME:
London, 1958, Ena recognises a woman who she exposed as a spy in WW2. Ena's husband, Henry, an agent with MI5, argues that it cannot be the woman because they went to her funeral twelve years before.

Ena, now head of the Home Office cold case department, starts an investigation. There are no files. It is as if the woman never existed. Suddenly colleagues who are helping Ena with the case mysteriously die... and Ena herself is almost killed in a hit-and-run.

The case breaks when Ena finds important documents from 1936 Berlin that prove not only did the spy exist, but someone above suspicion who worked with her then, still works with her now.

Fearing for her life, there is only one person Ena can trust… or can she?

SHE CASTS A LONG SHADOW
https://www.amazon.co.uk/dp/B089JDCR8D/

Preparing to expose the mole at MI5, Ena's husband Henry is abducted by Special Branch and Ena is thrown into a murder case.

All the evidence points to Henry having killed the mole, leading Ena to conclude that Henry is being framed. Close to finding out the truth, Ena is suspended from her job at the Home Office and the investigation is blocked by Special Branch. Only her sisters and her old friend Inspector Powell believe Henry is innocent.

Help comes from an untrustworthy character. A deal is agreed: A ticket to Austria in return for the names of the mole's associates, evidence to solve two of Ena's cold cases, and the proof that Henry is innocent of murder. The catch? Ena must accompany this character to Austria as insurance.

Printed in Great Britain
by Amazon